THERAPY WITH THE DEAD

THERAPY WITH THE DEAD

AN ALICE BRENNER MYSTERY

J.S. FOSTER

CHAPTER 1

WEDNESDAY, SEPTEMBER 18 VERY EARLY MORNING

The last time I wasn't stressed was last Tuesday night . I was snuggled down in my bed lulled by the soft music coming from the small speaker on the bedside table. My dreams were full of cozy gatherings of my favorite people. The bed was soft and warm. So comfy. I was content and happy.

The tranquility was shattered by the jangle of my cell phone. My clock said it was two in the morning. I sat up half asleep and unsuccessfully felt around for the phone. When I answered, the voice on the other end was frantic.

"Dr. Brenner? Alice?

I tried to respond, but she continued as though she hadn't heard me mumble, "Uh. Hello."

"Alice, I need you! I'm just unlovable. I always have been. This is no different. He doesn't really love me. It was all lies!"

Now I recognized the voice of one of my patients, Janet Ford. Janet was intense, with wildly fluctuating moods, and a flair for drama. She always made every small stumble sound as though she'd just fallen into the Grand Canyon. Her life was one continuous emergency. It was completely in character for her to call with a crisis at two in the morning. That made it difficult to know how seriously to take her when she was upset.

"Janet, I'm here. Take a deep breath and calm yourself. Remember how we do it in my office? Do that now." Often Janet couldn't calm on her own, but could with my help.

"I can't. I'm too upset." She began to sob.

"Alright. Focus on your breathing. Breathe in to a count of four. Hold it. Then slowly breathe out to a count of six. Just keep doing that. Let's do it together." Based on how my heart was thumping, I could use a little focused breathing, too.

I could hear her breathing begin to slow until she seemed to stop herself. "No! I can't calm down after what he did to me! I want to marry him, but he doesn't want me. How can I be calm!"

"Tell me what happened." I kept my voice soft and reassuring. .

"He'll be sorry! I'll show him! Nobody treats me that way!" Now Janet was yelling into the phone.

"Janet, breathe. Don't do anything you'll regret. Let's meet at the hospital emergency room in thirty minutes and talk about it." Normally I don't meet with my patients in the middle of the night, but this sounded serious. Meeting at the emergency room meant that I could get her hospitalized if need be.

"No. He needs a lesson. I'll show him, Alice."

The line went dead. Janet hung up. I didn't know where she was.

I sat there in the bed with a sinking feeling in my stomach. What should I do? My first impulse was to call the police, have them find Janet, and get her hospitalized for observation. However, in the state of Virginia, putting someone on an involuntary hold in the hospital requires they be an imminent danger to themselves, others, or both. I didn't know if that was the case.

If one of my less dramatic patients had said what Janet had said, there would have been no question about putting them on a seventy-two hour psych hold. But Janet was all hyperbole. For the most part, she didn't act on her statements. They were a way of letting off steam and calming her wild moods. Was this different? I wasn't sure. Janet was impulsive, but came from a very socially prominent family where proper behavior had been drilled into her. The most dangerous thing she'd done in the twelve weeks I'd been working with her was to throw a lamp at her bedroom wall.

In all likelihood, Janet was at home yelling at her cat and planning horrible revenge on her ex-lover that would never be acted on. But what if that wasn't the case?

What if Janet hurt somebody or hurt herself? I turned on the bedside lamp. In its glow, I could see my hand shake. I took a deep breath. The shaking was still there. Now I could feel it in my stomach.

Breathe. Calm down, Alice.

I needed something to settle myself so I could think clearly enough to make the right call. Someone could easily get hurt if I made the wrong decision. Janet might hurt someone else or could even get shot by the police. I didn't know what to do. The more I thought about it, the more uncertain I felt.

eMaybe tea and cookies would help. I got out of bed and shuffled to the kitchen. Peppermint tea would be just the thing. I nibbled on a biscotti while I found a tea bag and boiled water. The tea burned my mouth, but I no longer felt the frizzle of panic. Taking a tray of biscotti and tea, I went back to bed. After blowing the tea cool enough to sip, I reassessed my options.

If Janet had been set on hurting herself or someone else, she probably wouldn't have called me. It was more likely that she wanted reassurance that I cared. Being loved was an issue in all of Janet's relationships and she'd begun to act that out with me.

If I did call the police and ask them to find Janet and bring her to the hospital so she could be put on a hold, she could be in great danger. Cops aren't trained very well in how to deal with people with mental illness. Especially in small town departments, like ours. They have a poor track record in dealing with a person who is agitated and upset. It wasn't unlikely that the police would respond to Janet's drama and agitation with force rather than words. She could get shot. I was screwed if I didn't try to hospitalize her and screwed if I did.

By now it was three-thirty, and I'd decided that I didn't have enough reason to have Janet hospitalized. I set the tray aside and lay back down. I stared at my bedroom ceiling for what seemed to be hours, but I must have eventually fallen asleep. Because, in fact, I dreamed about her.

We were in my office at night, my lamps making pools of golden light around the room. Janet was staring at me.

"We're a lot alike, you know," she said.

"How are we alike?" I asked.

She smiled her sad smile. "We're both unlovable. We smile when we don't mean it."

The lights went off and blackness surrounded me. I could sense Janet was gone. I was alone in a cold void and couldn't breathe. The lonely darkness suffocated me.

WEDNESDAY, SEPTEMBER 18
EARLY MORNING

At seven the next morning, I crawled out of bed, shuffled to the bathroom, and shut the door. I was in a bad mood. First of all, I was still wasn't sure I'd done the right thing by not hospitalizing Janet. And there was the dream. I wasn't like Janet. Janet's life was a mess. I'd worked very hard for years to develop a life that functioned well. Janet was living a life of chaos. My life was structured. And if that wasn't enough, it was Wednesday. I hate Wednesdays.

Once ready for work, I found I had no coffee pods to feed my coffee maker. I hustled downstairs and onto the big front porch still debating whether I had time to get pods and come back or whether I should get a coffee on the way to work.

"There you are. I thought I heard you upstairs."

My best friend and landlord, Lucy, walked out onto the porch with a big smile and handed me a big mug of coffee.

Bless her.

"Come in." She held her door open and then headed for her kitchen. "We have time for bagels and lox this morning." My favorite breakfast and my best friend. *Heaven.*

When she finished her bagel, Lucy leaned back in her chair. "How are you, Alice? We haven't had much chance to catch up lately."

Lucy meant well. She knew I was lonely. At thirty-six I had no family, unless you counted my druggie brother, Mark, somewhere on the streets of Baltimore. I had no children, no spouse, only an on-again off-again boyfriend/hook-up, and Lucy. I would admit I wasn't dissatisfied. It was hard making friends and finding that special man when you lived in a small town like Fort Madison. Especially when you're a psychologist. So I spent a lot of my time with Lucy.

"I thought I heard you walking around up there in the middle of the night. Did you have a bad night?" she asked.

"Yes, I did." I frowned. "One of my patients called me in the middle of the night all upset. Apparently she'd had a fight with her new boyfriend and was feeling hurt and angry. Before I could calm her and get her to agree to meet me and talk it over, she hung up. I debated for a long time about whether to have the police pick her up so I could get her hospitalized. She's a real drama queen who always over exaggerates, so I eventually decided against hospitalization."

"Ugh. I hate situations like that. You never feel okay about it, no matter what you do." I knew that she knew what she was talking about. Lucy is a social worker in our group practice and has had similar things happen.

"Yeah. I had trouble going back to sleep."

"Are you okay with your decision now?"

"No. Not really." I sighed. "I guess I'll find out how she did. Hope she didn't get into trouble."

"Chances are that she just yelled, cried, and went to bed. She probably got more sleep than you did."

"I just felt she'd be okay without hospitalization. What if I made a mistake?"

"You don't make mistakes, girl." Lucy laughed.

"But I do." I shot her an exaggerated frown. Then I laughed, too.

We'd had this exchange many times over the seven years we'd known each other. Lucy swore that I had super intuition and that my hunches were right more often than not. That wasn't entirely wrong. I did often"know" things others didn't.

That's the way it'd been since I was a kid. Suddenly, I'd just know something. That's the upside to growing up with an alcoholic and abusive mother. I had to be on the alert for danger from her. I learned how to read nonverbal cues and to see patterns of behavior. Now I do it automatically. I'm not even aware of it. And, sometimes I can help others with my intuition.

It was like that when I first met Lucy. I was walking through downtown Fort Madison trying to get familiar with my new home. There weren't many people around. I liked that. One of the perks of living in a small town.

An attractive , nicely-dressed woman was walking toward me and a little behind her was a scruffy-looking man. As I casually glanced at them, I knew that the woman was in great danger from the man. Without thinking, I called out, "Lady watch out! He's going to hurt you."

The woman turned toward the man, jumped back, and ran to me. We could see the knife he held.

We both screamed, "Help! Police!" He stopped, then ran away. I guess two screeching women were too much for him. Remembering the shocked look on his face made me laugh again.

"What's so funny?" Lucy asked.

"I was remembering how we first met."

" Your intuition kept me safe. Thank you for the umpteenth time."

"That was another time I just knew something. When I saw that man walking toward you, I knew he intended you harm. That's why I yelled for you to watch out."

"Good thing you yelled like you did, too. He already had his knife out. If I hadn't jumped back, he would have cut me."

"Then I was blown away to see you when I walked into the practice on my first day of work."

"We were destined to be good friends." She always smiled when she said this.

"All because of my super power." And I always smiled back.

"? It's legendary at work."

That was new. "You're kidding."

"Not kidding." She laughed. "You're a therapist with a super power."

Well, damn.

CHAPTER 3

WEDNESDAY, SEPTEMBER 18
MORNING

Later, as I was driving to work, I remembered a disturbing session I'd had with Janet.

Janet was smart and talented. She and I had battled for control of the therapy from the beginning. Janet had seen a number of therapists before she came to see me. Most of them had diagnosed her as a person with Borderline Personality Disorder. Consequently, I'd read all my references on treatment for Borderline Personality Disorder and planned an approach. I'd identified that Janet needed to work on her self-esteem and would need lots of my support while she did that. Then we'd work on learning coping strategies for taming her stormy emotions. But first I had to help her develop trust. To that end I always did what I said I would, and was as nonthreatening and nurturing as I knew how. And gradually—very gradually—Janet was beginning to trust me a little. Baby steps.

Now she came to see me as scheduled, but liked to talk in riddles and make jokes that only she understood. Her confrontational attitude abated, becoming more approachable—sort of like a teen talking with an adult she liked, but didn't completely have faith in. All that was to be expected in therapy with a person with Borderline Personality Disorder or BPD. Janet had all the impulsiveness and stormy emotions typical of someone with BPD. All I had to do was be consistent, always tell her the truth, and be patient. That's all.

But then, after about seven weeks, she came in looking terrible. She hardly made eye contact and her voice grated.

"I never should have married Bill. He's such an ass." Janet pounded the arm of the denim chair.

"What happened?"

"He contacted me again. He knows I don't want to talk to him. He needs money. Again. His business is still deep in the red. He said I'd be sorry if I didn't help him."

"He's done this before?"

"Once before. I got scared and gave him ten thousand dollars." She scowled, a mixture of anger and fear. "This time he's after fifteen. He … he has pictures. From our honeymoon. Not the kind you share with friends and family."

"Why do you think he's doing this? Does he really need the money, or is it something else?"

"Besides making me upset or messing with me for divorcing him? I already told you. He knows I feel scared easily. Especially when I'm alone. Weren't you listening?" She started picking at the stitching in her chair.

"What makes you so upset about being alone?"

"I just don't like it!" She was yelling now. I chose to ignore it.

"Why?"

"I don't ever want to be alone. You never know what I might do." She watched me carefully as she answered.

"You mean you might hurt yourself?"

"Yeah. I might. I might just end it and then they'd be sorry. Bill wouldn't have his Money Bags around to finance him." She had that crazy little-girl smile of hers.

"Money Bags? Does he call you that?" I asked.

"Yeah. Sometimes when we're fighting."

"How do you feel about that?" By following this thread, I hoped she'd stop thinking about hurting herself. Unlike someone who is suffering from a Major Depression, a person with Borderline Personality Disorder can experience emotions that are fleeting.

"I didn't like it!" she yelled again. "Don't you even care I just told you I might kill myself?"

"Do you want me to care?"

"Yes, of course I do." She looked at me as if she'd like to chop me up into little pieces.

"I do care, Janet. Very much."

"Good." She seemed to relax, glares, scowls, and hard looks tucked away for now.

"How seriously do you take Bill's threat?"

"Very seriously. He's hurt people before. When he was angry, like in bar fights. He slapped me once when we were still married." Janet's foot hit the floor.

"Is that why you got divorced?"

"No. It was because he left when I got pregnant. I divorced him and moved back in with Mother."

"What about moving back in with her for a while now as well? If you're scared of Bill—"

"No. If I do, Mother will take over my daughter, Betsy, again. I may not be the best mother, but I *am* her mother."

"You've talked to the police about Bill's threats?" I reached toward her just a little.

"No. Should I?" Janet stiffened.

"Yes. Today. If he knows the police are involved he'll be less likely to try anything." I leaned back. I didn't want to scare her.

"Okay. I'll call them this afternoon." She was more relaxed now.

"Good. Now I want to get back to your fear that you might hurt yourself. Can you promise me that you won't hurt yourself this week?"

"I guess I can." She stayed relaxed. That was a good sign.

"Good. So let's think about what you can do to make sure that you don't hurt yourself."

She relaxed even more. This was familiar ground. We'd done it many times. "Okay."

I smiled, and meant it. "Let's look at things that have worked in the past. Then we'll find some new things to try. Are you willing to do that?"

"Yes."

By the time the session was over we had agreed on three things that Janet would do: invite friends over, have entertaining movies ready to watch, and stock up on her favorite foods.

Over the next three weeks Janet told me about the surface of her life. She was bored. She had a beautiful daughter and lots of family money, but also a controlling mother and an ex-husband who threatened her. Being the impulsive woman that she was, Janet fell in love with someone: her new running partner. She wouldn't tell me who, although she appeared to find my questions about the relationship amusing.

I wasn't worried. We were in the first few months of therapy. Janet hadn't decided to trust me yet. When she did, she would talk about what she was feeling and what she thought about the people and circumstances of her life. I had to be patient.

It was a Wednesday when it all changed. I remember it was a Wednesday because I hate Wednesdays. The last weekend has worn off and it's too early to look forward to the next. A hurdle that has to be jumped to get on with life. Of course it was a Wednesday.

CHAPTER 4

WEDNESDAY, SEPTEMBER 18
MORNING

That Wednesday began even worse than most. It had been raining all week and I managed to step in a puddle in the parking lot. My new shoes were soaked and my mood dripped darkness when I walked into the office.

Waiting for me in the reception area was Ron Margolis, a psychologist the partnership hired just last year. Over the last six months he'd developed an interest in the business aspects of running a group practice. He'd quote management texts on how a business should be run to be at its peak efficiency, and point out all the ways we weren't doing that.

Recently Mr. Big Business had begun to criticize my choice of jeans, tunics, and ethnic jewelry as not being professional attire for a therapist, like there was a manual about it that I'd neglected to read. We'd had a few run-ins when he'd tried to get me to dress more like Lucy, which would have been funny if it weren't so infuriating. I'd known since high school that my short, pudgy body would never be able to pull off the elegant businesswoman style that worked so well on Lucy's slender frame. Nor would my wavy brown hair have looked at all chic cut as short as Lucy's.

That morning Ron was trying to lean "casually" against the reception counter without creasing his sport coat. Georgia, our amazing office manager, greeted me as she took a file to the desk in back. Ron merely gave me a half-smile and nod. I'd seen him display that smirk before, his "I've got you now" look. Clearing his throat, he held out a folded newspaper to me.

"Good morning, Dr. Brenner. How's our famous schizophrenia expert today?"

"What are you talking about?"

He sniffed, offering me the paper. "Let me be the first to show it to you. It's about you and your shelter friends."

Suddenly the parking lot puddle didn't seem so annoying compared to what I'd just stepped into here. "Oh that," I replied, taking the paper. "Thanks for noticing." By now I had some idea of what Ron was trying to guilt-trip me about.

I moved closer to my office. "What's wrong, Ron? Don't you approve of the real mentally ill? Just want unhappy housewives and their children?"

"You know that's not true. I'm just more professional about it." He pointed at the newspaper picture of me sitting on the floor next to a homeless man with a graying beard, dark face, and oversized dirty sweater.

"Russ won't sit on chairs, Ron. He's afraid they'll eat him."

As I moved on I swear I heard him mutter, "Maybe you should both be back at the state hospital." Surely he didn't really say that.

What a jerk. I used to work at the state hospital where Russ had been a patient many times. "We're all people, Ron."

"Yeah. Some of us more than others." I couldn't believe he said that. I must have misheard him. He just wouldn't say that.

"Ron, you've totally convinced me that our practice needs a forward-looking branding strategy. When our clients know that we actively help the less fortunate, it's as if they're also contributing to positive change in our community. They feel good about us, and themselves. A win-win. Every partner should be working with a local charity, don't you think?"

Ron stared at me blankly. "That's a lot to think about."

Clearly this conversation hadn't gone as he expected. I broke out my own version of the "I got you now" smile.

"Okay. Good talk," I said cheerfully, handing him back his paper. "Gotta run now. Client waiting. Don't want to run overtime." I turned and headed toward my office.

I hurried down the hall and shut my office door behind me. As I stood there letting the office welcome me, I could feel my breathing slow. Ron and his misguided superior attitude faded. I sighed and put on a dry pair of shoes, which I had long since learned to keep on hand.

It was always like this. Coming into this room. Some therapists thought of their office as a consultation room, others as a workspace. I thought of my office as a sanctuary. I felt taken care of and calmed by this place. I hope my patients can feel it, too.

My office wasn't that special to look at. My couch was slipcovered in well-used blue denim. The dark wood coffee table came from my grandmother. The lamps came from long-ago flea markets. And I probably had too many books in there. But the desk … the desk was special. Elegant carved mahogany, solid and traditional. I found it in a Baltimore used furniture store just after I finished graduate school. I couldn't afford the three hundred dollars it cost, but I bought it anyway. It was a symbol of the rich professional life I would have.

That morning I looked at the reflections from the lamp on the deep red brown of the desk. The morning light danced on the brilliant red, gold, and blue of the Persian rug. The green life from my plants filled the room. I felt rich.

My office, my sanctuary, was calm and ready to hold my patients and me. It would keep us safe, a place to risk telling what hadn't been told before. Protect tender souls. Invite laughter. It was ready for business. And now, being here, I was too.

My first patient that day, Miranda Edwards, had also seen the morning's paper. Only she didn't want to talk about my work at the shelter.

"Did you see the front page?" She handed me the paper. "They identified the poor dead woman from Dolly Madison Park Monday night. Her ex-husband owns an art gallery near downtown. I can only imagine how he feels. Probably like I did after Howard died. Do you think it would be tacky to send him a card? Since I don't know him or anything."

What is she talking about? My breath caught as I read the headline. My patient didn't know the ex-husband, but I was well acquainted with him. I'd heard all about the guy from his just-dead ex-wife. Janet Ford.

I couldn't take it in. The paper said Janet was found dead yesterday morning. That just couldn't be true. I felt cold. Frozen.

"Alice, are you alright. You've turned white as a sheet. Can I get you something?" Miranda reached out towards me.

"No. I'm . . . I'm okay. I just felt dizzy for a moment. It's probably because I skipped breakfast this morning. Let's get back to your wanting to make new friends. How else can you find friends?"

I shoved my feelings about Janet down for the rest of Miranda's session. I don't think she noticed anything else was wrong but I couldn't remember what we talked about once she'd left.

After Miranda was gone, the shock of Janet's death came roaring back. All I could think about was Janet. I didn't believe it. She couldn't be dead.

Just to make sure I looked up our local paper online. There it was. "Local Socialite Found Dead in Dolly Madison Park."

Janet was dead.

CHAPTER 5

WEDNESDAY, SEPTEMBER 18 AFTERNOON

All I could think about was Janet. I'd discovered that she was intelligent, well-read, and had a dry wit that grew on me. She loved her daughter, Betsy, and was determined that she would have a better childhood than Janet, herself, had experienced. She had a strong sense of ethics, despite her temper and impulsiveness, and was active in the local Episcopal church. Janet was more complex than she had first appeared. In fact, I'd grown to like her very much. I'd hoped that together we'd be able to defeat the Borderline Personality Disorder that caused her so much pain.

Difficult, fascinating Janet, who had been so alive and in love just last week.

She'd come in awash in gold chains, wearing a wildly patterned empire top and a genuinely happy smile.

"Guess what, Doctor Alice. I'm going to cure myself. You'll be so proud."

I'd smiled back. "What will I be proud of?"

"Me and my wonderful realization that I can be the woman I'm meant to be. I'm not going to be bullied by Mother anymore. Or Bill."

"That sounds good," I'd said. "Tell me more."

"I'm in love," she'd sighed dramatically, "and we're going to tell the world about it."

"Is this your jogging partner from the park?" Maybe I'd finally get to hear more about him.

"Yes. We have the same interests and passions. All that, and he's such a wonderful person, too. Kind, funny, and a good listener. Being there, whether we're talking, making love, or just running in the park makes me a better person. Calmer, more responsible."

"That's what we've been aiming for." Were alarms sounding in my head? Yes, they were. Plunging headlong into a love affair with a man she met in the park was part of a pattern of impulsiveness that had plagued Janet.

"Yes," she'd laughed, "and I did it without Mother's money. I don't even care if she takes it all away. We'll be okay without it."

"It sounds like you're growing up. I'm glad."

Despite my attempts to get more information, she didn't tell me more, except that there would probably be screams coming from her mother's house that week.

"Don't worry," she'd said, as she left. "I'll tell you all the juicy details next week."

But I had worried. How could I not? Sudden love can fade just as quickly as it blooms. Dumping unwanted romantic news on your mother—especially if she's controlling—wasn't a good idea either.

This morning I had expected to see a defeated, depressed Janet. We would have begun work on how to repair the damage. Instead I was trying to reconcile the dead body in the park with the sunny, irresponsible, but very alive Janet.

That Wednesday morning, I just sat in my office going over the little I knew about the incident and about Janet after only twelve sessions. Sadly, it really wasn't very much. I thought back over her case. Had my work with her been good enough? Had I failed her in some way? I didn't think so. I'd had so little time to work with her, but I'd felt we were making progress. She was beginning to trust me, to take the process seriously.

I realized I'd been crying. I couldn't have red eyes when I saw my next patient. Checking my appointment book, I discovered Janet had scheduled a special session time to tell me about her lover. It was my next hour. I quietly cried some more.

I grabbed a tissue, wiped my eyes, and blew my nose. When I knew Lucy was between patients, I called her and told her about Janet's death. She was as shocked as I was. I ached to talk more with Lucy about how I felt and what this news might mean for the future, but I couldn't. Lucy had a patient waiting. We'd have to wait until after work. So I hung up and cried some more.

* * *

The police came to my office during Janet's appointment time. *How fitting.* Georgia buzzed me on the intercom, whispering, "Two police detectives who want to talk to you are out here. Ron volunteered to show them to your office. Sorry about the lack of notice."

"Thanks, Georgia. You did the best you could. I'll manage."

I was able to pat my cheeks dry and blow my nose before there was a knock on my door and Ron's voice saying, "Doctor Brenner? Have a moment?"

I opened the door. There was Ron, with an expression that managed to convey both sincere condolences and annoying superiority, like my client's death was somehow my fault. As if I hadn't been torturing myself for the past hour on that very question.

21

"Sorry to bother you, Doctor Brenner. These detectives are here about one of your clients. I assured them that we would cooperate in every way." That was big of him.

A tall woman with carrot-red hair was standing beside Ron, looking like she couldn't wait to get inside my office. A tall, dark, and handsome man stood behind her. I assumed he was her partner.

"Thank you, Doctor Margolis, I think I can handle it from here," I said, ushering the detectives into my office. Ron gave a nod and left. It dawned on me that he had expected to sit in on the interview. As if.

The woman spoke first.

"Doctor Brenner, I am Detective Rita Butler, chief investigator on the Janet Ford case. This is my partner, Detective Jay Manson."

I raised my eyebrows at the name.

"I know," he said. His voice was velvety deep. "And no, I am not related to Charles."

"You have better eyes." What a dumb thing to say.

He laughed. "Thanks."

My office had a couch and two comfortable chairs at one end, with my desk and two less comfortable chairs at the other. I led them over to the couch area so it wouldn't seem like a formal interview. And it didn't make sense to want my desk between me and Detective Manson.

Tearing my eyes away from the handsome detective, I addressed his partner, who seemed to be taking lead in no uncertain terms. "How can I help you, Detective Butler?"

Detective Manson was undoubtedly the sexiest man I had seen up close since college, though my vision was still a little blurry from weeping. He had deep brown eyes, short dark hair, and a body to die for. As I began to flush from the toes up, Detective Butler's eyes met mine. There was a twinkle that didn't fit my idea of a cop. I liked her already.

"We just have a few routine questions, Doctor, then we'll be out of your hair. You are the therapist working with Janet Ford, correct?"

"Yes. Janet was my patient."

"So you are aware that she's dead?"

"Just found out this morning." I sniffed.

"Word gets around fast."

I was beginning to realize that I wouldn't be able to talk about Janet for long without crying, not something I wanted to do in front of these detectives. Detective Butler seemed to sense this.

"Thank you for your time, Doctor," she said. "I know this is all quite sudden for you." I nodded and she continued. "It appears to be a homicide and we need to interview those who had contact with her recently. The deceased's mother told us that you were treating her daughter. For depression."

If Janet were alive I wouldn't even be allowed to admit that I was seeing her, and certainly not give details, unless she gave me permission in writing to talk to specific people. However, Janet was dead. I could talk now, but it didn't feel right.

"Not depression specifically, Detective," I answered. "I was treating Janet for Borderline Personality Disorder. One of her symptoms was depression. Mood swings were another."

"I see," Butler replied. "These mood swings, could they lead to risky behavior, poor lifestyle choices?"

"What does 'poor lifestyle choices' mean?" I didn't intend to sound snippy but that question came with large helping of judgment attached. Or was I being too emotional?

"I didn't mean it like that, Doctor. What I meant was, if Janet was prone to partying too much, hanging out with people that saw her as the heiress to a local fortune, not a real friend. That any clearer?"

"Yes. I see what you mean. When Janet first started her sessions with me, she told me that she liked to party. I took it to mean she had a group of drug-buddies she got high with. But that behavior seemed to stop once we established a good, working relationship. Getting high didn't fill the emptiness that comes with her condition. She also began taking a greater interest in her daughter, who was basically being raised by an army of nannies paid for by her grandmother."

"What about the depression? Do you think it could have come back suddenly? Given the circumstances, you may have been wrong, Doctor."

I felt myself stiffen. What did this policewoman know that made her so certain? "What circumstances, Detective? The paper said her body was found in Dolly Madison Park." Those alarm bells were starting to ring again.

"Yes, Janet Ford died beside the bandstand there. I can't get into specifics, but it looks like she was stabbed. So you see how we have to explore every possibility."

I felt sick as I imagined Janet's blood soaking into the ground by the bandstand. It was almost too overwhelming to contemplate. I couldn't help but think that her mysterious jogging partner must be involved somehow.

"Why didn't someone see anything? That area is well lit, isn't it?"

"Probably happened very early in the morning. We'll know more when we get the Medical Examiner's report back from Roanoke.

I'd forgotten that the closest state Medical Examiner was in Roanoke. This part of the Shenandoah Valley didn't have enough suspicious deaths to justify its own Medical Examiner. "When will that be, you think? The report."

"Probably later today or tomorrow. It comes when it comes." After they left, I sat my desk and cried some more. Then I began to think more clearly. *Was Janet killed? Or did she commit suicide? What part did I play in her death? Was it my fault? Did I make the wrong decision? Oh God.*

CHAPTER 6

THURSDAY, SEPTEMBER 19 EVENING

The next day at work the routine was, well, routine. I saw three patients before lunch and three after, with no surprises.

However, that evening there *was* a surprise.

I came home and Lucy was standing on our porch, just outside my front door. Something big and black was on the porch next to her.

Usually Lucy is very calm. Zen-like. Inside she's intuitive and sympathetic to the point that it sometimes gets her in trouble. She's almost perfect, if you don't think about her poor judgement about men and the eating disorder she struggles with. On the outside, she reminds me of Halle Berry. She's willowy with short curls and pale beige skin. Despite all that, today she was nervous.

"What *is* that thing?" I asked in horror.

"This is Sweetie." The huge, shiny dog-thing, which I now saw was a Great Dane, stood and turned its yellow eyes toward me. It didn't seem friendly.

"Hope you've got a good grip on that leash."

Clamping its teeth down on the plush mallard toy in its mouth, Sweetie growled.

I edged past to my door, hoping to get it unlocked before Sweetie decided to find out how I tasted.

"Well? What do you think of her? Isn't she neat?"

"Define 'neat.' And when did you decide to get a dog? What will Yew and Om think?" As if even Lucy knew what her spoiled, probably evil, Siamese cats actually thought.

"Oh, she's not mine." Lucy grinned. "She's yours."

"No way, no day," I replied, hoping that my definitive rejection wouldn't be ignored. The last thing I needed was a creature to take care of. I had enough trouble taking care of myself.

"Just listen—"

"No," I interjected, really meaning it. Lucy just kept smiling at me, but I was immune to that trick. We both used it all day long at work.

We're partners in a private practice group here in Fort Madison, near the center of the Shenandoah Valley. We share a wry sense of humor along with a weakness for fresh bagels, a rarity in Fort Madison.

Lucy owned a two-story duplex across from Starlight Park, and I'd moved into the apartment above hers. Our front doors share the same wide porch and its swing, wicker chair, and small table for our wine or Bloody Marys. We're best friends … except when she dumps an out-of-control dog on me. Why was she now burdening me with this big bundle of furry trouble?

Her smile still intact, Lucy turned and started up the stairs as soon as I got my shiny red door open. Pushing past her, Sweetie dragged her up the stairs into my living room. A dog like that could get you killed. I led a quiet calm life; I could do without a dangerous dog. Without a doubt, Sweetie was going back down those stairs when Lucy left. My friend could find some softhearted person to take her. It wasn't going to be me.

I was proud of my living room. The red Persian rug hugged the polished wood floors. The deep blue velvet of the sofa and the gold of my easy chair provided a counterpoint to the rug. Throw pillows with needlepoint designs pulled in the blues, reds, and gold around the room.

Sweetie looked very out of place. She was almost as big as my sofa.

"I've been volunteering at the SPCA. I was there yesterday evening. They were going to kill poor Sweetie because nobody would adopt her."

"No shit."

"Alice, all Sweetie needs is some professional help."

"I'm not a dog therapist. I work with people. They pay better."

Lucy's expression turned into a pleading one. "Please, Alice. I know Sweetie can be a good dog for you. Look at her. She needs love. And you need something to love. This Janet thing has rattled you. Loving a dog is a sure cure for that."

Sweetie pulled the leash out of Lucy's hand, ran across the room, squeezed behind the sofa, and flopped on the floor. It would have taken a tractor to pull her out.

"See. She feels safe here. You're just going to love her."

I shook my head. "She's an elephant."

"She's a purebred Great Dane," Lucy corrected. "She's a year old. She's been abused … only weighs eighty pounds."

"Meaning she'll get even bigger. That's not a selling point."

"She's spayed and house-trained. They promised."

"You have to take her back tomorrow. And as soon as I can get her from behind the sofa she goes down to your apartment."

"They'll kill her," Lucy reminded me darkly. "And it will be your fault, Alice Brenner."

"No it won't. I just don't want a dog."

"You told me you wanted a dog last weekend."

"That was the wine talking."

"Which is how I know you need a dog," Lucy replied. "And Sweetie needs a therapist. It's perfect."

CHAPTER 7

FRIDAY, SEPTEMBER 20 MORNING

I'd spent two years getting to know the patient who was in my office first thing on Friday morning. Short term therapy could get people through an immediate crisis, and sometimes that was all that was needed. But if the patient was dealing with a significant mental illness, such as chronic depression, or major issues like sexual identity, the therapy could take years.

Ben Asher was a thirty-two-year-old banker who came to me feeling depressed and with no hope for a happy outcome. He'd worked hard to get his depression under control and then began to examine what was and wasn't working in his life. Eventually he told me that he thought he might be gay. Whether he was gay and how to tell others about it topped the current issues we were working on in his therapy.

"Alice, I think I might have met someone," Ben announced as he settled onto the couch. He twisted the edge of his green T-shirt in his hands. His brown hair was tousled and dirty rather than the usual neatly groomed look. Even the T-shirt was different. He usually came straight from work in his dark suit and tie.

"Tell me about it." I wasn't sure whether the new someone was male or female. Ben hadn't fully accepted being gay. This might be a flight into normalcy to avoid the pain that can come with acceptance.

My room was sunny that morning. Sunlight polished my desk and coffee table, and brought a ruby glow out of the rug. I could almost hear my plants sucking up the light. A pretty place to discuss a painful reality.

"His name is Todd. He's in my spinning class at the Y. We got to talking after class and before I knew it we were having lunch or coffee almost every day. I … didn't want to tell you when it first started. Like it would jinx it."

"Did you think I would disapprove?" I inquired.

"Thought you might, sure. We're still talking about whether I'm really gay, so you might think this is too soon." His face was red and he wouldn't meet my gaze. His fingers continued to twist in his T-shirt.

Ben was projecting his feelings of wrongness onto me, making me the bad guy. That's part of what a therapist does. I sometimes represent the parts of my patients that they can't accept. Or I come to represent their parent or loved one. As in the case with Ben, this happens later in therapy after trust grows between me and my patient.

Sometimes this representation is so real that the patient feels towards me as they felt when a child with their parent or as an adult with a loved one. Thus they might rebel against me/parent or believe they are in love with me/loved one. That's called transference. Transference can be a useful tool to help the patient work through their issues.

If I should respond with anger/hurt in the case of the rebellion or with love/sexual attraction in the case of the love, that's called counter transference. And that's bad. Neither of us in that case is reacting to reality, but to the intense therapy experience. That's why it's unethical for therapists to treat family members or other people they interact with in their daily lives. Or to have sexual or other non-therapeutic relationships with their patients.

In small towns like Fort Madison, therapists sometimes encounter their patients outside their office. However, they are required to maintain confidentiality and boundaries of the therapy relationship. For example, I never acknowledge that I know a patient until my patient acknowledges me. I keep my distance or leave if I end up in a social setting with a patient. I explain all this to patients when we talk about the therapy relationship, but the burden is on me to maintain the boundaries of the therapy relationship. As the therapist, it's my job to keep the transference going in a safe environment so the patient can work through issues from their past that are interfering with their present lives. That's the magic of therapy. It's a mix of fantasy and a trusting, safe relationship with the therapist that allows growth to occur.

Ben wasn't aware of his transference that morning, but I was. It wasn't the right time to bring it up. Eventually, I would. But that day I said, "Ben, I think this is fine. You may have to experiment some with 'being gay' to know if it feels right to you." In fact, I had hoped that he would, but I didn't know if he had enough self-confidence to do it.

"Good. Because this does feel right. Todd and I have so many things in common. We both like to read and we both like biographies. We both have cats. And he's as into physical fitness as I am." He paused and looked up at me. "And, Alice, I feel so comfortable around him."

"You said before that you didn't know how you'd feel if another man put his hands on you. Has that happened? How was it?" Ben's father had only touched him when punishing him. He'd been isolated much of his adult life and wasn't used to physical contact. He thought that a man's caress might freak him out.

"We haven't had sex yet, but we've hugged and kissed. That's been fine. More than fine." He smiled at me and then went back to twisting his shirt.

"I'm glad to hear that. I'm also glad you're not rushing into sex." Ben appeared to be managing this well.

"Thank you, Alice. I really hope this works out. I feel so relaxed and comfortable with him. There's none of the tension I've always felt with women. Perhaps I really am gay." He blushed again.

"How would you feel about that?" This was what he'd come to discuss today.

"I'm not sure. I feel good about it when I'm with him. But sometimes, when I'm alone, I get panicked. Then I feel a twinge of depression. I just don't know how to think about that." His eyes bored into me.

"So you're still not sure about being gay?" Ben had never felt comfortable with women his whole life. He'd had multiple "crushes" on other boys growing up. I was convinced he was gay, but he wasn't. We'd discussed the pros and cons of being gay, whether he could choose to be gay, and how he imagined others would respond to him if he were. He continued to obsess about it. Eventually he would let himself accept that he was gay. But it didn't look like it was going to happen today.

"Yeah." He nodded. "I'm not sure and I want to be. But what if I'm not, even though I've started acting gay. What then? Can you take it back once you've declared yourself gay?"

I tried something new. "Maybe you're bisexual. Have you thought about that?"

In the quiet room, the sound of his ripping shirt was deafening. "My shirt."

"Looks like there's a lot of emotion behind your worries." I used my motherly voice.

"You think? I just can't let it go and let it be. I have to know in my mind and my heart. What if I say I'm gay and then discover I'm not? Change my mind, you know?" He was crying now.

I nudged the tissues across the coffee table. "You can always change your mind. You shape your reality by what you think. If you change your mind, you change your mind."

When Ben was learning how to manage his depression, he discovered that he could change his feelings by changing how he thought about things. I hoped he could use those skills in this situation.

"Yeah, that's right. But I'm not sure how I want to think about this." Squeezing his eyes shut, he rubbed them with his fists.

"Then it sounds like you need to just live with the question for a while." Eventually the discomfort of ambiguity would force a decision. I can't force patients to heal, just help them help themselves. Like the old therapy joke goes, the light bulb has to want to change.

CHAPTER 8

FRIDAY, SEPTEMBER 20 AFTERNOON

Detective Butler called me during my lunch break on Friday. I was expecting her to refer to Janet Ford's death, but instead she said, "Dr. Brenner, you do work at the Rescue Mission, correct?"

"If you're referring to a recent newspaper article, yes I volunteer there when I can. Is there a problem?"

"Not with the Mission, no, and I applaud your service, it's just that we have a man in custody—a suspect in the Janet Ford death—who won't talk to us."

A man from the Mission who wouldn't talk? I shivered, like I'd been doused with ice water. Of course I knew it could only be one person. We were newspaper buddies.

"And this man in custody, he's a serious suspect?"

"That's something we want to find out, but he won't talk to anyone except you. That's all he's saying that makes any sense. Mrs. Grimes from the Mission suggested you might be able to get him to open up. Said that he talks to you sometimes."

"There were several tight-lipped residents at the Mission, but I'm guessing you have Russ Logan. Won't sit on furniture."

"Is Russ Logan his real name? We can't tell for sure. And what's with the furniture?"

"You haven't heard? Chairs eat people. As for his name, Russ mentioned once he was a veteran. Maybe the VA knows."

Russ Logan was a psychotic black man who had befriended me at the Mission. Lately, he'd been dropping by my house with updates on the "agents" who constantly pursued him because of his special brain. Despite his psychosis, I felt I could trust him. We were becoming friends in a weird sort of way.

"So he's nuts." She laughed.

"Detective Butler, I'm glad we can both appreciate the potential for humor here. There's far too little of it in our respective jobs, I'm sure. So let me tell you that Russ Logan suffers from chronic schizophrenia. He has meds to control it, but clearly prefers not to. If he says he's seen something, it's likely to be a vivid hallucination. Do you understand me? He's afraid to talk to anyone in authority, especially if you've forced him to sit in one of those shark-chairs."

"Yeah, we noticed. We're letting him sit on the floor in the corner … at least for the time being. It won't be that way in jail."

"Jail? Not a psych ward?."

"Sane or psycho, he's our suspect in the Janet Ford murder."

"But Russ wouldn't do that!" How could I make her understand that beneath the craziness, there was a sweet man with a fine intelligence? I was sure he wasn't out of control enough to actually hurt someone.

"Doctor Brenner, I'm not calling to debate what Mr. Logan might or might not be capable of. We need help talking to him. If there's some rational explanation, your expertise can help find out what that might be. Will you help?"

If Russ were a therapy patient, I wouldn't have hesitated. Our communication would be privileged—in the office or in the police station. But Russ wasn't a patient, he was a friend. One in deep trouble, deeper than he probably realized. Did trying to make a homeless man's life a bit easier constitute a 'therapy relationship'? That was a debate I didn't think I'd win, at least not right now. And where did translating Russ's unique communication style for the police's benefit fit in? I could be "helping" Russ right into a cell for the rest of his life. But if he was involved in Janet's death, didn't I want to find out? For her sake, no matter what?

"Doctor?" Detective Butler interrupted my thoughts. "Are you going to help us?"

I let out the breath I hadn't been aware I was holding. "Okay. Sure."

Already I was regretting this.

CHAPTER 9

FRIDAY, SEPTEMBER 20 LATE AFTERNOON

By the time I got off the elevator in the basement of the Fort Madison Police Department, the humid air had turned my silk tunic into a limp rag. The back of my neck prickled with sticky moisture. The air smelled like sweat and industrial cleaner; it was almost too thick to breathe. Down the hall a phone was ringing. I walked toward the sound and found a large, windowless office with four desks and three people. A tall man in shirtsleeves answered the phone, then hung it up with a bang. The others ignored him and me. Nobody responded to my knock on the office door.

Detective Rita Butler sat at the desk opposite the door. Her denim jacket hung on the chair behind her, providing a blue backdrop for her carrot-red cloud of hair. Turquoise earrings and a silver pendent framed a face awash with pale freckles.

Despite the sweat sliding down the side of her face, the detective looked cool and relaxed. She was laughing at something, then winked at Detective Manson sitting beside her. An exaggerated wink, like a Victorian barmaid.

Detective Butler finally noticed me by the door. "Dr. Brenner. Nice of you to drop by." Like I had just wandered in by accident after dropping off dry cleaning.

Everyone seemed to expect Rita to handle the office greetings. If I hadn't known better, I might have thought she was their receptionist. Was Detective-Secretary a thing? I wondered how she felt about being put in that role.

"Come on in and let's talk a bit," she said, indicating a chair beside her and Detective Manson. The other detective returned to his previous activity, which seemed to involve studying his computer screen.

I sat down and was relieved to find that Detective Manson was just as handsome as I'd remembered. Not that I'd Googled the man or anything. Not me. Tamping down certain feelings, which were no doubt a product of the humid atmosphere of raw justice-seeking, I tore my eyes away from Detective Butler's partner and focused on her. "You called for a Russ-whisperer?"

Butler chuckled and Jay gave an amused snort. So far so good.

"That's right," Rita Butler replied. "We don't need a psychological profile or any therapy—just a translator. Hope that doesn't insult you." Her smile could have graced any movie star. I remembered all the movies and television shows I'd seen with a cop and a civilian partner. I wondered if we might have the beginnings of a partnership here.

Just in case, I smiled back.

I was tingling each time her silent partner inhaled and his muscles filled out his shirt. Very unprofessional. I'd have to talk to myself about that, later tonight … maybe. Taking a breath, I prepared to sound professional—but right as I was about to talk, a balding, middle-aged man in a gray suit walked into the den of detectives. He smiled at the room like he owned it. "Hello, everybody," he announced, then walked over to join us. "We ready to interview the suspect?"

"Not quite yet, Mr. Delany." Detective Butler turned to me. "Dr. Brenner, this is Tom Delany, our District Attorney. He's taken a personal interest in this case."

I suspected that this was Rita Butler's way of telling me that because Janet's mother was from one of Fort Madison's most prominent families, the District Attorney had been instructed by the mayor to get his "personal interest" up and running in short order.

"It's a pleasure, Mr. Delany. I recognize you from the news. You look even better in person." Jeez, I'd almost said "in prison." Talk about letting your Freudian slip show.

Mr. Delany laughed, very professionally. "Are we all ready, then?"

"I'm eager to help in any way I can," I jumped in. "However, I do have some requests." All three looked at me like I was a talking dog. I barreled on. "To have a conversation with Russ, I often have to sit on the floor with him. To get him comfortable. And he doesn't respond well to anger or aggression, so I'd like to keep it as friendly and low key as we can. He probably doesn't fully realize what is happening or how serious it is." I felt pedantic stating the obvious like that, but it had to be said.

"Of course, Doctor Brenner," Butler answered. "We all want a positive interview, but you need to know that your friend was covered with blood and had a bloody knife in his possession. Ms. Ford's body was laying beside the bandstand and looked like it had been moved. But there was enough blood at the scene that it looks like she was killed where we found her. The lab work isn't finished, but it'll be the victim's blood on your friend's clothing and the murder weapon, we're sure." At least she tried to appear sympathetic. DA Delany, not so much.

"So don't expect to get him off," the District Attorney advised me. "Russ Logan is guilty."

"Has he been arrested? Shouldn't there be a lawyer present?"

"He hasn't asked for one, and he hasn't been arrested," Delany practically growled. "If he is, he'll get one, don't worry. And this isn't Mr. Logan's first rodeo, Dr. Brenner. He's been cited before regarding his activities in that park." Wow. *That* was quite a switch in mood. I wasn't sure what to make of it.

I let his statement hang in the thick, sticky air as I considered if I should come back with a lawyer in tow. Except at the moment I wasn't on speaking terms with the only one I knew. That was a long, messy story. *Damn.* Was I being hopelessly naïve about this? It certainly was *my* first rodeo.

"I said I'd help Detective Butler communicate with Russ, and I will. But even if he is involved in Janet Ford's death somehow, the only thing he's 'guilty' of is having a debilitating mental illness. There are other people that would be more likely to hurt Janet. Her ex-husband, Bill, threatened her more than once and she was afraid of him. In addition she had a new boyfriend that she argued with. Why aren't you questioning them. Why this focus on Russ?"

Strong words, but all afternoon I'd been debating if Russ could have harmed Janet. Everything I knew about him, and my gut instincts, said no. But was it possible? I had to admit that under the right conditions, maybe so. I totally couldn't rule it out. But that didn't make Russ "guilty."

I knew I had to find out.

"I'll leave the three of you to it," Detective Manson said, adroitly breaking the awkward moment. "I'll go see about getting the autopsy speeded up."

While I stared at him like a lovesick thirteen-year-old, Detective Butler just said, "Okay," and turned away.

Could his spell wear off over time? I wondered. I wasn't sure I wanted to find out.

I stood watching Detective Butler pull on her denim jacket. Her face remained calm, but now there was a solid, determined line instead of a smile. No more twinkle in her eyes. Her body was tense with anticipation. She wasn't comfortable to be with anymore. Now she was a cop. Hardcore murder police.

"Let's go get a confession," the detective said to me and Delany. He nodded, and gave me a look I didn't need my PhD to interpret. Their agenda was crystal clear.

I had a bad-going-on-worse feeling about this.

*   *   *

Russ was sitting on the floor of the interrogation room when we opened the door. His weathered brown hands were stained with what might be blood. He looked older than his fifty some years. The tattered gray raincoat that he always wore was missing. He probably felt naked. He stood and reached toward me.

"Doctor Alice! Make them leave me alone. I want to go back to the shelter. They're mean here." Tears had left dirty smudges on his cheeks; his eyes were still red.

"It's okay, Russ. We'll get this straightened out. That's why I'm here." Seeing him like this, I felt like crying, too.

Detective Butler glared at both of us. "Sit down, Mr. Logan. I have questions for you."

"No! No more questions. Doctor Alice will take me home." Russ dropped to the floor.

I sat down more carefully. I couldn't help but notice the spit stains and ground-in gum beside my leg. *Good thing I have on my dark jeans today.* Russ didn't seem to notice the District Attorney standing in the room, his back to the wall. There was a large mirror on the far wall, which if my TV viewing was at all accurate, meant this interview was being recorded. I chided myself for not making sure earlier.

"You're not going anywhere, Mr. Logan," said the District Attorney. "Not until we get some answers."

Russ's eyes darted around the claustrophobic space. Another tear worked its way down his face. The man was a paranoid schizophrenic. Thought disorder and distrust—a real one-two punch of psychosis. Not likely that he'd ever be able to answer questions the way this horror show was going.

"Why were your fingerprints on Janet Ford's shoes, Mr. Logan? Why did you have the knife that killed her?"

Staring at the floor, Russ began to rock back and forth.

I couldn't let this go on. "Russ, did you see the dead lady in the park?"

He looked at me. "Yeah. I was hiding. From the agents."

"Can you tell me what happened?"

"She was laying there asleep. I snuck up, but she didn't wake up. So I thought she was drunk. Until I stepped in the blood. I ... I needed them, you see."

"Needed what, Russ?"

"Shoes. I needed shoes and hers were pretty with red and black on them."

"So what did you do?" I bet I knew.

"I took 'em." His eyes were focused right on me. "Then, when I tried to put 'em on, they wouldn't go on."

"Oh, give me a break," Butler injected. "She was a small woman. You're a big man. You knew her shoes wouldn't fit you." She appeared disgusted, maybe sick. I was having trouble seeing this angry cop as the woman I'd been laughing with just a few minutes before. Her rage seemed genuine, not just a tough cop act. Why was she so upset?

"No," Russ continued. "I wanted them and she didn't wake up. She was bloody and I knew if I took 'em she wouldn't care."

"So, Russ, what happened next?" I asked.

"I dropped the shoes and looked to see what else was there."

"Was there? What did you take?"

"Five dollar bills and the knife. I could sell the knife, I figured."

"Looting a dead woman didn't bother you?" asked Butler. "Why did you kill her?"

If I didn't know better, I'd think Detective Butler was smirking.

"No, no! I didn't! I didn't even know she was dead at first. Then I knew."

"Knew she was dead?"

"Yeah. By the agent that was lurking around the bandstand. I knew I should run 'cause more agents could still be around and then they'd catch me."

"What agents? Her body wasn't called in until dawn." Butler looked at me instead of Russ. I didn't know if that was a good sign or bad. Delany remained silent, trying to be inscrutable, but his body language was closing up. He wasn't happy.

Whatever. I needed to jump in. "Russ, tell me about the agents. What did they have to do with it?"

"You know, the Company agents. They wear black and have computer chips in their heads and super human strength. They killed that lady, but it's my fault."

Butler grinned. Delany perked up considerably.

"How is it your fault, Russ?" I asked, anticipating his answer. This was sounding like his usual delusions, reinforced by a very real tragedy.

"They were after me, not her. The lady must have gotten in the way. They want my brain. She just had a regular human brain. She just had red blood."

Butler took over, a very unladylike expression on her face. "Did you see the lady get killed?" she asked.

I could feel her tension. She really wanted Russ to be guilty, like the DA had said. As the lead investigator, she must be under a lot of pressure to get the case wrapped up, the quicker the better. I almost felt sorry for her.

"No," answered Russ, though he was looking at me. "The lady was cold when I got there. I took a nap at the shelter. I couldn't get the pillow I wanted. Having the right pillow is very important to the way your brain works. Would you believe the people at the shelter didn't even care? I have to take good care of my brain. It's special."

Slumping in her seat, Butler glanced at me. Delany was giving Butler some kind of city hall death stare. "Ask him why he didn't tell anybody," Butler instructed. Didn't even say *please*.

"I can hear her," Russ stated loudly. He was looking at me with that intense gaze he sometimes got. I didn't know how much longer he'd last.

Detective Butler's cheeks had turned an unbecoming shade of red. "Just answer the question, Mister Logan!"

Russ looked toward Butler for the first time. Adopting the tone most people use with small children, he patiently explained, "I can't use the phone. The Company would know where I am. So I told Betty at the shelter this morning during breakfast."

"Mrs. Grimes called us at eight o'clock," Butler confirmed, nodding at the file on the table. "Said he showed up covered in blood." She seemed more comfortable talking with me.

"The old 'she was already dead when I got there' story," Delany muttered. "How I love the classics."

I looked back to Russ. "How did the lady's blood get on you? Do you remember?"

"Do you know that they took my coat? I want it back … even if it does have the lady's blood on it. Maybe red blood will scare the agents. It might."

"Please answer my question. Don't worry about the coat right now."

"Oh. Okay. I hugged her. To tell her it was going to be all right. That she'd like it in Heaven."

With that Detective Butler abruptly left, leaving me staring at Russ. The District Attorney motioned for me to follow.

"Where are you going, Doctor Alice?" asked Russ, his voice rising. "I want my coat back."

Back in the detectives' bullpen, Detective Butler's face was still red, but she seemed to have calmed down.

Mr. Delany looked grim. "So, Detective Butler, do you have a Temporary Detention Order on him? Obviously, the poor man is crazy. Needs meds, whether he wants them or not."

"Yes. He'll be taken to Fort Madison General's psych ward. Standard seventy-two-hour hold. They'll medicate him till he's lucid enough to be put in jail."

"Jail? But he told you what happened," I said. If there'd been a soap box handy I would have jumped on it. "He doesn't need to go to jail. Can't you keep him in the psych ward? Punishing the man for his mental problems isn't going to make him get any better, or solve your case."

They both stared at me like I could use a stay at the psych ward, as well.

"Thank you for your time, Doctor Brenner," said District Attorney Delany, his political persona in full force. "Detective Butler, we'll be speaking later." Then he turned and left.

A few moments later, I did, too. Exhausted, and desperate for a shower. And a tall glass of wine.

CHAPTER 10

SATURDAY, SEPTEMBER 21
AFTERNOON

The next afternoon I called Detective Butler and reminded her that Russ needed to be in a psych hospital, not in jail. She wasn't interested. I was left feeling frustrated and depressed. That evening, Lucy and I had dinner together at her apartment. Later we sat on the front porch sipping the last of our wine. Sweetie joined us and curled up by the steps. I'd tied her leash to the railing to keep her on the porch. It was a clear, quiet night.

Lucy was in one of her pensive moods, rocking in the porch swing and staring out into the dark park. "Do you bring your patients home with you, too?"

"You mean, do I still? God yes, more than ever, probably."

"Who's at the top of your playlist this week?"

"I've got two patients and one semi-friend in heavy rotation. One is the man with schizophrenia I've befriended at the Mission. The police are holding him in jail when he needs treatment. Then there are a gay man getting ready to come out, and my client Janet, who died in the park." I gazed out into the night. Sweetie wagged her tail.

"I think about her, too," Lucy said.

"Who?" My voice seemed to echo in the still air.

"Janet."

"Why? What do you mean 'think about her'? In what way? Did you know her too? I don't think we've talked about her" I shifted in my seat, trying to get comfortable. But I felt uncomfortable. I didn't think I'd consulted with Lucy or anyone else at work about Janet. So why would she be thinking about her?

"No. The death. It's not normal for one of our patients to go that way when they're getting help." Lucy seemed so serene and comfy. I wished I could feel that way.

"That's true."

"I knew you were thinking about her." She smiled.

"How can I not? All the time I'm wondering if I could've done anything different. Could I have stopped her? What did I miss?" Sudden pains in my stomach made me flinch.

"You only saw her twelve times. That's not long. And don't play the *What If?* game; there's no way to win."

"I know. But what if …" My attempt at light humor was almost obliterated by the roar of a motorcycle passing bye.

"Have you thought about drugs?" Lucy didn't even seem to hear the noise from the street.

I just stared at her. I had to drag my attention from the motorcycle to Lucy.

"With Janet, I mean," Lucy clarified.

"Street drugs?"

"Any kind. You mentioned that she partied a lot. Could she have been on drugs, in a disinhibited state? Something like that could have been enough to turn a bad thought into a grim reality."

"I've thought of that. You're right, it could have happened." I admitted. I felt stupid.

"The Medical Examiner tests for drugs, I guess." Lucy seemed so calm.

"Yeah. Probably. I think … I think I'd feel better about it if that was the case." I felt warm even though the night was cool.

"Have you talked with Collier about this?"

"No." I could feel my cheeks grow warm. Collier James was my sometimes boyfriend.

"And why not?" Lucy was giving me that look she uses to get her patients motivated.

"It's complicated. You know that we're off and on all the time. We're off as much as we're on."

"Why is that? He's a catch. Handsome, funny, smart, and a lawyer. Most women would grab on tight. Why don't you?"

"I want to love him, but I don't. There's no chemistry."

"Poor sex life?"

"No." Now my cheeks were on fire. "It's good, but it's not special."

"I don't understand." She frowned.

"I don't feel any romance, no tingle. It's just flat. Our relationship is one of convenience. It's nice to have someone to go out with and to have sex with, but it's not love. We don't share important feelings or thoughts. That bothers both of us, I think. So one or the other ends it, then we get lonely and get back together."

"So you didn't talk to Collier about Janet's call and death, because. . ."

"It just never occurred to me to tell him." That made me feel sad. And lonely.

CHAPTER 11

WEDNESDAY, SEPTEMBER 25 MORNING

A few days later at work I was still tired from worrying about Russ. I didn't know what would happen to him in jail.

My phone interrupted this depressing train of thought. It was Mrs. Grimes, the Mission administrator.

"They pumped Russ full of meds and let him go after his psychosis cleared," she informed me. That was good news, at least.

"Were you able to give him an alibi?"

"Yes, thank God. He got to the Mission about nine that night, then left about four the next morning. Threw a real fit about a special pillow. Everybody remembered his stay with us very clearly."

"When do they think Janet was killed?" I asked.

"I overheard someone tell the lady detective that she was killed between midnight and two. Russ was over here sleeping off his pillow fight, you might say. So they let him go. Told him not to leave town. Like he would."

"That's really good news," I replied. "I didn't think Russ could have done it, but nothing I said did any good. The detective was determined to arrest him for the murder. I think she was being pressured."

"Yes, Mrs. Whitmire can be quite a force of nature, I'm told," Mrs. Grimes remarked. "But the Whitmire Foundation has contributed generously to the Mission over the years. It must have been trying for her when it looked like one of ours had killed her daughter."

"Well then, I'm really glad he decided to sleep here that night. Once again the Mission has come to the rescue."

Mrs. Grimes was laughing as she hung up.

* * *

My next patient of the day was a new one, a Mr. Louis Baldwin. He was a forty-five-year-old African-American man who complained of being depressed. When he called to make the appointment, he told Georgia that he'd been feeling depressed lately and didn't want it "to get any worse." I found him positioned against the back wall of the waiting room; sitting straight up with perfect posture, checking his watch even though I wasn't late.

"Mr. Baldwin?" I asked

There was a pause. "Yes?"

"Hi, I'm Doctor Brenner. Would you come with me, please?"

He followed me to my office. Once inside, he sat carefully on my sofa, then looked directly at me.

"Louis, what brings you here?" I asked. I usually start off with that. New patients often don't know what to do once they're in to see me.

"Didn't the receptionist tell you? I'm depressed. Can't get anything done anymore. I just want to sit. I'm sad all the time." His eyes challenged me.

"Interfering with your work, then?"

"Yes, that's it. I can't seem to do as much as I used to."

He appeared to be falling into the routine of answering my questions. Hopefully, that meant he was feeling more comfortable.

"How do you feel most of the time?" I prompted.

"Oh, I'm mostly sad." His eyes didn't look sad.

"Do you cry?"

"No. I was taught not to. It's not the thing for a man to cry."

This didn't surprise me. We sat there in silence a moment as he stared at me. My move, apparently.

Eventually I asked, "Louis, have you ever had thoughts of hurting yourself?"

"Yes." No hesitation.

"What kind of thoughts?"

"I think I'd be better off dead. Not that I'd ever do anything. My religion doesn't allow it." He gave me a cold stare.

"Good. I'm glad you wouldn't hurt yourself. Can you promise me that?"

"What?"

"That you won't hurt yourself," I answered.

"Yes, sure," he replied. "Why?"

"Part of my job is to help you keep you safe. I have to know that you'll be okay."

"Don't worry, Doctor Brenner. I'll be okay." He looked embarrassed, and a little irritated. "I told you my religion won't allow suicide."

"What religion is that?"

"Catholic."

"You attend mass weekly?"

"Yes." His eyes dared me to laugh.

"You came here to get help. I'm here to help you."

"Yes?" His voice was doubtful.

"And you can get help for this." I smiled. "Your life will get better."

"How?" He seemed almost belligerent. Like Janet had been.

"We'll both work hard to make you less depressed, and I'll teach you how to cope with the stress you have." I often said this to depressed patients. It was an easy-to-understand way to explain what therapy would be like.

"That sounds good."

The entire session went that way. Louis said little and the way he expressed himself contradicted what he said. I was getting more and more frustrated. Mr. Louis Baldwin wasn't going to be easy to help.

Finally I said, "Okay," and smiled at Louis. "How are you feeling now?"

"A little better." He sounded disappointed.

"Don't expect this condition to go away overnight," I said, "it's not like pulling a bad tooth. It probably took you a while to get depressed, and it will take time to get better. Today was a good start."

He returned to the cold stare. "Okay."

"I want to see you again next week." I glanced at my appointment book. "How about ten o'clock on Wednesday?"

"Sure," he said, sounding relieved.

That evening, as we took our walk, I told Sweetie about Louis Baldwin. "I didn't get the feeling he was depressed, even though he said all the right things. Something is going on, but it didn't seem like classic depression. Another mystery, eh, Sweetie?"

Sweetie wasn't impressed. I hadn't been able to figure her out at first, either. Not that I'd figured her out. Maybe I just wasn't good at figuring anyone out. *Some therapist you are, Alice.*

CHAPTER 12

WEDNESDAY, OCTOBER 2
EVENING

Janet Ford's death occupied my mind whenever I wasn't seeing patients. I just knew it wasn't a suicide and, from the rumors going around town, the Medical Examiner's report backed me up. But who could have hated her enough to kill her? And why stab her? Poor Janet didn't deserve it. Dying in the park. I teared up every time I thought about it.

I was intently contemplating these matters of life and death while I walked through the rain to my car Wednesday evening. And for the second time that day, I stepped in a puddle. Only this was a deep one. I felt my ankle turn. Pain scorched up my leg. I dropped my bag and fell right on my head. I thought I heard my head crack open and was about ready to go full panic mode when— "Oh my God! Alice, are you okay?" It was Georgia, bringing me back to reality. "Don't move. This looks serious." It certainly felt serious. I was so glad she was there I almost started crying.

For some reason I couldn't seem to get myself up; I just kept flopping around. With Georgia's help I got turned around and sitting in the parking lot, my legs straight out in front of me. My left leg throbbed, my head felt like someone had hit me with an anvil, and my butt was wet from the watery pavement. Was the universe trying to send me a message?

"I just want to go home," I whined. "I'm fine." I am a bad liar.

"No way, Doctor Brenner," Georgia assured me. While she dialed 911, she told me to sit there and chill out. Didn't sound so bad, the way she put it.

Soon there was an ambulance from the fire station down the street. The fire truck came along for the ride. I felt like an interesting exhibit at the zoo.

"It might be broken, miss. And we can't fool around with possible head injuries," the EMT said. "We're going to transport you to the hospital. Make sure you're okay."

"Oh, no," I wailed. "I have a dog at home."

"Oh, yes," Georgia declared. "I'll let Lucy know."

Things got blurry after that. I remember the ER. Lots of white coats and people rushing around. Eventually I came to focus on a handsome balding man in a white coat. Happily, I realized he was talking to me. He seemed to be about my age and was saying some doctor type stuff.

"You need a CT of both your head and ankle," he was saying, "but it looks like you'll be okay, Miss Brenner." *He knows my name!* "You have a sprained ankle and a mild concussion. Nothing major." The talking doctor smiled with twinkling blue eyes. "I'm sure your ankle and head hurt, but it doesn't appear to be serious. You'll probably be able to go dancing this weekend."

"Break dancing?" I couldn't resist.

He laughed, then looked wistful.

I wouldn't mind going dancing with you, I thought. Then before I could stop myself I blurted, "Why, Doctor, are you asking me out?"

We both blushed at the same time. "Um. No, but I was wishing that I had the nerve to get to know you better when you're not concussed and on pain meds. Guess it showed. Maybe when you're better, and if you want to, you could call me here. My name's Stan Wilson. Here's my card. It's got my phone number."

I felt flushed all over. I'd heard there was a new single doctor working at the hospital, but I hadn't even thought about dating since I'd been seeing Collier. Now Collier and I had broken up. Again. I guess we broke up. I wasn't sure. Maybe we weren't. But this doctor was really attractive and …

"Yes," I surprised myself by answering. I wondered if concussions made people bold. I thought that would make a good excuse when Lucy yelled at me for doing this. "Yes. I'd like to get to know you,"

We both smiled again and he left, saying he'd be back later. An orderly came to take me for my CT. Then I waited. And waited.

Two hours later Stan Wilson came back. "Hi, Alice. I was right. Only an ankle sprain and a mild concussion. You can use crutches if you want, but it's fine if you prefer not to. Just don't do anything that hurts. Expect your headache to last a few days. There shouldn't be any permanent damage. Maybe some minor memory loss. Take ibuprofen for your pain. I can prescribe an industrial strength version if you need them. And stay home while it hurts."

He looked sheepish. "Do you still want to get to know me? I won't hold you to it."

I could feel myself blush again. "Oh, I do want to call you, Stan." *Even if it does make me feel like a teenager.*

I am thirty-six with a PhD, I reminded myself. Too old to feel this way.

I called Lucy to ask her to come pick me up when she was free. She was already on her way.

CHAPTER 13

THURSDAY, OCTOBER 3 EVENING

On Thursday evening, as we often did, Lucy and I got together in her living room, usually enjoying a few cocktails or some nice wine while watching the local news. This particular evening, Lucy was more interested in getting information on my budding friendship with Stan than in watching television. I thought it was ridiculous, since Stan and I had only talked once since meeting in the emergency room.

"What kind of person is he?" She asked

"He's nice. funny, and really devoted to his job."

On the screen Sue Turner, the Channel 3 star reporter, was standing in front of the Fort Madison Police Department building.

"Look at that, Lucy. Sue Turner has a new haircut. Looks nice"

"Shush! Don't you want to hear this?" Lucy waved at me.

"It has just been revealed that the Fort Madison police called in a local psychologist to help them interview a person of interest in the Janet Ford case."

Lucy choked on her Bloody Mary. "Alice! She's talking about you."

"If she doesn't mention my name, maybe Ron won't freak out."

"A police spokesperson would neither confirm or deny the participation of psychologist, Dr. Alice Brenner. However, sources tell me that the person of interest, a Russell Logan, was taken from the police department and admitted to Fort Madison General's psych ward. In an interesting twist, Dr. Brenner has not only worked with Mr. Logan at the Rescue Mission …" Now the screen was filled with the picture of me with Russ at the Mission that ran in the newspaper. "… but she was also treating the murder victim, Janet Ford." Now they showed a formal portrait photo of Janet that I had never seen before. "Perhaps they needed a psychologist to determine the need for treatment." Was she insinuating something? Why did I feel so uneasy?

Turner flashed a smile, wrapping up her remote report. "Police are still looking for a homeless man, Jim Summers, said to have left town. They believe he may be able to shed some light on what happened to Ms. Ford. More tomorrow in our morning show."

I was stunned. I realized I'd been naively expecting my small contribution to the wheels of justice to go unnoticed.

"Wow!" Lucy giggled. She was almost through with her drink.

"Yeah. I don't like that. Psychologists shouldn't appear on the news in a criminal case … it's bad for business."

Lucy headed into the kitchen. "The only thing to do about that is to have another drink, and maybe some pita chips. You'll be fine. The police don't usually go after white women."

Her remark unsettled me. Mostly Lucy and I ignored the whole race thing. We related as young professional women. Sometimes I even forgot she was black. Apparently, she didn't.

Nonetheless, the three of us—Lucy, Sweetie, and me—had a nice evening. Us humans had two more drinks. Sweetie didn't have any, being our designated driver, or rather, walker. Taking her out to do her business at the end of the evening proved to be kind of unsteady, so we each held on to Sweetie's back. She was a good sport about it.

Hours later I woke up in the middle of the night. My heart was pounding, Sue Turner's words were replaying in my mind. What had she meant, linking me with Russ and Janet? It bothered me. I wasn't sure why.

*   *   *

Stan and I agreed that for a first meeting coffee sounded right. The next afternoon, I met him at the Beanery down by the old train station. It was a basement coffee shop known for it's baked goods. I'd been craving one of their cheese Danishes for weeks, so I was excited to be there for two reasons.

My shoes *thunked* on the shiny wood floors. Stan stood until I was seated. *Nice.*

Somehow, I felt very comfortable around him. Maybe because he'd seen me with my clothes off already (in a hospital gown). Or maybe it was his sweet manner.

After we ordered, the serious talking began.

"Um, Alice, you seem a little distracted. You all right?"

"Yes. I'm fine. But you're right, I am a little distracted. One of my patients turned up dead a couple of weeks ago."

"You don't mean Janet Ford, do you? She was your patient?"

"Don't you watch the news? Yes, she most certainly was."

"I saw her mother on the TV news last night offering a $50,000 reward for information that led to a conviction of her daughter's killer."

"I saw that, too. I wonder if it will help the police or just bog them down with lots of eager people with useless information."

"I don't know, Alice. But I knew Janet Ford, too. Sewed her up once in the ER after she'd cut herself. Couldn't she have just as easily killed herself by accident? Maybe she tried to force someone to rescue her."

"It's possible, I guess," I replied. "But if that's the case, why didn't that person rescue her? If they could have and chose not to, isn't that almost the same as murder? Criminal disregard or something? I don't know the term, but I'm sure it's something. You're not supposed to just let people die." I paused to take another bite of my luscious danish. Stan tried to hide his smile. We were being serious, after all. "But, Stan, I did want to ask you about Janet Ford. Can you tell me much about attending her?"

He studied the blue-checked tablecloth. "Yeah. I guess confidentiality doesn't apply now that she's dead. The first time I saw her was over a year ago and I just remember that she'd cut her arm with a razor blade. Two of the cuts required stitches and the rest were scratches. The last time was a month or two ago. I stitched four of the cuts that time."

I remembered the bandages on her arm. We'd had an emotional talk about her cutting.

"Remember anything she said? How she was acting?"

"Not really. It was early on a day when I was on call. She was dressed for running and so was her friend. But I can't remember anything she said. The friend did seem familiar, but I couldn't place her."

Janet hadn't told me anyone was with her at the hospital.

"Think. Was there anything else?"

"Just that I thought they were two beautiful ladies. I didn't see anyone as pretty in my ER until you came in."

He made a reach for my hand, but I pulled it back. It seemed too soon for us to hold hands.

"Two ladies?" I mumbled as I took a bite of pastry. God, it really was delicious.

"Yeah. I think the cutting incident happened before they actually ran."

"Did you tell the police?"

"You know I don't report people for injuring themselves. We're only required to report gunshot wounds."

"I mean after Janet died. Her jogging buddy might be a lead on her boyfriend. She must know something. And the ER has security cameras, I saw them. Have the cops take a look."

"I never thought of it like that. Think I should tell them?"

"Yes, I do. Please, Stan, call them. Detective Rita Butler is in charge of the case. Tell her what you know."

"I'll call when I get back in the car. Now, can we talk about you?"

"Okay. I guess we've been serious enough for today." I smiled and looked into his eyes. "How'd you end up in Fort Madison?"

"The job."

"Same here. I came for a position at the state hospital in Staunton years ago, discovered Fort Madison, and fell in love with the place. Never thought I would like a small town so much. I grew up outside a big city."

"As did I," Stan said. "I grew up outside of Chicago. Where'd you spend your youth?"

"In the Baltimore suburbs."

We both smiled.

"How did you become a psychologist?"

"The way most psychologists do," I replied. "Trying to fix my family."

"Is that possible?"

"In theory. My father was never around and my mother was an alcoholic. I tried to do something about it." *How could I be telling him this on a first date? Jeez!* He seemed to make it so easy to trust him. He'd probably have made a great therapist.

"How did you get to be a doctor?" I asked.

"Oh, that's easy. My father is a doctor. A family practice doc. I always knew I'd be a doctor. My immediate passion for emergency medicine surprised us all. I'm pretty sure my dad thought I'd take over his practice. Now it looks like my little brother will."

"Three doctors in the family?"

"Yes. I have two brothers. The middle one is a writer."

"Oh, so you're an eldest child, too," I said.

"Yes. We tend to want to control things, don't we?"

"Not always. Sometimes we like to let someone else control for a while." We both laughed. "This was a good idea, Stan," I said. "I haven't been here for some time."

"I like the ambience," he stated.

I glanced around the dim room at candles flickering and the flowers on each table. Romantic and trendy.

"And I like the company," I said, trying not to be too flirty.

He took my hand in his. "I do, too."

"That's a little thick, Stan." I took my hand back.

"I hope I didn't embarrass you."

"No permanent damage," I reported. I studied the orange flower at our table. I didn't know what kind it was, but it made me happy.

We both laughed.

This time, when he grabbed my hand, I let him.

The next evening Lucy and I were sitting in my living room. I was curled up on the sofa and she had the wing chair and ottoman. We'd shared dinner and were finishing off the dinner wine. I was a little tipsy. I'd taken a thirty-minute break when Stan called. Now that I was back, Lucy was curious.

"What's Stan like?" Lucy asked.

"He's a second-generation doctor from Chicago. And he's a really nice guy," I answered.

"Great. And?"

"He plays guitar and saxophone, mostly blues music, when he has time. Big into what he calls 'the classic Chicago sound,' of course." Though Willie Nelson was my favorite music artist, I could relate to a good blues band any day of the week. I was looking forward to having Stan teach me more about it.

"Is there chemistry?"

"A little. Some maybe."

Lucy seemed disappointed.

"I'm kidding," I laughed. "There's more chemistry than I've felt in a long time."

CHAPTER 14

MONDAY, OCTOBER 7 AFTERNOON

On Monday Stan called again. "I've been thinking about you," he said.

"Me, too," I replied.

"Good. Would you be interested in having dinner next week? I can't this week. We're short staffed and I'm working double shifts ."

"I'd love to." I hoped my voice didn't betray the idiotic smile on my face.

"Super. Let's aim for dinner on Saturday. I'll pick you up at seven-thirty. "

He just said "super." That was so cute.

"Alice," he said, becoming more serious. "Are you feeling better about your patient who died?"

"Yes, but I'm still wondering if there was anything I could have done."

"I knew Janet Ford, too. She was difficult to help. You did what you could."

A few minutes later, after we said our good-byes and hung up the phone, Sweetie jumped on my lap. She had become much more affectionate over the last weeks. Especially after I gave in and admitted that I was going to keep her. She had a way of looking at you that was so soft. I thought she might love me. You couldn't send someone who loved you off to be executed. Besides, Sweetie was a really good listener.

She'd just started to lick my face, when I heard Lucy calling my name and pounding on the door. By the time I dumped Sweetie off me and got to her, Lucy was yelling.

"What?" I didn't really feel like talking to anybody.

"Open this door right now. We've got to talk!"

I clumped down the stairs to let her in. Reluctant or not, you couldn't shut out your best friend.

Once we were seated in the living room, Lucy shoved a newspaper in my face and asked, "Have you seen this?"

"I have a feeling I'm going to."

"Laugh while you can. Look!" She held up an article at the bottom of the front page.

The black print blurred as I read:

Local psychologist blamed for Ford murder! Mrs. Doris Whitmire told reporters today that her daughter, Janet Ford, would not be dead if her therapist, Dr. Alice Brenner, had provided competent treatment. Mrs. Whitmire will be reporting Dr. Brenner to the state licensing board. "I don't want this woman's incompetence to endanger other patients," Mrs. Whitmire said. Her lawyer, Collier James of Black, Wiley, and Coos, stated that Mrs. Whitmire was determined to get satisfaction. Dr. Brenner was unavailable for comment.

I practically collapsed onto the sofa. As the paper fell to the floor, Sweetie made herself scarce.

"Collier's trying to take my license!"

Lucy gave me that look she reserves for stupid friends. "Didn't you know that Mrs. Whitmire was his biggest client? And you were seeing her daughter in therapy. What were you thinking going out with him anyway?"

The deep blue of his eyes and that cute little smile he gets flashed through my head. "I was thinking he was pretty cute, and since we'd already seen each other naked during college, I wouldn't have to break him in. This is a small town and Collier is a very low maintenance boyfriend with hardly any bad habits."

"I'd call stabbing you in the back for Mrs. Whitmire a bad habit. A good boyfriend could've warned you."

"We're supposed to go to that United Way fund raiser tomorrow night," I said. "We usually call a truce for such events, even if we aren't currently seeing each other."

"I wouldn't count on it."

I was staring down at the floor between my feet and Sweetie was finally beginning to crawl out from behind the sofa. Did I mention that Sweetie hates conflict? Hides every time.

Lucy had a deliberately cheerful expression and I'm sure she was about to lecture me about cheering up when my cell phone rang.

I'd started to push myself off the sofa to walk across the room to pick it up, when Sweetie sprang from the sofa and tried to crawl behind the little table where I'd left the phone. The table was too little and Sweetie was too big. The table fell, scattering the phone and a bouquet of flowers across the wood floor. I slipped in the water from the vase of flowers and landed on my back beside the phone. Lucy screamed as I grabbed the receiver. It was wet.

"Alice, is that you? You don't sound like yourself. Are you okay? And who is that yelling in the background?" It was Collier.

"How did you think I'd be, Collier? I'm upset! I thought you cared about me." I felt like a kid whose birthday had been forgotten.

As complicated as our relationship was, I had always been sure that Collier loved me.

"I'm sorry. It's part of my job … And just so you know, I tried to dissuade her. I don't want to hurt you. I do care about you. Deeply and truly."

"But the job comes first," I muttered. I was going for *angry* but barely managed to avoid *pathetic*. What was that lump of concrete doing in my stomach? I couldn't feel anything but the heaviness. Maybe it was shock.

"Doesn't yours? It's true for both of us." He sounded surprised.

Yes, our jobs come first. And that said what was wrong with our so-called relationship. We cared when it was easy. Maybe that was the root of the uneasiness in my stomach when I was with Collier. Maybe it had been time to let go and I hadn't wanted to face it. I still didn't want to face it. I wanted to feel loved. I felt like crying, but I wouldn't. Too much effort.

Guess I didn't even have a part-time boyfriend anymore. At least I had other options. I figured that Collier did, too, with those deep blue eyes and cute smile.

After I hung up, I looked at Lucy and said, "Collier and I aren't an item anymore."

"Again?" She had that I-wish-I-could-strangle-you look that she gets when I tell her about problems with Collier

*   *   *

That evening Lucy and I gathered for happy hour and the local news. We'd agreed to drink just V-8 juice, because we both had hangovers that morning and were grumpy. Sweetie approved.

Again, Sue Turner was talking about the Janet Ford case as soon as we turned on the television. "It's been a busy day here at the Fort Madison police department. The police issued a statement saying that Russell Logan is no longer a person of interest. The police apprehended a drifter, a Jim Summers, who they say was in the park about the time Ms. Ford died. Detective Rita Butler quoted him as saying that he saw quote 'a man bending over Ms. Ford'. Detective Butler went on to say that the police are not convinced the man is a reliable witness and that they will continue to hold him in custody for now."

Sweetie sat on my feet and licked my knee. There was a big wet spot on my jeans. "Lucy, I don't want V-8, I want a real damn Bloody Mary. This whole thing is making me freaking anxious."

Lucy sighed. "Me too. Do you think we're drinking too much?"

"Not us. We're just under a lot of stress right now. Besides, who's going to know? We're here in the privacy of our home. Not driving anywhere. But better hide the phones."

"Yeah. Right. Let's have some real drinks."

I could have sworn that Sweetie rolled her eyes as we headed into the kitchen to make up some Bloody Marys. Just what I needed, my dog judging me. That's what cats are for.

CHAPTER 15

THURSDAY, OCTOBER 10
MORNING

On Thursday morning I was stopped in the hall by Ron Margolis and Marvin Lane, the group's psychiatrist and main partner.

"I saw the paper yesterday," Ron said. "Why haven't you informed the practice about the complaint to the licensing board? You know we're damaged by the publicity, too. It affects everyone, even staff."

"I'm sorry, Ron. You're right, of course. I just got the letter from the board today. I was waiting to talk with their investigator, but I should've written a formal memo to the partnership first. I have to admit that I'm pretty shocked. It's all new to me."

Marvin had the grace to look embarrassed as Ron continued. "I understand, Alice. But you might want to think about what would be best for the practice. Maybe you should consider stepping away for a time, before more publicity hurts us all. Or maybe you can settle this quietly."

Marvin spoke up. "Ron, that's enough and rather inappropriate. You are not in a position to suggest what Alice should do or not do. She's been with us a lot longer than you have."

Ron gave us both incredulous looks, then walked off without another word.

"Thanks, Marvin," I said. "Our boy wonder got a little carried away. You know that I'd tell the group if anything comes of this."

"I know, Alice. Don't worry about it." He walked down the hall back to his office shaking his head and muttering to himself. That was one of the little things that made him so cute. If we didn't work together and if he were't married, I could be interested in Marvin.

That's the story of my life. Most of the men I was attracted to were unavailable.

Once in my office I thought about what Ron had said. What he meant was that I should leave quietly if I lost my license. That wasn't likely. The claim was clearly invalid; I'd done the usual and expected things in treating Janet Ford. But even a dismissed nuisance claim could destroy my practice. Fort Madison is a small town. And a therapist's reputation is everything. Patients get nervous when their therapist is investigated. I wondered if that was Mrs. Whitmire's intention all along. Was she really that vindictive?

That afternoon I received a call from Mrs. Whitmire's secretary, Heather Thorne. Ms. Thorne informed me that I was expected at the Whitmire estate promptly at 6:00 p.m. At first I was shocked, then angry that this arrogant old lady had the nerve to order me around. I rang Lucy when I knew she was free.

"Whitmire wants to talk to you? I thought you were her enemy."

"I know, Lucy. How dangerous do you think she is?"

"She's in her sixties and seems dignified. So not at all physically dangerous. But she is a powerful force in this town. She is dangerous to your reputation and ability to work here.."

"So what does she want?"

"You're the therapist. Find out."

"Come with me. Please."

"You're really that scared of her?"

"Scared. Frightened. Wary. Let's not get sidetracked with labels. Mrs. Whitmire is trying to get my license pulled, and if only ten percent of what Janet said about her was true—"

"Okay, okay," said Lucy. "Sounds like it could be the most interesting thing to happen in Fort Madison in years."

CHAPTER 16

THURSDAY, OCTOBER 10
EVENING

We got there right at six. It was dead dark when we drove up to the Whitmire manse. As a Fort Madison founding family, the Whitmire tribe had taken the high ground and erected a Gothic-inspired Victorian pile with *Downton Abbey* aspirations, quite befitting of an old line family that thought of themselves as rural royalty. The estate commanded a rolling hilltop and was surrounded by parkland which, while less extensive now, still impressed us common folk.

After being buzzed in at the front gate by Heather, we drove up a tree-lined, serpentine drive, eventually arriving at a large courtyard with a fountain. There were two other cars there, parked over next to a detached garage. Before us the Whitmire estate rose out of the night in all its Gothic glory; a gloomy monument from the Gilded Age. Especially for a small town like Fort Madison, our own mini-Hearst Castle was quite a thing.

"Janet Ford grew up here?" Lucy asked.

I parked a short distance from the entranceway, a set of wide steps leading to two large doors. "For a time, yes."

Now Lucy and I were waiting inside this relic. Heather Thorne had greeted us outside and showed us to the living room. She appeared to be in her mid-fifties, and tastefully dressed. I so wanted to ask her what working for Mrs. Whitmire was like but I hadn't dared.

"Please wait in here," Thorne had said. "Mrs. Whitmire will be down shortly."

Fifteen minutes passed. I smelled a tactic being deployed.

"I wonder how they managed to preserve the Old World atmosphere when the Whitmires refurbished back in the eighties," I commented.

"Shhhh, they're probably watching. Using scanners and stuff."

I couldn't tell if she was kidding. Sporting jeans and an embroidered top—was I underdressed? Should I have put on more makeup, any makeup?

"Two can play this waiting game," I whispered. "Let's book it out of here."

"Sit tight, girlfriend," Lucy whispered back, like she knew something I didn't. I gave her a long appraising look, searching for clues, but Lucy was calm and relaxed, like she'd lived surrounded by oppressive opulence in some former life. Maybe there was more to Lucy than I knew. I just felt uncomfortable.

So we waited some more, listening to the slow ticking of the antique grandfather clock. I admired its rich wood and ornate face. We were perched on a down-stuffed sofa upholstered in deep gold velvet, our feet on a glowing red Persian rug worth ten times more than mine, maybe twenty. The sparkle of a cut-glass vase with its carefully arranged roses and the glow of the well-polished silver tea service on the coffee table gave the room a rich, cultured feel.

After about twenty-five minutes of forced lounging, the doorbell rang. I could hear Thorne answer, but couldn't see who came in. Had Mrs. Whitmire double-booked us? The secretary showed whoever it was into the library on the other side of the big entrance hall, resplendent with a curved staircase and intricate marble flooring; both imported, no doubt. Almost immediately, I heard someone come down the staircase and go into the library. Five minutes later the library-dwellers came out and swept into the living room where we waited.

A small, gray-haired woman in a tan cashmere pants-suit leaned on the arm of a handsome man that I knew well. Before I could react, Mrs. Whitmire said, "I am Doris Whitmire. And this is my lawyer, Collier Jackson. I believe you know Mr. Jackson." She turned cold eyes on me and smiled a viper's smile.

"Hello, Collier." I could barely breathe. With all that had been happening, I hadn't taken time to sort out how I felt about my former sometimes, now definitely, ex-boyfriend supporting the enemy. I'm sure that at some point Collier had told me about his being the Whitmire family lawyer. Janet had certainly made a point of telling me who her mother was, but I had never made the obvious connection until it was standing in the same room with me. If this was the effect that Mrs. Whitmire was going for, she'd certainly succeeded.

"Alice, it's good to see you," Collier said, acting like this super-awkward meeting was the most natural thing in the world. I guess that's why he earned the big bucks. Then he smiled that special smile that made my toes tingle. Damn, he was good.

Me, not so much. I couldn't say anything. It seemed that I had forgotten how to talk.

After an exquisitely uncomfortable pause, Collier and Mrs. Whitmire sat in the blue velvet easy chairs opposite us.

Picking up on my sudden loss of speech, Lucy began talking for both of us. "It is nice to see you, Collier. You're looking well."

She turned to Mrs. Whitmire. "Mrs. Whitmire, my name is Lucy Henderson. You have a lovely home. Thank you for inviting Alice to meet with you. I am a partner with Alice at our therapy practice, so anything that affects her professionally, also concerns me."

"I understand," Mrs. Whitmire replied.

By now I had recovered enough to risk a few words. "I hadn't expected to see you here." I gave Collier a meaningful look. That meaning being *Why didn't you warn me, you creep?* "Why did you think you needed a lawyer, Mrs. Whitmire? " I asked.

"Why? For protection, my dear. Both yours and mine. After all that has happened, Mr. Jackson's involvement was only logical."

I had to admire how she made it sound like she was looking out for my interests.

Lucy leaned forward. "Mrs. Whitmire, I'm sure everyone wants to find out what happened to Janet. See justice done. That is only logical, too."

"Your friend there is responsible for my daughter's death," Mrs. Whitmire said flatly, her eyes measuring me for an orange jumpsuit. I could feel myself blush.

"I assure you that Dr. Brenner did what any therapist would have," countered Lucy, keeping her voice even. "She is not responsible for Janet's death. Don't be so eager to rush to judgement."

Collier spoke into the silence following Lucy's statement. "Again, Doris, I'm not sure you should be talking to them. This could be seen as interfering with a police investigation."

"Please, Mrs. Whitmire," I said, "Janet was my patient. I cared about her very much. If I don't find out what happened, it will haunt me." I hadn't expected to be so melodramatic. It just popped out that way.

"Janet had mood swings and could certainly get depressed, but she never presented as being suicidal. She was very upbeat during our last few sessions, in fact. You probably know that even severely depressed people can hide that depression from friends, family, and even their therapists. It often takes months before patients trust their therapist enough to reveal just how severely depressed they are. You wouldn't have summoned me here if you thought you needed protection from me. Why am I here? What do you want?"

Mrs. Whitmire glared at me, but I could see the wheels turning behind those cold eyes. "Jackson and Miss Henderson are no longer needed," she suddenly decreed. "It's obvious that neither of us needs protection. Dr. Brenner, please come with me."

As Mrs. Whitmire rose and made her way to the library, the three of us just stared at each other. *Did that just happen?*

"Dr. Brenner, are you coming?" Mrs. Whittier's voice was still cold as the vast marble floor in the hallway.

Taking a deep breath, I followed her into the library. She motioned me to a wing chair beside the fireplace, where a small pile of glowing embers had no effect on the room's penetrating cold. After a few seconds of panic, I noticed a man sitting on the sofa opposite me. I took in his graying goatee, dark hair, blue eyes, and intelligent expression. He smiled at me and rose to his feet, fully aware that I was trying to figure him out.

"Dr. Brenner, this is David McGinty, my private investigator."

McGinty and I shook hands while Mrs. Whitmire continued her speech.

"I retained this gentleman because the Fort Madison police are hopelessly incompetent in these matters. As your friend said, I want to find out what happened. It's either suicide or murder, and I must know which."

"Mrs. Whitmire, I had nothing to do with Janet's death," I said, starting off on a line of thought I hoped would lead somewhere useful. "And even if it does turn out to be suicide, which I sincerely doubt, I reject your assertion that I would be somehow morally responsible. I feel for your loss; it's a horrific situation, but lashing out at me, threatening my career and reputation, isn't going to get you the answers or satisfaction you're looking for." I had the feeling that most people didn't speak to her eminence like this. There was probably a very good reason for that.

Mrs. Whitmire glared. I glared back as best I could. "Now, why am I really here, Mrs. Whitmire. Why did you summon me to your home?"

Mrs. Whitmire replied, "Mr. McGinty seems to think you could be useful. And I believe that our goals are aligned."

"Oh really? How so?"

Mrs. Whitmire looked like she'd just taken my queen and put me in check. "We both want to find Janet's killer. I agree with you that suicide is unlikely, though if she had been taking drugs that night I am less convinced." I had been thinking the same thing. This was getting interesting.

"Janet liked you as a therapist, and for that I thank you," Mrs. Whitmire continued. "I am withdrawing my complaint to the licensing board."

Wow. Was that an apology? Not what I expected. Maybe my reputation could be salvaged after all.

I turned to McGinty. "So you're to do the job that Fort Madison's finest don't seem capable of? That's fine, but how could I be useful to you? I'm no detective. And I have a full-time workload." It all sounded suspicious to me.

Mrs. Whitmire gave him a nod. "First of all," he said, "as Janet's therapist, you probably know almost as much about her as her mother. Second, you likely know things that her mother doesn't. And since your patient is dead, confidentiality no longer applies. Third, you seem to have an in with the police that I don't have."

"And, my dear, we need to keep this investigation discreet," added Mrs. Whitmire. "The two of you working together can unearth more useful information without being suspicious. When the time is right, the police will be brought in."

"Not suspicious? This is a small town. If I'm seen with your private investigator it'll look very suspicious."

"Oh, Mr. McGinty has a plan for that," she said. The coldness had finally left her voice. A welcome change.

"Yes," he agreed. "I'm not here as a private investigator; I'll be an antiques dealer doing an appraisal of the Whitmire estate. Now that Mrs. Whitmire's granddaughter is the sole heir ..." He let the sentence trail off.

I hadn't thought about what would happen to Janet's daughter, Betsy. I imagined the ex-husband would try to assert his rights, with an eye on the sizable trust account he would administer. *Is Bill a likely suspect?* I wondered. Plausible.

I realized that McGinty was still talking to me. "... you and I will be dating. Our hearts brought together by tragic circumstances."

Yikes! What had I missed? I took another look at him and decided that a few innocent dates, even pretend ones, didn't seem all that bad.

What I said out loud was, "Oh. Really." I was pretty sure Whitmire and McGinty wouldn't realize my mind had been elsewhere.

"Again, I can't stress enough the need for discretion," Mrs. Whitmire stated.

I felt she still wasn't being totally forthcoming, and it was starting to annoy me. I had the distinct impression that this woman had been playing me in ways I wouldn't discover until far too late.

The more I thought about it, the angrier I became. "Hold up here, folks. Mrs. Whitmire, why should I help you? As incompetent as they might be, this is still a police matter. I'm confident that suicide will be ruled out eventually. Besides that, you accuse me of being a bad, even reckless therapist, you try to get my license pulled, and then you expect me to go all Nancy Drew for you, participate in a charade just to protect your reputation? No thank you. And you can sue me all you want. The partnership has insurance for that and you'll lose in the end."

McGinty's eyes twinkled. At least someone was enjoying the show.

The patented Whitmire glare returned in full force. I felt pinned like a butterfly. "I thought you wanted to find out who killed Janet," she said softly, the glare suddenly muted. "Don't you care about giving her peace?" Taking a lace-edged handkerchief out of her sleeve, she dabbed at her eyes. "You tried to help her when she was alive, can't you finish the job now that she's dead? No matter what you decide, my complaint to the licensing board will be withdrawn."

My stomach twisted and I could feel my heart pounding. Mrs. Whitmire knew my fear that I hadn't done enough for her daughter. The logical answer that I did all I could in the short time I'd worked with Janet had no credence in my heart. Somehow I was guilty, even if someone else had murdered her. Mrs. Whitmire knew it and had just offered me a way to redeem myself, and I couldn't refuse. I had to know what had really happened to Janet. Deep down I wanted to wipe away the guilt that I felt. What else could I do?

"Okay. I'll do it. But only if no one finds out about it. I'm with you on that front. I have enough issues at work."

"Good," said McGinty, looking pleased. "You won't regret it. Let's have lunch on Sunday. Maria's at one, say? We'll set things up then." He shook my hand and patted my arm. I had a good feeling about him.

"Come along, my dear," prompted Mrs. Whitmire. "We need to collect your friend." She escorted me from the library, leaving Dave McGinty, Private Investigator, to his own devices.

Upon returning to the living room, Mrs. Whitmire straightened her back and gave Lucy and me a piercing look, like a Greek goddess gazing down at us puny mortals—and finding us lacking in some tragic way.

"Please understand that this meeting is private and privileged information," she said.

"We understand," I replied.

Collier stood as Mrs. Whitmire left the room and headed up the stairs. With the audience concluded, the room suddenly felt warmer. "Well, ladies, that's enough for today, don't you think?" He had a "welcome to my world" look of apology that I couldn't help but feel a twinge of sympathy for. But just a twinge.

"One last thing before you go," Collier said.

What now? I wondered.

From his leather briefcase, which I had not noticed him carrying earlier, he produced two sets of papers, one to each of us. "Standard NDA form. Nothing to be alarmed about. I'm sure you've signed them in the past."

Unbelievable. So the old lady wanted us to sign non-disclosure agreements. Wow. Somehow, I wasn't surprised, though I had to wonder how Collier knew to have one already made out for Lucy. Guess he's a good lawyer.

As Lucy and I exchanged eye-rolling looks, Collier silently offered me his fountain pen. A six-hundred-dollar Mont Blanc. I knew because he gave it to himself last Christmas and kept bragging about how expensive it was. It was a sign that he'd "arrived."

After we reluctantly signed and Collier stowed away the forms, he presented me with a manila envelope. "Your copy of Mrs. Whitmire's letter to the licensing board formally withdrawing her complaint."

She had it ready the whole time. Amazing.

We walked with Collier to the door. I was about to follow Lucy out when he took my hand. "Alice, we need to talk. I miss you. Maybe we can work this out."

"You want to talk about our 'relationship' now? Collier, be reasonable." I wanted to jump into his arms and hit him at the same time. Instead, I just stood there, looking up at him, holding his hand. *What's going on?*

Leaning down, he kissed me on my cheek. "I'll wait as long as it takes."

"You could've warned me, you know?" I said. "This play she staged to get me to do what she wants. What kind of relationship is that?" I was working up my version of the Whitmire death-stare.

"I know, I know. I'm really sorry, but I couldn't contact you. Now that we're working together—"

I kissed him hard on the mouth, whispered in his ear, and ran for the car.

CHAPTER 17

THURSDAY, OCTOBER 10 EVENING

In the car, we both started talking at once, while the Whitmire mansion was safely receding in the rearview mirror.

"What was that I just saw?" Lucy asked sternly.

"He kissed me," I said. "I kissed him back and gave him a little something to think about. No one kisses me without consequences. Now he's spoiled for other women."

Lucy gave me another one of her "straighten up" looks and said, "Have you lost your mind? That's the dumbest thing I've ever heard. Now, straighten up and tell me what Lady Voldemort said to you in the library."

"She thinks we can make up and play nice." My face was burning from her dumb comment, but I was going to ignore it.

"Was there someone else in the library? Who was it?"

I couldn't respond to that either. I was too obsessed with Collier. "Collier kissed me and said he was sorry. And I liked it."

Lucy sighed. "Okay, we'll talk about Collier. Did you like the kissing or the apology? And what did you whisper in his ear? Don't think I didn't see that move."

"Like I said, just a little something to think about."

"Such as? Something X-rated?"

"That I knew voodoo and had a pincushion at home with his face on it."

* * *

That night when I took Sweetie out for the last time she was tense, walking stiff legged and rolling her eyes. At one point she growled and stared behind us. I didn't see or hear anything, but she didn't respond to my attempts to calm her. Once home, she paced through the apartment muttering to herself for about forty minutes. By bedtime, we were both spooked and it took a long time before I could fall asleep.

It was 2:00 a.m. when the phone rang. I fumbled to answer, remembering that call I got from Janet. This time it was Lucy. Because she's my best friend, Lucy gets to drop in unannounced or uninvited—sit on my sofa eating popcorn and watching movies when I'd rather be doing something else. *But she doesn't call me in the middle of the night.* With that thought, I was wide awake.

"Alice," Lucy whispered. "There's a man down here on the front porch. I don't know what to do."

"Call the police."

"No. It's the man from the article about you at the Mission. He's asking for you. Listen. He's saying, 'Dr. Alice. Oh, Dr. Brenner. It's your man Russ. Come on down!' Over and over. I didn't want to call the police if it was one of your patients." She hesitated. "I'm afraid to open the door."

"Is he black?" I asked.

"Yes. With scruffy hair and a great big sweater." She took a big breath. "He looks like a patient who escaped from a hospital."

85

"That's Russ. Remember I told you I had to go to the police station about him. He's harmless. Just stay in and I'll come down."

"He doesn't look harmless to me."

"You don't know him like I do."

I threw on a sweater, jeans, and moccasins while I muttered to myself about why Lucy, a social worker, was scared of sweet, harmless Russ. Sweetie looked at me expectantly. "No midnight walks for you," I told her. "Stay put like a good dog for a change."

I ran downstairs. Russ was there to greet me.

"Russ!" I exclaimed. "What are you doing here? Been okay since the police released you? I worried about you. Nobody seemed to know where you were. And do you know what time it is?"

"Hey, Dr. Brenner. You came on down just like I said," he laughed. "I'm Russ, the Powerful."

"What did you expect? I should have called the police on you." Out of the corner of my eye, I could see Lucy watching us through the window. "Why are you here, Russ?"

"It couldn't wait till morning, Dr. Alice. It's important." He was serious now.

"What is?"

"The agents are watching you. I got you in trouble with them. Now they're watching you. Very sorry about that."

"Russ, nobody is watching me. I've been very careful."

"Yes they are. Tonight, I saw one of them walking behind you, just far enough back that you wouldn't notice. When you took that big black dog out. The dog knows things."

I sighed. Russ might be becoming a patient after all. "Russ, those thoughts you have about the Company and their agents, you know

I don't believe that's real. They're a symptom of your schizophrenia. You need to stay on your meds."

"I know I have symptoms, I know it. But that's not one of them. The agents are real. This one is." He frowned. "I'll show you. I'll catch this one. This one doesn't seem as experienced as the others. I can catch this one. I'll show you. You'll see."

"No, Russ. Just go back to the Mission. Get some sleep. We can talk about this later."

"Okay. I'll go. But you be careful, Dr. Brenner. They want to hurt you. Keep that big black dog with you. That's why I'm going now, you have that dog." He ran down the porch steps, across the street, down the hill, and faded into the darkness of the park.

Lucy came out of her apartment and hugged me. "Thank you. Next time you see him, tell him he can't be on our porch in the middle of the night. Tomorrow, I'm going to call a security company and at least get some security locks put on. That was scary."

"I can try." I smiled. "Russ is his own man. He doesn't do things like other people do. And he likes Sweetie. Says she knows things."

When I went back upstairs to bed, I found Sweetie standing at the living room windows wiggling and whining. She knew her friend, Russ, had been downstairs and didn't understand why she didn't get to play with him. Maybe we did need to beef up the security around here.

I had trouble going back to sleep. Then I dreamt I was falling into a deep, dark pit that laughed in Russ's voice and said, "I told you. But you wouldn't listen. I told you." I woke and knew he was right. Why wasn't my intuition working?

CHAPTER 18

SATURDAY, OCTOBER 12
MORNING

The Saturday paper featured two stories on the front page: a local drug dealer was acquitted due to a missing witness, and the victim of a fatal accident on Afton Mountain had been identified. There'd been at least four drug acquittals due to some kind of problem in the last year. Each time I read about it, my irritation with our little police force increased exponentially. Why couldn't they get their act together? It's not like they were under-funded.

I wasn't up for another account of small town ineptitude, so I drifted over to the article about the wreck. As I read about the car that had gone off the road at one of the many bad curves Afton Mountain is known for, I visualized the scary hairpin turns and steep grade of I-64 coming down the mountain into the Shenandoah Valley. The scenery was beautiful: mountains stretching off to the right side and the tree-covered slope to the left. The interstate curved out over deep valleys with nothing but the guardrail between you and series of deadly drops down the sheer mountainside. My inclination when I drove that mountain was to slow my car to a creep, but it was an interstate and the traffic was usually going closer to seventy-five than thirty-five. It was scary, and at night dark and treacherous.

The accident had happened late last night as the driver was coming back home after an evening in Charlottesville. The car was twisted and crumpled. The driver, listed as Dr. Stan Wilson an ER doctor at Fort Madison General, was dead at the scene.

No!

I was numb. I read the article three times, but Stan was always dead.

When Lucy knocked on my door, I was trying to drink coffee and sob at the same time. *She must have read about Stan*, I thought. *How like her to come up to comfort me.*

"What's wrong, Alice? You're not ready for our walk." Then she saw I was covered with coffee and tears. "What happened?"

Lucy was neatly dressed in khakis, a pink polo, and clean white walking shoes. I looked down at my coffee-stained gray tee, ripped jeans, and bare feet. Then I followed her without comment into my messy living room. Lucy sat me on the couch and picked up the scattered magazines on the floor, stacking them neatly on the coffee table. "What happened, Alice?"

"It's Stan." I picked up the crumpled paper and shoved it at her. "He's dead." About the same time I remembered that I hadn't brushed my hair, I could feel my nose begin to run. I brushed my hair down with one hand while I pulled a tissue out of the box on the table.

"Oh, honey, this hasn't been a good month for you and the people around you."

That said it all.

*　*　*

Lucy stayed with me the rest of the day. It turned out to be one of those warm Fall afternoons that deny the calendar. We spent most of it on the front porch. I was still in shock.

"Lucy, how could this be? One minute he's Stan and the next he's dead. I won't ever talk with him again. He won't ever play his blues music again. It's just not fair."

"Of course it isn't. It never is when somebody dies young. But you still have Stan in your heart. You have your memories of him," she answered.

"The few there are," I sniffed. "We were just getting started."

"What about dinner the other night? You never told me what you talked about."

"We talked about a lot of things. How he learned to play the saxophone. And how his mother coped with a house full of men." I smiled. "Apparently, she is quite the drill sergeant. Oh, and the fact that he stitched up Janet Ford when she cut herself."

"That's one of the perils of a small town," Lucy noted. "Everybody's connected to everybody. So did he know anything useful?"

"As a matter of fact, he did." I paused. "He saw Janet with her running friend."

"The guy she was so in love with?"

"No, this was a woman," I replied.

"There's a friend that Janet ran with other than her lover?"

"Yeah. She was with Janet the last time Stan saw her."

"Wow. Did Stan know her?"

"No," I said. "But he could identify her. I told him to call Detective Butler and tell her. There's cameras at the hospital, so maybe they have video. She might know something."

"Or she might have done it. It seems strange that she hasn't come forward," Lucy said. "Unless she did it. Alice, that's just too much of a coincidence. Stan was able to identify the girlfriend and then has a fatal accident. Did he ever call the police?"

"He said he'd call as soon as he got to his car," I said.

"Contact Detective Butler and check it out. Maybe they should investigate Stan's death as a homicide, not an accident."

"I bet there's a leak in the police department. The killer could have found out that Stan knew something."

I reasoned that a leak could mean the police might somehow be involved. I wondered if McGinty had the same suspicions. Was that why Mrs. Whitmire wanted our private investigation kept that way … private?

*   *   *

It was almost evening when I was finally able to get Detective Butler on the phone.

"Thanks for returning my call, Detective," I said quickly. "I don't want to take up your time, so let me get right to it. Did Stan Wilson call you last week?"

"No," she replied. "Are you talking about the Stan Wilson who went off the mountain? The one in the paper?"

"Yes. We were friends. He told me on Thursday that he could identify the woman Janet Ford was running with. Maybe her friend knows something. I told him to call you."

"Sorry for your loss. He never called me."

"Is his death being investigated as a possible homicide?"

"I couldn't say. Afton Mountain is out of my jurisdiction." Her voice hardened. "Are you going to get involved in that case, too?"

"He was my friend," I answered. "I'm concerned." I was thankful she couldn't see the tears coming to my eyes.

"You seem to be associated with a lot of possible criminal activity lately. Let the police do their job and stop interfering," Detective

Butler said. "You're going to get yourself in trouble, Dr. Brenner. I suggest you drop it."

We were still sitting on the porch when Russ appeared. He'd been around a lot. I was beginning to wonder why. It was kind of creepy

"So, Russ," I began, "besides agents, what's going on?"

"I came here today at great risk to myself to tell you about that man friend of yours."

"Which one?" Lucy cracked helpfully.

"The one who got killed up on Afton Mountain."

"That was Stan," I said. I could feel the tears begin to fill my eyes again. Lucy patted my shoulder and Sweetie gave me a sympathetic look.

"Stan," he said, as if trying to classify the name somehow. "I know what happened to Stan. The agents got him."

"Russ, the agents aren't involved in everything." This was getting to be too much.

"They were involved in this."

Lucy seemed troubled. "What makes you think that?"

"I saw the same agent who follows you following him. The same one."

"When?" I didn't really believe a word but wanted the details anyway.

"The day Stan your man died, I saw him stopping at the dry cleaners and I saw the agent watching him. The agent was still there when he picked up a pizza at Louie's Pizza and got in his car with it. The agent followed him when he drove off."

"How did the agent do that?" I asked. Like I said, I wanted all the details.

"In a car. Agents can't fly or anything." His sarcastic tone of voice reinforced his "you poor innocent" expression.

Now I saw that Sweetie was also favoring me with a very pitying look. *Okay, I get it. I'm naive.*

"What kind of car was it? Did you get the license number?" I asked. Even childish innocents liked facts.

"Of course not." Russ laughed. "Agents can change those. Why bother?" With that, he walked away. Sweetie was still giving me that pitying look.

Later that evening, I couldn't get Russ out of my mind. He kept saying the agents were after me. He'd said the same agent who had been following me also followed Stan, "proof" that the agent had killed Stan. These ideas were most likely symptoms of his illness, but what if it was true? What if someone were really following me? What if they had killed Stan? Did that mean I was next?

CHAPTER 19

SUNDAY, OCTOBER 13 AFTERNOON

My first meeting with Dave McGinty was on Sunday. He was already at Maria's Pizza, seated at a table. He stood while I sat down.

"What happened to you? You look like you've been run over by a truck."

"A friend of mine was killed Friday night in a wreck on Afton Mountain."

"What? The one in the paper, the ER doctor?"

I nodded. I could feel tears filling my eyes. This was not how I planned to start our "date."

My pretend boyfriend seemed genuinely sad. "I'm so sorry, Alice. It's hard losing someone suddenly like that. Why don't we do this some other time?"

"No, it's okay. I think it might help to concentrate on something else for a while. And I think the two might be connected."

"Really? How?"

"Stan attended Janet in the ER recently. She was there with another woman. Someone she jogged with. I asked him to call the detective on the case, Rita Butler, and tell her about the woman. She might know something, right? Stan said he'd call Butler that evening. Two days later, he's dead. That's too big of a coincidence."

"You think whoever killed Janet didn't want Stan talking about this mystery woman? Sounds like a conspiracy."

Was I going off the deep end now? Making connections where none existed?

"That Afton road has some dangerous spots, especially on the Valley side. All it would take is a hard bump at the right time. Stan's car was so badly damaged I doubt they could tell if he'd been pushed or not."

"It does make sense that it might be the same person, but it might not be. We'll have to see."

What was that? A non-committal endorsement?

We were interrupted by the waitress. After we ordered a pepperoni pizza, we just stared at each other.

Before it got too awkward, I said, "Where do we begin, Mr. McGinty?"

"First of all, call me Dave."

"Okay, Dave." I tried a smile and discovered that I could still do it.

"Okay if I call you Alice?"

"Of course. Especially if we're dating." I smiled again. It was a little easier this time. Science says that smiling makes you feel better, in spite of yourself. Stupid science, with its data.

"Tell me about yourself, then. Where did you grow up? Where do you live? What's important to you?"

"Well, I grew up just outside of Baltimore. I never knew my father and my mother passed away when I was in college. I have a brother in Baltimore, but we don't have much contact. I live in my friend Lucy's duplex across from Starlight Park. And recently, I got a big dog named Sweetie."

"What kind of dog? How big? I love dogs."

"Great Dane. Black. About a hundred pounds now, though it feels like more in the morning."

"Wonderful. May I meet her sometime?"

"Sure, though she's not very well-trained and will probably jump on you."

"Would you like some help training her? I've had some luck with it."

"Yes. Thanks. However, she's quite a handful."

He laughed and I noticed how much his eyes twinkled. Like an Irish Santa Claus.

"How about you?"

"Grew up in Boston. A case brought me to Virginia and I fell in love with it, just like the ads used to say. I live in a small apartment just over the mountain toward Charlottesville. I have an MFA in Creative Writing and I hope to be a novelist someday. Crime, naturally, like every other PI in America. And," he paused with a smile, "I have a black and tan Dachshund, named Pluto."

I laughed and said, "I don't know if a short Dachshund would be much help. At least a big dog like Sweetie might scare the bad guys."

"True, but in my experience, brains count more than size." He lifted his beer to me and took a big swig.

"I like both brains and size." I tried to smile my most seductive smile, but I suspect it looked rather sickly, given how red my face felt.

Dave laughed so hard that he choked on his beer and I joined him (in the laugh, not in the choking).

I felt better than I had all weekend. Clearly, this McGinty was a complex and interesting man.

"On a more serious note, I do have some information … by which I mean I heard a few deep, dark rumors."

I leaned forward. McGinty was getting more interesting by the minute.

"You should understand that most detective work is basically research," McGinty began. "Real research, the 'go to the library or check the archives' kind of work, not surfing the web while enjoying a cold-brewed beverage."

"Skip the lecture, professor. Give," I said.

"Okay. Some of my research suggests that the Whitmire family may have been involved in some shady activity back in the day. Maybe Janet's death is involved somehow."

"Really? That sure beats my conspiracy theory," I said admiringly. "But Mrs. Whitmire always had money. She'd have no reason to be involved with something illegal. Besides, she's not the criminal type."

"Every great fortune usually has a crime of some kind behind it, and I'm betting that *keeping* a great fortune during a recession or two has its dark side as well. And how do you know she's not the criminal type? If that audience at her estate the other day wasn't some masterful scam to get you to do what she wanted, I don't know what is."

"Okay, you got me there, but you know what I mean. I really liked Janet, but she could be manipulative, couldn't keep a secret, and was diva-level dramatic. All of that is more likely to have ended in a bad outcome than Mrs. Whitmire's arrogance and sense of entitlement. Or some sketchy rich person stuff from her past."

"You're wrong." His smile was brilliant, beaming. We'd have to swap notes on technique.

"No, you're wrong." I could feel myself blush as I realized that I was enjoying this way too much.

After a moment of mutual staring, I asked, "How are we going to do this? How will we find out things? Will we interrogate suspects?"

He laughed. "No. I'm not *that* kind of investigator. That's more like a fictional private eye. I investigate by asking questions and finding the answers … mostly through research. For instance, what was Janet doing in the park with a knife? Was it her knife? Or did it belong to someone else?"

"Are you asking me?" I felt uncomfortable.

"Yes, I am. How would you answer those questions?"

Reluctantly, I answered, "The news said that it might have been her own knife because one was missing from her kitchen. So I think she went into the park with the knife. Maybe there was someone with her. It wouldn't be out of character for her to threaten herself with the knife to get someone to do what she wanted. I didn't think she was suicidal, so I'm more comfortable believing that someone else was there and they stabbed her."

"Okay. Do we know where she was stabbed and how many times?"

"I don't."

"I don't either. So let's talk about Russ Logan. Did he see anything? Would he have stabbed her? You were there during the interrogation, what do you think?"

"No, I don't think he saw anything. He found her after she was dead. The detective seemed to want to prove that he did it and got mad when it was clear that he didn't. If Mrs. Grimes at the Mission hadn't been able to give him an alibi, he'd be charged and probably convicted of murder."

"Sounds like they went overboard. They didn't seem to care about his rights."

"Yeah. Right. I don't know you, but you don't seem like someone who'd do something like that."

"I wouldn't. I started out being a cop, but kept letting the fact that suspects were people get in my way. Finally, I left the job and became an investigator. It suits my personality better."

"Good. I like the idea of a researching private investigator."

"However, this time we'll be doing a bit more." He smiled a devilish smile. "We, my dear, are going to break into Madam Whitmire's house and do some exploring."

"I thought you said that investigating was mostly research."

"It is. Just this time it's on site."

"Oh." I was having a hard time getting my head around this. I'd always tried to be a good girl and breaking and entering wasn't my idea of a good girl. We could get arrested!

"Why me? Can't you do this yourself?"

"I need a lookout and helper. This is a two-person job. I don't have anybody else that I trust to do it."

He trusts me? What's wrong with him? He knows I've never done anything like this before.

"You have a problem with this? Too adventurous?" Dave was looking at me quizzically. I guess I'd been silent too long.

"Well . . . yeah." My cheeks were burning like I'd already been caught doing something wrong.

"Let me tell you the plan. You'll see that it's less risky than you think. First we'll park out of sight of the . . . ' He stopped abruptly as a waiter came to the table with our pizza.

"Thank you. It looks great." I stammered as he put the pie down in front of us.

"Can I get you anything else? he asked.

"No. This is all we need." Dave replied with no stammer, appearing as calm as usual.

I waited until the waiter was half way across the room before saying, "How do you stay so calm?"

"Practice." The smile was back.

"Back to the plan. Go on."

"Okay. We'll park out of sight and go on foot around to the side and enter that way."

"Isn't it fenced all the way around her estate?"

"Actually, no it's not. The fence and security are just around the drive. It looks like Mrs. Whitmire is too cheap to fence the whole thing."

"How do you know that?"

"I checked it out this morning." He looked annoyingly pleased with himself.

"How do we get in the house? Won't there be people inside? What if we're caught?"

"We'll figure all that out at the time. Loose planning always works better. We'll plan as we go."

"That seems like idiocy to me. Shouldn't we firm up the plan more than that?"

"How many times have you broken into and searched other peoples houses?" Again that annoying look.

"Never. How many times have you?"

His face was stony as he replied, "More than you have."

I was afraid to ask more. I really didn't want to know what was behind that face.

"Well . . . okay if you really think you know what you're doing." I couldn't believe I'd just said that.

"I do." His face was not as hard as it had been. In fact his eyes were warm as he said, "This will be good for you. You're afraid of adventure. Of taking risks. You need to learn how to be really alive."

"And what makes you think you know me. This is only the second time we've met. How dare you presume to know me!"

"I have very good intuition about people. And, unlike you, I trust myself."

There was that smile again. He was one of the most exasperating people I'd ever met.

"Since you seem to know it all, tell me how we're going to do this dating thing like you told Mrs. Whitmire *and* break into her house."

"It's easy. We'll pretend to be dating, talk on the phone every day, and get together twice a week to share information and to keep the pretense that we're into each other. I'll keep Whitmire informed of any developments while 'appraising' her antiques. Then on Tuesday night we'll go into her house and see what we find."

We talked for about another half hour then left. When we said good-bye, he kissed me on the cheek. This investigation might have its perks after all. But I couldn't trust it. *Remember, Alice, Mrs. Whitmire and her employees are not your friends.*

* * *

Later that sunny Sunday afternoon, Lucy and I were sitting on the front porch watching the steady stream of walkers and joggers go by. Most weekends, we just sat there and admired other people's willpower. Then Sweetie would get restless and share some of her enthusiasm with us for a jog-walk around the park. No matter how tired we were, we just couldn't refuse her.

This Sunday I wasn't even thinking about exercise. I stared at Lucy's pots of flowers in cheerful red and pink bloom. They didn't know that the weatherman was calling for frost that night. They were doomed. I was feeling so down that Lucy's eating a whole bag of chocolates didn't even register with me. Ordinarily I'd be worried. Chocolate was a trigger for her binging and purging. But today, I was focused on me.

I've never been one of those calm, secure therapists with no self-doubt. Therapy is such a vague, almost mystical process. Two people get together and talk. The power of words shifts one or both of their world views. Out of that shift comes awareness. The awareness brings pain. And with the pain comes healing. A new person leaves the therapist's office and the therapist is enriched by the experience. Now how do you explain that?

I was beginning to wonder if Ron was right. Maybe I should quit. I was still young enough to do something else for a living, right?

"Lucy, I think maybe I should quit. I'm feeling like I'm not any good at therapy anymore. Maybe I'm better suited to something else."

"Girl! That's the stupidest thing I ever heard. You. Quit? Not gonna happen. You don't know how to do anything else. You're too experienced to quit." Lucy hugged me.

"Maybe I did mess up," I continued after a moment. "Maybe Janet's mother is right. Could I have prevented her murder?"

Lucy frowned "No. Even if she was looking to get killed, it wasn't your fault."

"Could have tried to influence who her friends were."

"Janet hadn't gotten past the 'poor little me' stage yet, had she? It was way too early." Lucy studied me for a moment. "That is unless you psychologists know something we social workers don't."

I appreciated the pep talk, but was still not convinced. It was my pity party and I'd wallow if I wanted to.

"I thought things were going well in session," I admitted. "In the last few weeks she started to trust me a little. Her behavior was more focused and positive." In her last session she said she'd met a man and was in love. She wouldn't tell me that day who he was, but promised she'd tell me all the details the next time." But there hadn't been a next time.

There was a crash inside the house. From up in my apartment. *When did Sweetie leave the porch and go upstairs?* Lucy and I found Sweetie on the couch in my living room. The coffee table was on its side, and there were books and broken coffee mugs scattered around the room. Sweetie had my cell phone in her mouth.

"Damn it, dog! I can't leave you alone for a minute. Give me that." I was yelling loud enough for the neighbors to hear me. While I took a couple of deep breaths to calm down, Sweetie dropped the phone, jumped off the couch, tucked her tail under her, and wouldn't look at me.

"Your phone okay?" Lucy asked

"No. It doesn't look like it." It was covered in dog slobber. There was a dial tone, but the case was twisted and had tooth marks in it. I'd need a new phone if I wanted to read it as well as talk.

"How about your text messaging?" Lucy asked.

"Well, she might have texted somebody, but it probably wasn't in English."

Later that evening I remembered something else Janet told me. She wasn't going to let anyone take her child. Ever. That was part of the reason she'd let her mother force her into therapy. Apparently, "Mother" had threatened to file for custody based on Janet's drug problem. I wondered if Bill would have fought Janet for the daughter if she had stopped giving him money. Probably. She was an only child and would have inherited the family fortune. Now that Janet was dead, the estate would go into a trust fund for the daughter. As the father, Bill would probably be the administrator. And we were talking about millions, real money. He looked like a good suspect to me.

CHAPTER 20

TUESDAY, OCTOBER 15 MORNING

On Tuesday, I met with the state licensing board's investigator, one Mrs. Deeds. For a wild minute or two I had fantasized that Mrs. Whitmire withdrawing her complaint against me would halt any further action, but strangely enough, the licensing board does not work for Mrs. Whitmire. Once a complainant initiates an investigation, the process marches ahead, regardless. However, I was pretty confident that with the facts on my side, and Mrs. Whitmire's letter, I could expect a speedy and positive result.

Mrs. Deeds had sent a registered letter to me at the office on Friday, the same day I had my audience with Mrs. Whitmire, stating that I was being investigated and she would be in Fort Madison to interview me at nine Monday morning. Pretty short notice if you ask me, and they hadn't. If I chose not to meet with her, the investigation would proceed without my input. Needless to say, I was there to greet her at nine on the dot, though it wasn't easy rearranging my schedule so last minute. We met in my office. She was dressed like she was ready for court.

"What a pretty space," she said. "It's so comfortable."

"Thank you, Mrs. Deeds. How can I help with this investigation?"

"May I sit here at the desk so I can take notes. If you sit here on the chair next to me, we can get started."

After we arranged ourselves, Deeds glanced down at her notebook. "As you know, the mother of your deceased patient, a Mrs. Doris Whitmire, contacted the licensing board to register a complaint. She stated that you had been ineffective in changing her daughter Janet Ford's behavior and yet continued to see her. She says that her daughter would not have been the victim of a crime if you had done your job correctly."

"Yes, that's pretty much what she said in the newspaper." I felt my face getting as stiff as my words. But this was a formal investigation. It was probably better to be stiff than to be too relaxed. "Mrs. Whitmire blamed me for her daughter's death, whether it was suicide or murder. She has since changed her mind about filing the complaint."

"Yes, I have her letter. Even so, we take every complaint seriously, especially those where the patient dies while in treatment." She gave me sympathetic look. One I used several times a week. "Let's start by getting the facts down. You were seeing Janet Ford in therapy?" Mrs. Deeds continued.

"Yes."

"What were her diagnoses and symptoms?"

When I told her, she said, "What kind of therapy do you practice?"

"Mostly Cognitive Behavioral, with some Dialectical Behavior Therapy thrown in."

"And how long and how frequently had you been seeing Ms. Ford?"

"Once a week for twelve weeks."

"So," she looked up at me, "you only saw her twelve times?"

"Yes. Twelve times."

"What about medications? Did you think she needed anti-depressants or mood stabilizers? Something to help her focus?"

"I didn't feel that medication was appropriate."

"So, you didn't send her to a specialist for any prescriptions?"

"No, I did not."

"Hmm. Do you have a statement that you wish to make to the board?"

"Yes. Janet Ford was a difficult patient who had a history of going to therapists. If she could have continued with me, it probably would have been for a period of several years. As it was, I only saw her for twelve weeks. I did nothing wrong and was treating her like any other therapist would have. Her mother had unrealistic expectations about how quickly her daughter would improve."

After she finished writing, Deeds sat back in my chair and said, "I wouldn't worry about this, Doctor Brenner. It seems fairly obvious that this is a grieving woman striking out at you. Twelve weeks is certainly not long enough to have changed this patient's long-held habits. Then there's the whole issue of your general competence - Cognitive Behavioral and Dialectical Behavioral Therapy are the usual and customary therapies for Ms. Ford's diagnosis. However, this complaint still has to go before the board. They are the only ones who can render an opinion on this. But as I said, I wouldn't worry about it too much." She closed her notebook and put her pens away. "It seems obvious that you did nothing wrong."

So that was good news. "When should I know something official?" I asked.

"It usually takes between one and three months. All depends on how much is on the agenda at their next meeting. November's meeting is next week, and there's no meeting in December."

"So the next time they meet after next week is January?"

"Is that a problem?" asked Deeds, knowing it must be.

"It's just that Mrs. Whitmire has been quite vocal about her dissatisfaction with me. I'm still waiting for the press release recanting her accusations. Last week I lost three patients, and I haven't gotten any new ones. This is more serious than a bad Yelp review. What should I do?" That came out sounding more pitiful than I expected, but suddenly I could see how my reputation could be damaged beyond repair, especially if I didn't get some support.

"I am sympathetic, Doctor Brenner," said Deeds after a moment, "but the licensing board can't advise you in that area. You need to consult with a crisis specialist or a PR company. Those would be my suggestions. And best of luck."

I thanked her for her time and showed her out. As she left, Deeds turned to me and said, "You know, if Martha Stewart can rehabilitate her reputation, I'm sure you can."

I had to admit that the woman had a point.

CHAPTER 21

TUESDAY, OCTOBER 15 EVENING

After work, I went to Staples to get a new phone. I was feeling particularly proud of myself, because I was taking care of my cell phone problem as soon as possible. Usually I let chores like this pile up for months, then I feel like a bad person. And even when I do get it taken care of, I still feel bad because I waited so long. Today was different.

While I looked at the display of phones, Dave walked up the aisle to stand next to me.

"Hey, Alice, I'm glad to see you. I tried to call you this morning, but your phone just kept ringing. No voicemail. No nothing. So now I run into you while I'm daydreaming about buying a new laptop. It's fate"

His soft voice filled my ears, while I gazed into endless blue eyes. He wore a black T-shirt today. I hadn't noticed how fit he was before. Helping him work for Mrs. Whitmire might not be so bad.

"Dave. It's nice seeing you. Sweetie ate my phone. That's why I'm here. I'm getting a new phone," I said. I don't know why that would make my cheeks burn, but they did.

"That explains why I couldn't get you. Now that we're both here we have some business to attend to." He grabbed my upper arm and half-pulled me into an empty aisle. "Remember. We're going to explore Whitmire's house."

"Tonight?" My heart was pounding as I pulled my arm from his grasp.

"Surprise." That irritating smile was back.

"Why didn't you warn me? I can't just drop everything and go break into houses." Who did he think I was, anyway?

"I did warn you, Dr. Brenner, a few days ago. I didn't say anything else, because you overthink everything and you would have been in a tizzy by now." He looked so superior that someone should just punch him.

"Why don't you leave managing my moods up to me, Mr. McGinty. I *am* the mental health professional here." My jaw was clenched sop tightly that I was getting a headache.

"I'm glad you made that clear, because I'm the professional investigator here. It's my professional opinion that tonight's just the right time for us to go exploring in the Whitmire house."

"Why?"

"Because almost no one is home."

"And how do you know?" I smirked at him.

He smiled again. "I investigated."

"Yes. You *are* the investigator."

"Yes. And we're wasting time. Let's go." He reached for my arm again.

"Alright." I turned away from him and began to move for the door, preventing him from actually touching me.

In the parking lot he walked me to my car and said, "Follow me to the estate and park behind me. That red SUV over there is mine."

Without waiting for a reply he walked to his car and drove off. I had to hustle to keep him in sight. Once parked to the side of a wooded portion of Mrs. Whitmire's drive, he motioned me to be quiet and follow him into the trees. I wished I'd known we were going to do the break-in that night when I was getting ready to go to Staples. I wouldn't have worn my ballet flats. The fragile shoes weren't made to stumble through dark woods. It was a little better when we got to Whitmire's wall. I tried to keep my hand on it for direction and balance.

Eventually we came to the end of the wall. It just stopped by a big oak tree. If we walked past the tree, we'd have been only about a dozen yards from the back of the house. The windows were dark and the only sound was a faint lilt of music from the guard station at the drive.

McGinty leaned toward me and whispered, "See the last window on the left? That's where we can get in. When I scouted the place, I noticed it looked like a storage room. It's not likely that anyone will hear us breaking in."

"And what if they do?"

"Then," he smiled. "then we run."

"Very funny," I replied. But he didn't hear me. He was already on his way across the back yard. I hurried to catch up.

The actual break in was surprisingly easy. Dave took off the screen and broke the glass in the window. I cringed, waiting for an alarm to go off, but nothing happened. "Why isn't there an alarm ?" I asked.

" I observed gaps in their security system the first time I was here. Later it was obvious that they didn't bother to alarm the storage room window. Easy pickings." He smiled.

"Now what?" I asked. I didn't know why his smiling was so irritating to me. But it was.

"Hey! Stop daydreaming." Dave snapped his fingers in front of my eyes. "I was talking to you and you didn't hear a word I said."

"Sorry." My cheeks burned. I was sure he could see how red they must be.

"As I was saying, we'll start in her study. I want a look in the secretary in the corner and her computer. If we have time, we'll look at the bookshelves."

"What're we looking for?" I asked.

" Anything interesting. You'll know it when you see it."

"I doubt it." I muttered. What made him think I'd have any idea of what was interesting? But, like a dutiful child, I followed him into the study, while Dave closed the door silently. *He must have done this kind of thing before.*

I opened the first drawer in the secretary, and began to look through the messy pile of papers inside. Dave booted up the computer and began trying possible passwords. It only took about five passwords until he hit on the right one and the computer opened.

"Lucky for us, Mrs. Whitmire isn't very imaginative." He gestured toward the keyboard. "She used her birthday as the password."

"How do you know her birthday?"

"I always research my employers." He smiled at me. I looked away, my cheeks suddenly warm.

"Ah ha! Already things are interesting. Financial records right up front." He muttered to himself as he scrolled through them.

"Go get her, Mr. Investigator." I smiled, too.

There wasn't anything interesting in the first drawer, so I opened the fold down desk and found neatly organized cubbies filled with correspondence. "Looks like you didn't get the drawers organized, Mrs. Whitmire." Now I was talking to myself just like Dave.

The first three cubbies held current bills and looked normal for what I imagined a large house like that would require. The other cubbies were more personal correspondence. Nothing in the first two, but the last looked older and might yield something. As I reached to pull out the stack of letters and cards, a male voice spoke just outside the study door. I jumped at least a foot.

Dave, too, had stopped staring at the computer monitor and seemed to be looking for a place to hide. Why hadn't I thought to do that when we first got here? My heart was pounding and I was gasping for air. I didn't have the focus needed to find a hiding spot. All I could think of was to hide behind the door if it opened. I started to move toward it when Dave motioned me to stop.

The voice was growing fainter. The man was moving away. I let out the breath I'd been holding with a soft whoosh. Dave motioned for me to continue my snooping. All was quiet, except for the pounding of my heart.

My still shaking hands flipped through a stack of cards until I saw it. On a return address. Craig Fletcher. I'd seen that name in the newspaper. He was some kind of criminal. I pulled the card out of its envelope. A birthday card dated about five months ago. It read, "Happy birthday to my favorite cousin. Love, Craig." *Cousin?*

"Look at this, Dave." I whispered. "It's a card to Mrs Whitmire from a crook." I waved the card at him.

When Dave saw the card and envelope, he whistled softly. "Do you know who this is?" He asked.

"No. Just someone I've seen in the newspaper. Who is he?"

"He's just the biggest drug lord in the entire Shenandoah Valley."

"Wow. They're cousins! I bet she doesn't want anyone knowing that."

"I imagine not. See. I told you'd know it when you saw it." He smiled and for once I wasn't irritated. "I wonder why Craig sent that? Psychopaths aren't warm people. He must have wanted something from her."

I shrugged. Imagining what motivated a psychopath was always hard for me.

After a pause he said, "Keep looking."

Before I could begin, loud footsteps sounded in the hall outside. They were getting closer. I ran for the large desk across the room and slid under it just as the door opened. I didn't know where Dave was. I could hardly breathe. I peeked around the end of the desk.

There were two of them. Maids with sour expressions on their faces.

"Hawthorne knows we cleaned this room yesterday. She's just being petty." The fat one complained.

"Yeah," the blond one said. "She's really got it in for us. Just because we forgot to change the sheets last week." My heart was pounding so loudly, I could barely hear her.

"Mrs. Whitmire was really mad about that." *I'll bet.*

"She's spoiled." The blond shrugged. They both settled down on the yellow chintz sofa, leaving their cleaning supplies lying on the carpet.

"Yeah and she got more upset by the sheets not being changed than she did about her daughter dying."

"That's a cold woman."

"Very cold. But have you noticed how jumpy she's been. Like she's afraid of something."

"Maybe she did it." I wasn't sure I heard that right. My pulse was beating so loudly in my ears

"Did what?" *Good. That's what I wanted to say.*

"Killed Janet. That obnoxious bitch certainly asked for it."

"No. Mrs. Whitmire is hard to work for, but she wouldn't kill her own daughter. She wouldn't want the bad press of a Whitmire being murdered. It would be too embarrassing."

"Ha! You're right about that." She laughed. I almost groaned, because my left leg chose that moment to cramp. Badly. Unfortunately, the maids chose to badmouth Hawthorne and the Whitmire family for another thirty minutes. I had to hold my hand over my mouth to stop myself from screaming in frustration.

"Well." The fat one stretched. "Do you think we've spent enough time in here to satisfy Hawthorne?" *Yes! Please leave.* My leg was killing me.

"Yeah. Let's go." The blond stood up. *Thank God.*

They gathered their equipment and left without another word. I crawled out of my hiding space and tried to stand up. My back and legs screamed in protest. I was shaky and dizzy. Leaning on the desk, I looked around for Dave. About the time I got the cramp out of my leg he crept out of the closet.

"Did you hear all that?" I asked him.

"Yeah. Very interesting. I wonder what Mrs. Whitmire is afraid of?"

"That would be a good thing for you to find out, since you have access to her." I smiled my sweetest smile.

"I'll try. Meanwhile, let's get back to it."

There wasn't anything else in the computer or secretary, so we moved to the bookshelves lining the wall around the fireplace. This time it was Dave who found the interesting thing. It was an old scrapbook with yellowed pages and curling photos. There was a picture of a white couple and a young boy with a big smile. Standing next to them was a smaller black boy with sad eyes. Written on the page next to the picture was "Cousin Gabby and her family (taken just two months after adopting Craig)."

Dave took pictures of each piece of interesting information with his very expensive tiny camera and returned the item to its place. No one would ever know we'd been there.

We crept out of the study, around the corner and down the hall to the storage room. No one saw us. My breathing slowed and I began to relax my tension-cramped muscles.

"So now we just retrace our steps and go home?" I asked.

"Yeah, but just in case we're sighted, run like Hell and meet me at Kathy's after you get away."

"Oh. Okay." Why did he have to bring that up? I was just starting to slow my heart rate.

Very quietly, Dave raised the storeroom window and helped me through. I waited with my back to the building while he crawled through the open window and replaced the screen. We were about half way across the lawn when there was a shout from the side of the house.

"You there! Stop or I'll shoot!" I looked over my shoulder to see a large man with a gun. Dave grabbed my hand and ran. I was dragged along until my brain caught up with my body. Then we both ran as if our lives depended upon it. They did.

I ran downhill, following a faint path that had probably been made by deer. It was clear that I was going to get caught. Most of the security people followed me and they were steadily gaining. Just then I noticed a big tree to my right that had low hanging branches. Maybe I could climb it. *Dumb idea, Alice. You haven't ever climbed a tree before. ,What makes you think you can do it?*

Since I couldn't see any other way I pulled myself up the tree with much slipping and scraping myself on the tree's rough bark. Just in time, I made it up to the lowest branch about seven feet above ground and lay along its length.As I lay there, trying not to breathe so loudly. three security guards ran to the tree and stopped. I was sure I'd be pulled down any minute. But I wasn't.

"How did she get so far ahead?" the tallest one said

"I thought we were gaining on her," the red head said.

"Well I don't see her. Did she turn off the path?" The tall one looked to either side of the path.

The third, plump, guard just stood there, panting. I hoped the noise he was making would mask the sound of my breathing.

None of the three looked up. After a few minutes of trying to decide what to do, the guards turned around and went back up the hill to the house.

My heart was pounding and I'd been holding my breath so long that I had black spots in my vision. I gasped for air and looked down. It was a long way. I wasn't sure how I'd made it up the tree, let alone how to get down. I lay there too afraid to fall for a long time. Eventually I slid down the rough tree trunk, falling the last three feet. I pulled myself up while every muscle hurt and limped back to my car.

Almost an hour later, I limped into Kathy's trying not to look guilty. Dave was already seated in a booth.

"Took you long enough. What have you been doing?" He asked.

"I had trouble getting away. You sent me down the hill while you went up. They went down. I had to climb a tree to escape."

"I'm surprised you know how to climb trees."

"I learned on that one. I was just lucky that Whitmire's security people didn't think I could climb trees either. They never looked up." My heart skipped a beat as I remembered how close I was to being discovered.

"So." He smiled. "What took you so long?

"I had to figure out how to get down out of the tree." His superior smile irritated me again and I was angry that my cheeks were burning. He didn't have any right to know that I was embarrassed.

The smile deepened. "I'm impressed you weren't caught. You sounded like a herd of hippos going down the hill."

That did it. Not only was he making fun of me in a terrifying situation, he compared me to a hippo. A herd of hippos.

I smiled sweetly. "That's not nice. You don't have to talk to me like that."

"If the shoe fits." The smile never wavered and his clichés drove me nuts.

"Just shut up, you jerk." My hands clenched into fists and my cheeks burned. This was about as angry as I ever let myself get.

"How do you feel now?"

"Angry!'

'Yes and how does your body feel?"

I hadn't noticed my body since I got so angry. I did a quick survey and was surprised to see that I felt good. No heart pounding. No shortness of breath. No shakiness.

"I . . . I feel good. Even calm now."

"Good. It worked."

"What worked?" I glared at him. "Did you deliberately make me mad at you?"

"Yeah. It got your focus off of being scared." He looked self-satisfied.

"How dare you manipulate me like that?"

"You needed it. You came in here looking like a panicked squirrel."

"I don't like being treated like that."

"It was necessary. People were going to ask you what was wrong. I didn't think you'd be able to handle that."

"Don't treat me like a liability. We're working together. I have as much to add as you do."

"Not in today's situation." The smile was back.

I just couldn't stand to sit there and be talked to like that a second longer. It reminded me too much of talking to my mother when she was in one of her drunken moods. I never wanted to deal with that again.

So I left without saying another word. I went home and sat on the floor hugging Sweetie. She was the only person I could ever trust. I told her so.

Sweetie agreed and licked my face.

CHAPTER 22

THURSDAY, OCTOBER 17 AFTERNOON

On Thursday, I saw Louis Baldwin for the third time. When I went out to bring him back to my office, the waiting room was crowded. As I walked across the room to Louis, a disheveled looking man rose and grabbed my arm at the wrist. I tried to pull away, but he tightened his grip.

"What are you doing?" I asked. I glance around the room. Most of the waiting patients looked away. Except Louis. He was watching intently, a strange expression on his face.

"You've got to promise me that these meeting are confidential," the man holding my wrist said.

"They are unless you're a danger to yourself or others. Ask your therapist about it. They can tell you more." I tried to look friendly, but my wrist was hurting.

I tried to slip my wrist loose, but he just tightened again.

"You're not telling me the truth. I'm not letting you go until you do." His eyes didn't look psychotic. Instead they were cold.

Louis stood and walked to my side. *Don't agitate him, Louis. My wrist can't take much more.*

Instead, Louis smiled and said, "Sir, please leave. You're hurting her."

The man looked up at Louis and his eyes widened. He let go of my wrist and walked out the front door, never looking back.

"Thank you, Louis," I said.

"You're welcome," he said.

On our way to my office, I asked Georgia, our office manager, to find out who's patient the aggressive man was and to let them know what happened. Maybe we needed to talk about waiting room safety in our next staff meeting, but I couldn't think about that then. Louis and I had to talk.

Once in my office I asked, "Do you know that man?"

"No."

"What do you make of his backing down?"

"I have no idea."

I was left with another mystery about Louis. This one felt creepy. He continued to be puzzling, maintaining he was depressed and had suicidal thoughts. I really didn't see it. If anything, he seemed more narcissistic to me. He was too self-assured to be depressed. My "super" intuition was alarmed.

"How did the week go, Louis?"

"It went well, of course. Defeated a business rival with little trouble."

"And you feel good about that? "

"Naturally." He appeared to be perplexed.

"I'm glad you were able to feel good. Enjoy your success."

"Oh. Yes. Well, that I did. Certainly."

"I'm happy for you."

"You are?"

"Yes, I am."

"Thank you." Was there a tear in his eye? It looked a little shiny. Of course, I might have imagined it.

"Louis, you'd tell me if something else was going on, wouldn't you?"

"Of course." I didn't see any evidence of tears now.

"Okay. Good."

"Going on how?" He raised his eyebrows.

"Emotionally. Something that could be causing you stress. Other than business rivals," I replied, smiling my "I'm on your side" smile. One of my best.

There was an uncomfortable silence. Louis seemed to have smile immunity. I was determined to wear him down. I knew he had more to tell me.

"I don't have any more to talk about today," he said. "I think I'll leave a little early, if you don't mind."

"Okay. As you like. This is your time."

He gathered his coat and left without a backward glance. He had twenty-five minutes to go on his session. Usually there's a bit of drama involved when people leave early; this was a puzzle.

*   *   *

That evening, I arrived home to find Lucy sitting in the porch swing. She had two full glasses of wine. "I got off early and decided to wait for you," she said, handing me a glass. "We haven't talked for a while."

"Didn't we talk last night?" I took a meaningful sip.

"I mean," she said, matching me sip for sip, "we haven't talked about how things are going for you."

"Ah. You want to practice therapy techniques on me," I laughed.

"No, but I am worried about you, Alice."

"I'm fine." I sipped my wine and felt some stirrings of discomfort. Lucy could be relentless if she sensed hidden problems.

I tried to distract her by mentioning Louis. "Let me tell you about something creepy that happened in our waiting room today . . .. '

"You're changing the subject, Alice, and I'm not going to fall for it."

At that point Lucy's phone rang and she hurried inside to answer.

Literally saved by the bell. I took advantage of this brief reprieve to refill my glass and scrunch around in my chair to get really comfortable. Since Lucy put the puffy cushions on it, the big, white, wicker chair was more comfortable than any of my living room furniture.

Lucy returned to our porch with a strange expression on her face.

"What's wrong?" I asked, instantly alert.

"That was Rachel, from down at the newspaper. You know the woman I met in that knitting class?"

"Made a sweater for her cat, you said."

"Yeah, that's her. She knows we're friends 'cause I was knitting you a scarf for Christmas."

"What scarf? You didn't give me a scarf last year."

"Had some construction issues." She grimaced at a memory I could only imagine. "Anyway, she just called me to tell me the Medical Examiner ruled Janet Ford's death 'Undetermined'. And no street drugs were found in her system, just prescribed medications. It'll be in tomorrow's paper."

"Well, I owe her for the heads up. And how could someone kill Janet like that? How could Janet kill herself? I saw her just four days before she died and she seemed to be doing better. I don't get it."

"Something could've changed. You know how impulsive Borderlines are. Maybe she said the wrong thing to the wrong person."

I reached for the bottle and Lucy filled my glass. *Is she counting?*

Sighing, Lucy took another sip of wine, closed her eyes, and relaxed into the porch swing. She did that sometimes, just went away.

While Lucy swung and sipped her wine, questions of life and death were running through my mind like over-caffeinated squirrels. Could the police be right and Janet killed herself? If Russ Logan wasn't the killer, then it looked like suicide. There must be other forensic evidence to support it. I didn't think it was a suicide. But I couldn't believe someone would stab Janet to death like that. Was it something she did? Was it someone she knew or a random stranger in the park? Or *did* Janet commit suicide, a bad impulse that got the better of her? Could I have made such a bad mistake? It was a question I knew I had to answer or it could drive me crazy.

CHAPTER 23

TUESDAY, OCTOBER 22 NIGHT

It was eight by the time I made it home on Tuesday. It had been a long, hard day. Sweetie was asleep on the sofa. She seemed unusually quiet and I was pleased to see her looking so … well, sweet. Then she burped and opened her eyes. When she saw me, she jumped off the sofa and stood before me with her tail tucked under her and her head down.

"Sweetie, what's wrong?" I asked. Sweetie didn't say anything, but slunk over to the far corner of the living room and lay down with her big head on her paws. She wouldn't look at me. I had a sinking feeling. Maybe she hadn't been so sweet. I swept my eyes around the room.

"Damn it dog!" I yelled.

There was raw wood showing on one of the coffee table legs. And fresh teeth marks. On my pretty coffee table. And the rug. The end of the corner by the sofa was gone. Eaten.

"Sweetie, I'm going to kill you. Come here. Right now!"

Sweetie whined, but she wouldn't look at me. She licked her lips and scrunched down even tighter. We were at a standstill. I muttered curses at Lucy for bringing that dog to me, and at Sweetie for being the dysfunctional canine she was. I assured her in no uncertain terms that she would be driven back to the SPCA at the first opportunity.

It didn't make me feel any better. Eventually I went into the kitchen. There wasn't anything good in the pantry and nothing but lettuce and apples in the refrigerator. Here I was with a chewed coffee table and rug, a crazy dog, and nothing for me to eat. I couldn't do much to make things better, but I could get something to fill my stomach. That's something my mother taught me. When upset—eat. Or drink. Right now I preferred the food option since I hadn't eaten all day.

I grabbed my purse and keys, ran out the front door, and slid into my car before I even thought about what I was wearing. Fortunately, my Central American embroidered vest, white tee, and blue jeans looked fine. I didn't even think that Sweetie needed a walk.

I didn't have to think about where to go—there was only one place in town to get a world-class pastrami sandwich. And they were open for at least another hour.

The New Brew was officially a coffee shop, but they had a good selection of deli sandwiches, and a cheesecake to die for. I ate there often. I like to sit at the big window up front and watch the people parade by outside.

I was savoring the spicy greasiness of my pastrami when Detective Rita Butler walked in.

"I thought you might be here," she said.

"Yeah." I smiled. "You're the detective."

"Good at it, too. Mind if I join you?" she asked.

I was surprised she was seeking me out, and at this time of the day. She must work long hours. "Go ahead. I like to talk to people."

She grinned this time. Probably her "I'm not here to bug you" look. I have one of those, too. "Talking to people and learning their stories; we have that in common. In some ways our jobs are similar."

"Yeah. Except then I try to help them cope with their problems." I took another big, decisive bite of the sandwich. *Mmm, pastrami.* "You make people's problems worse by locking them up."

"Only if they're guilty. Don't forget that."

"Pretty sure of yourself, aren't you?"

"Yes." She was serious now. "I have to be. By the way, do you usually eat dinner out? Shouldn't you be home with that big dog of yours?"

"Oh, I went home. My dog chewed up my coffee table and ate the corner of my oriental rug. I needed food. Actually, I needed pastrami."

She laughed. "I had a dog like that when I was a kid. Ate everything! I guess we kids were lucky he didn't eat us. My parents eventually took him to an obedience school and he came back cured. Maybe you should try that."

"That's a good I idea. I'll see if I can find one for her." I sipped my ginger ale. I wasn't in the mood to tell her about having to wait for the obedience class to start.

Rita had a wistful look, almost lonely. What was that about? "It's good to see you here," she said. "I don't like always eating alone."

My stomach rolled over and I felt like I might throw up. Maybe a greasy pastrami wasn't the best choice on an empty stomach. I put down my sandwich. "Me neither. It's nicer having someone to talk to."

She smiled a vaguely amused look and sat down across from me

"You know," I began, "I'm glad you're here. I wanted to talk with you again."

"Oh?" Despite my serious tone, the detective still had that amused expression.

"I've been thinking a lot about Janet Ford's murder. I can't accept the suicide theory."

Detective Butler didn't seem so amused anymore. In fact, she looked downright not amused. "You know I can't talk to you about police business."

"You said our jobs are similar, and like yours, I can't talk about official business, namely my patients. It's just that I know some things, and luckily for you patient-doctor confidentiality does not survive death. Don't you want to know what Janet Ford told me?"

I could see that I had Detective Butler's complete attention. It didn't take her long to reply.

"Okay. But you'll have to come down and give an official statement or the DA will be pissed," she said. "At both of us."

"Yeah, I figured. Not a problem."

Rita Butler took out small notebook. "Anytime you're ready, Doctor Brenner."

"Janet told me that she was having an affair. That she loved this man and she was going to marry him. She said her ex-husband had been paid off for an uncontested divorce, but he could still get control of the daughter's trust fund if she died. Her remarrying would prevent that. So, the ex-husband had a good motive for murder, yes?" I smiled. Seemed so obvious to me.

Detective Butler appeared thoughtful. "You're right about the motive, and ex-husbands are always likely suspects. But this one has an alibi. He didn't kill his ex-wife, and we don't think he hired someone to do it for him, either. If he was responsible, he'd be arrested by now."

"But he can't have an alibi. He has to be the one. Who else are you looking at?" I asked.

"I can't discuss an open case with you."

"But you just did."

"Yes, I just did. I don't know what's wrong with me tonight. Must've been working too long today. I better go home myself."

She got up to leave and I watched her go out the door. The whole conversation felt weird, like she had a reason to seek me out that didn't have anything to do with police business. Maybe she wanted therapy but was too embarrassed to say so. That happened sometimes.

Just then I noticed the guy behind the counter was staring at me. Probably wanted me to go so he could close up. It was about time and I was the last customer.

When I got up to pay, I found I was wrong.

"You look familiar," he said. "Oh, I know—I saw you in the paper yesterday." There was a stack of well-thumbed papers at the end of the counter.

Offering a free paper to read in today's digital world was one of the New Brew's quaint charms. Not so quaint was me on the front page of yesterday's paper with the story of Janet's death and that her mother had blamed me. That was publicity I definitely didn't need.

He smiled as I rushed out, my face as red as the red velvet cake in the cooler.

CHAPTER 24

WEDNESDAY, OCTOBER 23
EVENING

After work on Wednesday Lucy and I hung out. We were both famished, so we went to out to eat—taco salads at Casa Mex. Sweetie was waiting for me when I got home. She wiggled her butt, wagged her tail, and grinned engagingly. I knew she was trying for cute, but she was about as cute as a hippo. She was trying, though, and I couldn't resist. We hugged and spent the evening sitting on the sofa, ignoring the canine-caused destruction in the room while we watched car chases on TV. I didn't particularly like them, but Sweetie got all excited when car chases and ambulances were on, so I always tried to find her some. I have to admit, they're a lot more fun with a dog howling along.

Afterwards, it was time to take Sweetie out for her bathroom break. The books featuring cute puppies don't tell you how many times you have to walk your dog outside so they won't pee on your rug. Sometimes Sweetie didn't seem like she was worth all the work. But tonight, after her therapy dog help in the morning and howling at the ambulances on TV together, I was feeling particularly close to her. She was definitely worth it. Guess this was how dogs squirmed their way into people's hearts.

Once outside, we headed for the park and the big trees dominating the area. Sweetie found a duck feather blown over from the pond and I studied the patterns the roots made burrowing into the soil. Leaves crunched underfoot and a cool breeze lifted my hair. I was hoping Sweetie would hurry up so we wouldn't get too cold when the sound of crunching leaves pulled at my attention. They were too loud. And out of sequence. I looked around, peering into the dark shadows around the trees. Nothing but darkness. Maybe I was imagining it. But Sweetie stopped and growled softly. Maybe she noticed something, too. I jerked on Sweetie's leash.

"Come on, girl. That's enough," I said.

We turned back toward home. I could hear the out of sync crunching of leaves until we reached the path. There were no other walkers in our part of the park, but the leaves had sounded as though there were.

As we walked away from the trees, my back felt like a target and I wanted to run home, screaming at the top of my lungs. But I couldn't. What if I was wrong? What if nobody was following us? What if the sounds I heard were someone else out walking his dog? Running screaming through the park is not the image a therapist wants potential clients to have. In a small town, image and reputation were everything to a business or practice. I could walk calmly and risk getting bashed over the head, or run screaming and risk my livelihood if the wrong people saw me.

I opted to act like the professional I should be and walked calmly … with the target on my back burning a hole through my shirt straight to my heart.

Sweetie stopped again, went rigid, and a low growl rumbled deep in her throat. I tried to continue walking, but she wouldn't budge.

"Come on, dog. I mean it!" My voice was not calm, but not screaming either. It was the best I could do. This animal was going to get me killed.

Sweetie lunged at the end of her leash and almost pulled me off my feet. Her hysterical barks shattered the night. She looked like she wanted to eat anyone who came near.

A police car pulled up beside us, and a young cop stuck his head out the window. "You all right, miss?"

"Yes, I think so. For a while it sounded like someone might be following us," I answered.

"Probably just kids," he said, like that explained everything. "They think it's funny to scare people."

"Well, they just got a big laugh."

"Looks like you're heading out of the park. Have far to go?"

"Just five houses up the hill." I pointed.

He smiled as he noticed me shivering while Sweetie jumped around, tail wagging, eyes bright. "I think I'll stay right here and light your way until you get home," he offered.

I could have kissed him. Instead, I shivered all the way home, locked the house up tight, climbed into bed, and hid under the covers until I finally fell asleep, Sweetie beside me. Later that night I awoke to Sweetie scratching at the front door. I didn't turn the light on, but crept up to the front window and peered out. I couldn't see my door because of the porch roof below, so I waited, hoping to see whoever it was leaving. I never did see anyone. After a while Sweetie stopped scratching and I crawled back in bed. It was dawn before I fell asleep again.

The next morning I found Sweetie asleep at the foot of the stairs, right beside the front door. Outside, there were muddy tracks on the porch. On my doorstep.

THURSDAY, OCTOBER 24
MORNING

I was freaked out about the tracks—they were much bigger than any I would have made. And why did Sweetie think she needed to sleep by the door and not with me? I asked her about it, but all she did was wiggle and lick my face. I assumed that meant "Everything's okay, boss." But it didn't feel like that to me.

I paced around the kitchen, drinking my second coffee while Sweetie gobbled her artisanal kibble. I wanted someone human to talk to about it. Since this was a work day, there wasn't anybody. There were the people at work … not that I'd be comfortable telling them that I'd wanted to run screaming across the park last night. Some of them already thought I was bad for business, the sketchy therapist with the dead client. Telling them about the almost-screaming episode might convince others to adopt this view. Besides, I'd taken today off to recover from my scare last night.

If I had close friends I could tell them, but I didn't have many close friends. Lucy was the closest and she had probably gone to work already. This couldn't wait until she got home.

Detective Butler kept coming to mind, but I didn't know if I wanted to make an official police report. She seemed competent and kind. Unless you were a suspect. Underneath the tough cop, I thought I could see a caring woman. A woman who'd had a lot of the same kind of struggles in getting recognized as a professional as I had. Probably more.

I dialed the number she'd given me back when she wanted me to come in and help them talk to Russ. A man answered and told me she wasn't working that day. He said to leave a message on her cell phone and hung up. Luckily, I had her number. She gave it to me when I helped translate Russ for them. The call went straight to voicemail and I assumed she'd probably get back to me tomorrow.

Sitting down on the kitchen floor with Sweetie, I hugged her. "Great. Now I've made a fool of myself and didn't get any help. What an idiot."

We went downstairs to the porch and sat in Lucy's swing, watching people walk to the park and leaves fall from the trees.

An hour later a black SUV pulled to the curb in front of the house. The windows were tinted and I couldn't see who was driving. In fact, I didn't register that it was Detective Butler until she jumped out and was halfway up the sidewalk.

"Hi. I just called you a while ago," I said.

"I know. That's why I'm here." Smiling, she sat in the wicker chair next to the swing.

"I didn't expect to hear from you until tomorrow." I think I was blushing. My face felt sort of hot.

"Well," she smiled again, "I thought I might as well come over and see what your problem was."

Problem? So that's what she thinks of me. That I have problems. One of those irritating, demanding types with one problem after another. Now I knew my face was hot.

"I'm sorry to bother you. It probably wasn't anything. I was just feeling a little worried." I hoped I looked cooler than I felt.

She gave me a serious look. "It's okay, Alice. Just tell me what happened."

Alice! Is she talking down to me, trying to relax me, or does she really think of me as Alice? I was speechless.

She smiled again. "Well?"

"Uh … there was this sound in the park. When I was walking Sweetie in the trees last night. It sounded like someone else was walking in the leaves. But I didn't see anybody. Then a police car came by and scared them away. The officer said it was likely kids." I took a deep breath. "Then this morning Sweetie was sleeping down by the front door. She never does that, and there were muddy tracks on the porch. They hadn't been there before. See, they're just over there going to my door. I know it's silly, but I'm really on edge. I'm probably just worrying, but those muddy tracks—they're real."

Rita went over and stared at the tracks. "I'm glad you told me about this. I don't know if it's anything. It might not be, like you say. But walk … Sweetie is it? Walk her where there's other people around for a while. Try not to go anywhere isolated. Okay?"

"Okay." There was no reason for me to feel better, but I did.

I expected her to leave and go back to whatever she'd been doing before I'd interrupted her day, but she didn't. Instead, she said, "Mind if I stay and enjoy your porch a while?"

"Of course not. Do you like porches?" That was a dumb thing to say, but it came right out.

She sat back down. "Yes I do. I don't have one on my house. So I always enjoy sitting on other people's. Watching people go by, just like now."

"We both do that," I blurted.

"Do what?" She seemed confused.

"Watch other people. We're observers. Sometimes I observe more than I live my own life."

"Yeah, you're right about that. Especially when I'm working a tough case, I seem to retreat from others," she said.

"Yeah." It felt comfortable to just sit there. Sweetie lay on the sun-warmed floor twitching as she dreamt. I rocked in the swing and Detective Butler watched the joggers pass.

"Is this your house?" she asked.

"No. I rent. I have the upstairs and a social worker from work has the downstairs."

"How old are you?" She had a quizzical expression that made her question less rude.

"I'm thirty-six," I replied, thinking she appeared to be about the same age.

"Why don't you own a house?" She looked at me. "As a professional you make enough—and you're old enough."

I felt my face go red again. "I … just don't want to have to be responsible for it. To make repairs, to be here any length of time, to …"

"To make a commitment?" She looked sympathetic.

"Yeah," I sighed. "To make a commitment. Since my divorce six years ago, I haven't been much for commitments."

"I know what you mean. I've been divorced eight years. Eventually I decided I loved my job more than being married."

"Did you have any kids?" I asked. Somehow it felt okay to be nosey.

"Yeah, a boy. He's ten now and lives with his father over in Charlottesville. How about you?"

"No. We were only married a year. Hadn't gotten around to kids." It had been a really stupid thing to do. Just thinking of marrying him made me feel like an idiot.

"Is that okay?" she asked. She seemed not to notice the affect this conversation was having on me.

"No," I answered. My face burned.

"I don't own a house either. It's not just the commitment thing, though that's part of it. It's also money. I don't make much at the police department. Sometimes I wonder what I'd do if I had lots of money."

I cocked my head to the side. "Would money make much difference?"

"Only in the sense that I'd be able to be who I really am rather than just a workaholic cop."

"Who would you be?"

"I don't really know," she laughed. "I'll let you know if I ever get the chance to find out."

Then we sat for a while listening to Sweetie's snores.

When Rita left she said, "Thanks for the quiet company. That was really nice, Alice."

I took a deep breath. "You're welcome, Rita. Come again."

"Thanks, I will." She nodded and got back in her black SUV.

I sat swinging on the porch for awhile, thinking that I might be making a new friend.

* * *

That evening I had dinner with Dave McGinty. Was I a multiple dater? Maybe. But the "date" with McGinty wasn't real … was it? Thus, I was not a slut. At least not technically. Nonetheless, I felt

137

funny walking into the Clock Tower to meet him, thinking about Stan. Poor Stan.

"Are you okay?" It was McGinty. "You have a strange look on your face."

"Do I? I was just thinking about Stan Wilson."

"Oh. The man who you think was run off the road and killed?"

"Yeah." I could feel tears in my eyes.

"Seems like you miss him."

"I do. He was a nice man. He didn't deserve to die like he did."

"Of course he didn't. I'm sorry for your loss." His smile was kind.

I felt too exposed. "Well, it can't be undone," I said, terminating that conversational thread. I sat down and leaned in, role-playing the all-business Alice Brenner. "What have you found out since our last meeting?"

To his credit, McGinty took the abrupt shift in stride. "A couple of things, as a matter of fact. First, have you noticed how many drug cases are getting dropped or thrown out of court?"

"It's not something I pay much attention to, really. Is it more here than other small towns?"

"It sure is. And witnesses keep disappearing."

"Okay, that sucks. Now tell me why I care."

"Because there's a well-organized criminal enterprise called the Consortium, which distributes most of the heroin and meth in the valley. It's the organization that Craig Fletcher runs. To be so successful they must have people in the police departments and the DA's offices leaking information so they can either scare off witnesses or kill them outright."

"So the cases get dropped and the drugs stay on the streets. I've seen enough cop shows to get that," I said, still wondering what this to do with Janet, besides Fletcher being her cousin.

"Right. Now in your town, the Fort Madison Police Department has some of its best officers forming a task force dedicated to shutting down this particular operation. That includes not just decapitating the group's leadership, but also identifying and indicting the organization's moles in the police department. It's a very sensitive situation."

"Wow. I didn't realize that it was so organized. Sounds like the Mafia."

"It's not. In the big scheme of things, the group is strictly regional, but still a significant problem."

At that point our server, Dominick, came to take our orders.

"All right," I said to Dave after Dominick retreated, "as you were saying?"

"Yeah, here's where it gets interesting. It turns out that our local drug lord is, in fact, a cousin of none other than Mrs. Whitmire."

"I know that. We found out about that last week."

"I knowe," Dave assured me. "She doesn't know that I know. I was tracing some money Janet sent to someone in Winchester. Financial transactions can reveal all kinds of things, and I couldn't find what the payment was for, if it even was a payment. But Janet kept detailed financial records."

"Janet was a closet CPA?" I could hardly believe it.

"Took after her mother in that regard," Dave laughed. "She noted in the checkbook's register that the money was for 'Cousin Craig.' The police and FBI have identified the head of the Consortium as one Craig Fletcher."

"He's the cousin."

"Yeah. I contacted a friend of mine in the FBI and learned that Craig Fletcher is a thirty-seven-year-old African-American gentleman who was adopted by a wealthy white family in the city of Winchester when he was five years old. Master Craig was raised to be rich—best schools, all the right activities, impeccable manners. The works. And," he paused for effect, "the wife of the couple was Whitmire's first cousin."

"So we have further proof that Craig Fletcher and Janet Ford were cousins. Now why would a kid raised to be rich become a crime boss and not a money manager or corporate pirate? I mean, who sells drugs if they don't have to? It's pretty dangerous."

"Exactly. Who does that? You're the therapist, maybe you can find out why. All I know is that the couple's other son, Roger, resented Craig. He wasn't adopted and apparently felt that Craig should defer to him, some sibling crap like that. Needless to say, this sentiment wasn't reciprocated."

"Not surprising. Healing the scars left by family issues is a large part of my practice." I resisted the temptation to elaborate but I didn't want to interrupt Dave's story, and our food had just arrived.

By unspoken agreement we took a short food break. Dave clearly enjoyed his trout fillet and garlic mashed potatoes. My clam chowder was certainly tasty. After my last sip of soup, I put down my spoon and asked Dave to complete Craig Fletcher's biography. He didn't seem to mind that he still had some mashed potatoes left.

"So, like I was saying," Dave resumed, "there was always tension between the two Fletcher boys. And it turned out that Roger was able to break their father's will, which had left most of his estate to Craig. Apparently, Dad didn't trust Roger to maintain the family fortune properly. Which turned out to be an accurate assessment. But on top of that, Craig only received a relatively small amount from the mother's will, nowhere near what he'd been raised to expect. An unbalanced accountant was responsible for that, though I don't know the details, but a Russian mail order bride was involved, and his suicide. You can sketch in the rest."

"Now, maybe Craig was not a very nice man to begin with, or these betrayals and setbacks changed him for the worse, but reading between the lines it's obvious the whole thing enraged him. He might have been raised to be rich, but he wasn't prepared for the backstabbing, fraud, and legal tricks used against him."

"Wow. That is … it's amazing. Why hasn't this information been leaked by now?"

"None of it is in the public record. Being at the Whitmire estate gave me access to private family files. See what I mean about most investigative work being just basic research?"

.I placed my hand on top of his on the table. "B, ut at least we know that this crime boss, Craig Fletcher, knew Janet. She sent him money for some reason. Any theories?"

"Not really," David replied. "Maybe for drugs, though that seems unlikely. Pay back a loan. The amount was nine thousand dollars. This was five years ago. He might have been doing something else for her. Janet didn't mention anything to you?"

I shook my head. "Not that I can think of right now. I'll go over my notes."

"That would be good. In any case," David continued, "you'd have to assume that Fletcher knew about Janet's faults—her impulsiveness, manipulativeness, inability to keep a secret, and enthusiasm for drama."

That made sense. "Yes. And if Janet knew anything about her cousin's drug business it could make him very uneasy. Logical, right?"

"Totally. But Janet's shaky personality would also be a red flag to a man who has to keep his life private. I very much doubt that he'd let her know anything about his illegal activities. Despite her sending him a check, it doesn't prove they were close."

"Proving a negative like that is impossible, but maybe someone who didn't know all about Janet's faults let something slip."

This was getting interesting, so when our waiter wanted to know if we'd like coffee and dessert, we told him we did.

"You might be onto something," Dave remarked later over his double-latte. "If Fletcher found out that Janet was hip to his drug hustle, he could very well have had something to do with her death."

I frowned. "But don't drug lords make sure the bodies are never found? Cement barrels in the bay, that sort of thing. A public park seems too random … amateurish, somehow."

"Maybe. Maybe not," Dave said, trying to sound wise in a joking way. "Drug lord behavior is not my area of expertise, but I see your point. It does seem like Fletcher would hire a professional killer; no way would he get *his* hands dirty with it."

I knew we wouldn't solve this murder mystery over dinner, but maybe I could get to the bottom of how my tiramisu disappeared so quickly during our conversation.

"I'm very impressed by your diligence, Mister McGinty. Your employer is clearly getting her money's worth. Did you ferret out any other pertinent information while roaming through the Whitmire private records?" I was trying to sound sophisticated.

"Not really, but it's still early. Nothing jumped out after I focused on the Winchester angle. And there's a big hole in the timeline that I need to fill. A pampered young man becomes a major drug distributor in the same area where he grew up …" Dave paused, as if contemplating this. "Though technically he's a silent partner in a string of dry cleaners and laundromats. His neighbors probably don't know what he really does for a living."

"Laundromats to launder his money? You're kidding."

"That's what I thought, too." We grinned at each other.

"By itself, getting screwed out of his inheritance doesn't explain a life of crime," I offered. "Whatever befell him, it didn't take away his education, the friends he made at those fancy boarding schools, or the other advantages he had. It's an intriguing question and we don't have any answers."

"I'm getting a current picture of Craig Fletcher from an FBI source. That'll have to do for now. When I get it, I'll share."

As he wiped the last traces of lemon custard from his lips, I thought, *I could help him with that.*

I wondered if that was all Dave was thinking of sharing. If this had been a real date we'd probably be nearing the "your place or mine" stage, but instead we hugged briefly outside. I got a quick peck on the cheek in case anyone was watching, and then we went our separate ways.

That was fine. I didn't need any more complications. And besides, he worked for Mrs. Whitmire. He wasn't likely to be my friend.

That's what I told myself.

CHAPTER 26

TUESDAY, OCTOBER 29
AFTERNOON

I treated myself to lunch right after my eleven o'clock patient left. It was Tuesday, and that meant my favorite lunch—a sesame seed bagel with green olive cream cheese.

I was sitting by the front window of the Daily Brew Coffee Shop aimlessly watching people walk by and savoring every bite. I must have been really caught up in the savoring because I didn't notice Rita Butler come in until she walked over to my table.

"Mind if I join you?" she asked.

"No, of course not." *Why is she always catching me with food in my mouth?*

"Looks good." She nodded at my half-consumed bagel.

"Yeah. It's my favorite. What're you having?"

"Ham and cheese on a poppy seed."

"That's good, too," I said.

We both smiled and then laughed.

"Dumb conversation, huh?" she said.

"Yes and no. Yes, the content is inane, but the nonverbals are good." I smiled again. A "we're having fun hanging out" number that Lucy was familiar with.

Her face suddenly got red. "Are you flirting with me?"

"No! At least not in a romantic way." *Wow. I guess I overdid it.* I explained, "I think there's a certain amount of platonic flirting involved in becoming friends. And I guess that's what I'm doing without really realizing it."

"Oh." She took a big bite of her sandwich.

I felt myself get sweaty as I waited for more of a response. Had I just made a fool of myself or was something else happening?

Finally, she swallowed and said, "So you feel it, too."

"Yeah," I answered, "I'm starting to think of you as a possible friend."

"Me too." Her smile was warm this time.

Breakthrough!

"Oh good." It wasn't just me. I flashed a quick grin, then settled into a normal, comfortable smile.

"It seems strange to talk about it like this," she stated. "I don't think I've ever done that."

"Me either … but I usually don't talk to people other than patients when I'm working." In fact, I make a point of not "doing therapy" around my friends. People can feel it's invasive, a psychological form of rape, and I'd rather not have anyone think of me that way.

"Are you working now?" Rita looked serious.

"No. Not right now," I replied. "It's just that during my working day I find it easier staying in my therapist mode, focused on my clients. I usually bring a salad to work and eat in my office."

"Oh." She seemed doubtful.

I could see the fear of my "analyzing" her growing in Rita's eyes. If I didn't reassure her then our friendship might die in its infancy. "What I do at the beginning of my day is to sit for a few minutes and meditate about the patients I'll be seeing. What they're working on and what they might need from me that day," I explained. "Then before I go home I meditate again and mentally close the office."

"Do most therapists keep such a distance between their private and their professional lives?" she asked.

"Probably. Most therapists that I know do some version of it. You can't let the job consume you, so that's how I prevent it. I sleep better that way," I said. "You know, therapy is not sorcery, it's more like a partnership. The patient has to participate or there's no point to it." Not strictly true perhaps, but close enough.

"I'm sorry if I got that tangled, but I'm glad we both want to get to know each other," she said. The fear in her eyes had disappeared.

"Yeah. Me too." Maybe I was about to have a new friend.

We ate our lunches in comfortable silence.

"I know you're not supposed to talk about a case," I began as we got ready to leave, "but have you really checked out Janet Ford's ex-husband?"

"As you said, I can't tell you anything about my investigation." Smiling, she leaned toward me. "But if I did, I might say that he was in Alexandria for a business meeting and didn't check out of the hotel until the morning after Janet's body was found. But I didn't say that, so everything's fine."

I smiled. "Thanks for not telling me. I appreciate it."

The rest of the day seemed to fly by, and I didn't feel my private and professional lives were tangled at all.

CHAPTER 27

TUESDAY, OCTOBER 29
EVENING

The evening passed slowly and I couldn't seem to get my mind off food. My usual TV dinner didn't do it at all. I ate an apple for dessert, but kept thinking about Tastee Freeze chocolate milkshakes. They're very thick—just how I like them. Maybe the problem with losing weight wasn't what I had for lunch, but what I ate when I felt stressed out, which was usually some kind of carb-rich stomach-filler, like bread or pasta. Professionally, I knew that stress eating was common. Personally, I knew I was stressed.

Making new friends isn't easy for me, and Rita Butler's outspokenness wouldn't let me pretend that it wasn't happening. And then there was the whole blackout business and all the scary unanswered questions that went with it. All in all, I really needed a chocolate shake.

At about seven I gave up and loaded Sweetie into the car. We went to the Tastee Freeze down by Dolly Madison Park. Not only was it the closest, but I thought their shakes had more chocolate than the one on Richmond Avenue.

On the way back I took the shortcut through the park. Even in the fall it was lovely at night. Quiet and mysterious. The road snaking through it had widely-spaced lights that left long stretches of shadow. Tonight's half-moon lit the ball field and golf course, making the shadows in the woods seem even deeper. There weren't many people in the park either—just a lone car some distance back, and a couple walking a dog off in the distance. I drove slowly past the stark trees. Sweetie was curled up in the backseat. I enjoyed the quiet as I sipped my milkshake.

Suddenly there was a bright glare in the mirror followed by a loud *crunch* as the car behind me rammed into lmy car. We lurched forward and I stomped on the brakes in panic, fearing another sudden impact. However, the car sped off before I could think to get a good look at it. Sweetie scrambled up from the floor where she'd been thrown. I looked around in the dark car and invited Sweetie into the front passenger seat. Her tail was between her legs and her eyes were confused. My milkshake was splattered all over me and the steering wheel. This couldn't be happening. People didn't have wrecks in the park. I couldn't tell how much damage had been done. My hands shook as I searched for my cell phone.

Before I could find the phone and call the police, the car returned from the other direction. It parked across the street, not another vehicle in sight. The driver came out of his car, a hooded sweatshirt pulled over his head.

Just a kid, I thought, *just a kid.*

Sweetie began to growl. He approached quickly. I was staring at a masked face—all but the eyes covered. Something metallic glinted in his hand; it appeared to be a knife. Sweetie snarled and charged the window, leaping into my lap. I slammed my foot on the gas pedal, the car roared … and nothing happened.

My heart stopped for that second as he raised the knife. Sweetie was going crazy, her paws stabbing my legs. I screamed and jammed the car into gear. The car leapt forward, gears grinding, Sweetie barking, blocking my view. With strength I didn't know I had, I shoved Sweetie back onto the passenger seat with my right hand while driving as best I could with my left. After almost swerving off the road, I was able to regain control. I stole a glance into my rearview mirror but the other car was gone. I didn't slow down until I was out of the park and we were at the well-lit gas station on Thornrose Avenue. My house was on the other side of the park, my dog was hysterical, and my insides wouldn't stop shaking. So I called the police.

The police weren't too happy with me, which I thought was odd. One officer kept saying I shouldn't have left the scene of an accident. His partner took pictures of the car with his cell phone. I repeated that I was being attacked, carjacked, or something, but the officer clearly wasn't buying it. His patronizing attitude was really getting to me, and even in my half-hysterical state I could see a serious confrontation brewing. I might have been moments away from a trip to jail when Rita Butler rolled up in her black SUV. She took the officer aside and his mood immediately changed. Now he was apologetic and offered to escort me home. I let him. Rita gave me a wink and drove off.

As soon as Sweetie and I were back home, I locked us in and called Lucy.

She was knocking on my door almost as soon as I hung up. "Oh, Alice. You're a mess!"

"It's just a chocolate milkshake I was enjoying before we were hit." I tried to be adult, but I felt myself begin to dissolve as the reality of the assault began take hold.

"Are you hurt?" she asked.

"Yes and no. Sweetie caused most of the damage jumping on my lap, and I have bruises from the seatbelt. Mostly I'm just scared.

The knife …" I started to cry like a five-year-old with a boo-boo on her knee.

"Here, honey." Lucy hugged me despite all the sticky chocolate. "You're going to be okay. Perhaps we need to get you cleaned up before we talk more."

"Okay," I wailed.

Lucy pushed me out at an arm's length and inspected me. "Can you take a shower by yourself? I'll help you if you need me to."

"No," I sniffled. "I can do it."

Twenty minutes later, wrapped in my pale blue fuzzy robe, I felt like a grown up again.

"Okay," Lucy pointed to the steaming mug on the coffee table, "here's some hot tea, fixed just like you like it. Snuggle into the sofa and get comfortable." She patted the cushion next to her.

"You're so nice to me," I whispered.

"Yes I am," she said, glancing at the smudged chocolate on her turquoise tee. "Now tell me everything, from the beginning."

After I had given Lucy a blow-by-blow account of what happened, she hugged me again and said, "Why'd you do such a dumb thing?"

This was not the encouraging words of sympathy I expected. "I just went for a milkshake. Part of my stress-eating."

"You drove through a dark, deserted park after you thought someone was following you. You're not acting smart."

"It's hard to be smart when you're scared."

"You weren't scared when you decided to go on a milkshake run. That's what I mean: don't deliberately do things that can make you more scared—or hurt."

"Sweetie was with me. She started growling before I even saw the mask or knife."

"Good for her." Reaching down, Lucy gave Sweetie a pat. "She recognizes danger better than you do."

"Yeah." I hugged myself and the shaking eased.

"Alice, I'm worried about you. Can't you just stay home until the police sort this out? You've been in the paper, you're on Facebook, LinkedIn, and professional sites. You're more vulnerable than you realize."

"I'll shut down the online stuff, but you know I can't just stay home." I hugged myself tighter. "Too many sessions have been canceled as it is, and I'm not getting new clients. I have to work. I *like* to work."

"At least start taking Sweetie with you." Lucy reached out to me.

Dislodging my hand from my robe, I took her hand. "Okay, Lucy. I'll take Sweetie. She'd enjoy that anyway."

After Lucy left I locked the door and went around to each window, making sure they were all locked, too. It didn't do any good. I lay awake listening to Sweetie's snores and wondering why someone wanted to kill me. Did I really know something I shouldn't?

CHAPTER 28

WEDNESDAY, OCTOBER 26 MORNING

I still felt shaky the next morning. The bright sun didn't make it seem less real. The more I thought about the night before, the more certain I was that Hoodie Man would have killed me. I just didn't know why. This time I didn't have any hesitation about calling Rita.

She was in her office, but her tone wasn't friendly. "Are you feeling better?" she asked with a puzzling lack of empathy.

"I'm just as scared, so no." I waited for Rita to respond. Nothing. "He would have killed me, Rita. I know it."

"You can't be sure." She was sounding like a cop, not a friend.

"Yes, I can."

"It was cold last night. Maybe you mistook a scarf for a mask."

"No. It was a ski mask. Looked like a skeleton head. The guy didn't just have a cold face, it was a skull. Did you find the scene?"

"Glass and metal, just where you said they'd be." Her tone was turning alarmingly official.

"What's with this new attitude, Rita?"

"There is no attitude. I'm just telling you—"

"Yes, you do have an attitude. You sound like you don't believe me."

"Alice, no one else saw it."

"What about the glass? What about the damage to my car?"

"People have been known to do that to their own cars."

"People? This is me we're talking about. Don't you believe me, Rita? Your friend." Though just now she wasn't acting like one.

"Like you, I find it's easier to keep my head focused on my cases when I'm at work. I have to be professional about this. The official view is that there may have been an accident and that you left the scene. You'll get a ticket for that."

"A ticket! If I'd stayed at the scene you'd be investigating my homicide now."

"I'm sorry, Alice. Sorry for what your insurance company will say, and sorry because I can't support you. There's just not enough hard evidence."

"Evidence!" I shrieked.

"Yes, Dr. Brenner. Evidence. I know you've been under stress. It just got to you last night. Or maybe you'd been drinking. You should take a short vacation or something."

I didn't bother to reply, just hung up. So much for new friends.

The day went downhill from there. I couldn't get Rita's cold tone out of my mind. How could she not believe me? My car looked like it'd been rear ended. Wasn't that evidence enough? Did I need my own accident investigator? My life was the pits. Someone tried to kill me and nobody believed it. Could my life possibly get worse? Well, I guess having my life taken away violently would be worse. Was that where I was heading?

* * *

Russ was sitting on the porch steps when I went down with Sweetie to give her a bathroom break. He looked pretty good today; cleaned up, not fidgety.

"I knew the agency would try to get you," he said when he saw me. His lopsided smile managed to look serious. "Didn't I tell you?"

"Russ, that wasn't the agency. There is no agency."

"You know there is. You saw them. I've been telling people that I've got evidence now because Doctor Brenner saw them. People will have to believe me because everyone believes you." I feared that Russ's confidence in my "evidence" was the reason he was so calm today; I reinforced his delusions.

"I don't need your help, Russ," I said. That's all I needed, a mentally ill man as my "proof" that *I* wasn't off the deep end.

"Yes, you do." Russ continued talking. "Yes ma'am, you do. The agency has you under surveillance again. Without me around they'd kill you." He shrugged and walked away muttering to himself.

After Russ left, I leaned back in the comfortable wicker chair and almost dozed off.

I jerked awake as my phone rang upstairs. Luckily, I grabbed it just before the answering machine picked up.

"I'll get you the next time, bitch. You're dead." It was a muffled voice. It sounded vaguely familiar.

"What?" My voice squeaked. "Who are you?"

The line went dead. And I slid to the floor. Sweetie was delighted to sit on me. "Oh God, Sweetie. I'm dead. He's going to kill me."

Sweetie licked my face and wagged her tail. It was the best she could do.

CHAPTER 29

THURSDAY, OCTOBER 27 AFTERNOON

Dave called me before work on Thursday. "Alice, we need to talk," he said. His serious tone sent a shiver up my back.

"Okay. Can we talk at lunch today? I don't have any afternoon patients so we can take as long as we want."

"Good. I'll see you at Kathy's at noon." He hung up without saying another word. He was usually much more talkative. It was odd.

At noon Dave was already there, seated in the back booth with his back to the wall. I slid into the seat opposite him.

"What's going on?" I asked.

"I found a bug in my apartment."

"A bug?" Didn't most rental apartments have bugs?

"Yeah. Not an insect. A listening device." He looked grim.

"What did you do? Did you call the police?"

"No. I didn't do anything. I don't want whoever is spying on me to know I found the bug."

"Oh. Okay. So what do you make of this?"

"We've rattled somebody."

"Well Duh! Remember someone's been following me in the park and then tried to kill me the other night."

"Yeah and now they're spying on us in a more sophisticated way. There's probably bugs in your home too."

"Ugh! That's so creepy." I really didn't like the thought.

"We'll leave yours alone, too. Best that they don't know that we know they're there."

"So what now?"

"Now we figure out what to do about our watchers." He was serious. Almost as serious as I'd seen him look.

"What watchers? You mean cameras?"

"No. We've been under surveillance since just after I got here. There are three of them. Two are at that booth over there and one is sitting at the end of the counter." I started to turn, but he hissed, "Don't look. We don't want them to know we've spotted them."

"Oh. Okay. What do we do?" I was feeling overwhelmed.

"We pay our bill and leave. Calm. Laughing. Maybe flirting a little. Act like we don't have a care in the world. We'll lose them on the road."

Once in the car I could see the three watchers hurry out the door and head for a dark blue Mustang.

"They're driving a muscle car. Can we lose them?" I asked.

"Yeah, of course. It's more about the driving, not the car." He smiled. "And I am a superior driver."

"Oh you are? Well, prove it." I smiled back, almost forgetting the watchers.

Dave squealed out of the parking lot, before the watchers'd started their car. We were down the road and turning off onto a side road that led to the county before the watchers'd gotten onto the main road. I thought sure we'd lost them, but they followed us onto the country road. Soon we could see them way back behind us.

"Don't worry," he said. "I can go around curves faster than they can. There's a lot of curves coming up."

"Be careful."

"Hump!" He gave me a glare before focusing back on the road.

Dave was right. The two-lane road curved around hills, cornfields, and cute white farmhouses. We couldn't see how close our pursuers were, but at least they weren't on our tail.

Suddenly Dave made an abrupt left turn onto a long gravel driveway that wound its way up a hill. At the top was another farmhouse and a large detached garage. We drove past the open garage doors, screeched to a stop, Dave jumped out, and closed the doors. As I climbed out of the car in the dark, he grabbed my hand and said, "Come on." He led me through a side door and onto a brick path leading to a similar door at the back of the house. Once inside the kitchen, Dave yelled, "Hey Larry!"

"Who's that?" A deep voice answered.

"It's me, Dave, and a friend."

"Hey Dave. It's good to see you, buddy. A large man with a red beard, dirty overalls, and a big smile walked into the kitchen. "Who's this?" He extended his hand to me.

"I'm Alice Brenner. It's nice to meet you."

"Likewise" His blue eyes twinkled. I wondered if he thought we were being too formal. He seemed like a very casual guy.

Dave interrupted. "We're being followed, Larry. I think I lost them by hiding the car in your garage. Can we stay here for a while to give them time to give up?"

"Sure. I was just about to make some chili. Wanna help me eat it?"

"I'll help you cook it, too," I said.

So we spent the afternoon with Larry. Turns out he has a University of Virginia Ph.D in American history, but chose to return to run his family farm. It was a fun three hours and when we returned to town, I was feeling relaxed. But it didn't solve the problem of our being spied upon. Did it?

CHAPTER 30

FRIDAY, OCTOBER 30
MORNING

I began to take Sweetie everywhere. To the grocery store, to the dry cleaners, and even to work.

"You can't bring an animal in here. This is a business. What are you thinking, Doctor Brenner?" Ron Margolis didn't approve of my decision to have Sweetie with me.

"Sweetie might help some of my patients loosen up. A canine co-therapist. You know the research."

"We'll see what the others have to say about that."

I stood tall and led Sweetie through the waiting room. Out of the corner of my eye I could see Georgia give me a thumbs up. The rest of the week Sweetie and I went back and forth to work together.

I tried to call Rita Butler about the threatening call, but she wasn't available. At least not to me.

And though Rita didn't return my call, a colleague of hers did. He was a slow-speaking man with a deep country accent who introduced himself as Detective Gibbs. I don't think he liked me. For one thing he kept calling me "Miss" instead of Dr. Brenner or Alice. Just "Miss." For another, he didn't seem to take the threatening phone call seriously. Said it was probably kids.

"Detective Gibbs," I said, trying to maintain a professional, non-hysterical tone, "kids, as you put it, wouldn't know to call me just after someone tried to kill me. My number is unlisted. It wasn't a random teenage prank."

"Yes. There's that," he agreed.

"What do you mean 'that.'" I could hear my professional tone slipping. "Don't you believe me? I am being targeted by someone. Women are killed by stalkers every day. Is it department policy to ignore reality?"

"No, Miss, we don't ignore reality. And we don't make it up either. We never found another car. No one has tried to get a car with that kind of damage fixed. And you didn't stay where you say it happened."

"I was in danger. Of course I left. Somebody was going to stab me, whether you believe it or not," I snapped. This was getting absurd. "And you found the broken glass."

"Maybe it happened like you say, maybe it didn't," he remarked.

"What do you think happened?" I asked.

I could almost hear him smile. "I don't know. I just know that you're awfully involved in this murder case of Rita's. Maybe too involved."

"I didn't ask to be involved. Janet Ford was my patient. Detective Butler called me to help with your first suspect."

"A suspect that you have been spending an awful lot of time with," he said.

"Exactly. That's why I could help with the interview," I answered. "But Russ just comes and goes. I can't control his behavior."

"As you say."

"Please make sure that Detective Butler knows about the threatening phone call." I wondered if he'd bother.

"Oh, she does, Miss. She does."

I had another of those sleepless nights wondering why Rita hadn't called me and how Detective Gibbs would react when my mutilated body was found. At least Sweetie was sleeping well.

* * *

Ben was my first patient on Friday. I wondered if he had been able to tell his two friends that he was gay. He didn't look happy.

"How are you today?" I asked.

"Not so good," he answered.

"Tell me about it."

He sighed. "I tried telling Jeff and Bill about my being gay."

"And?"

"Well, I played golf with Jeff on Saturday, and at the sixteenth hole I told him that I wanted to talk to him about something important. He was about to take his turn and seemed a little irritated about stopping, but I went on anyway. Perhaps I should have picked a better time. He stopped and picked nonexistent lint off his pant leg."

"It didn't go well?"

"It could have gone better. At first, he was surprised and then said it was okay and that it wouldn't change our friendship. Then he hit his ball off into the woods. And on the seventeenth hole he ended up in the woods again. At the eighteenth hole, he told me it did bother him. That he liked me, but my being gay creeped him out and he needed to think about it. He passed on burgers and beer afterwards and left right after the game. I've been afraid to call him."

"I'm so sorry, Ben. I know that wasn't the response you wanted."

"Yeah. Jeff and I've been friends for ten years. His response really hurt." There were tears in his eyes.

"It's possible that he'll come around and remember what a good friend you are to him."

"Maybe, but I'm not going to count on it," he sighed. "It's just that I don't have many friends, and to lose two over this really hurts." The tears were sliding down his face now.

"You may have to make new friends." That would be hard for Ben. He tended to be a loner.

"I don't know if I can. It's so hard when you're out of school." He looked at me with defeated eyes.

"Yes. It can be harder, but you can do it if you put in the effort." I deployed a reassuring smile. "We'll work on that. There are strategies."

"Okay." His voice was both hopeful and doubtful.

"What happened with Bill? Did you call him?" I changed the subject back to his current crisis. We needed to deal with that today. Later we could work on making friends. Today was just planting a seed for him to think about.

"Yeah, I did call Bill. I thought he'd take it even harder than Jeff because he's a banker and fairly conservative politically."

"And?"

"And he was okay with it. Said that he'd wondered if I was gay and that he was happy for me. Even thanked me for sharing with him and that it wouldn't hurt our friendship. He said he had a gay friend at work and he knew that coming out must be a big relief for me as well as terrifying." He was smiling and crying at the same time.

I handed him the box of tissues. "Sounds like he had more experience with gay men than Jeff and Tom."

"Yeah, experience. He really was okay with it. I feel so grateful." He wiped at his tears, blew his nose, and stopped smiling. "What does all this mean about work? Bill is a banker and was okay with it.

Jeff is an artist and wasn't okay about it. Now, I don't know what to do about telling people at work."

"Bill may be a banker, but he lives in a big city, which tends to be more gay friendly than small, Southern towns. You might want to be more circumspect here in Fort Madison. But again, it's your decision. One way or the other, whatever you do is fine with me."

"You said last time that I might want to tell my family before I take on work."

"Yes. In your case that might be easier. You don't see your family much, like you do people at work. Also, it sounds like your family is fairly liberal and openminded. They might be able to accept the news. But I'd probably tell my brother and sister before my parents."

Ben was still undecided about what to do at the end of the session. After he left, I found out more about the investigation into Janet Ford's murder.

My third patient told me that the police were investigating his cousin because she was Janet Ford's neighbor. He said the cousin had an autistic son who screamed a lot and Janet had called the city's Social Services Department to report child abuse. The cousin was investigated and cleared, but she and Janet had been at odds ever since. The cousin had invited him to a dinner to celebrate Janet's death. They had lasagna and a big cake. Sounded rather ghoulish, and in very poor taste.

As interesting as that was, I knew the female cousin hadn't had anything to do with Janet's death. It was a man who called me. And a man who rammed my car. He was out there free while the police investigated the probably loony mother of an autistic boy.

CHAPTER 31

MONDAY, NOVEMBER 2 MORNING

Early Monday morning I got a call. I hoped it was Detective Butler. Instead it was Dave.

"You need to call in sick this morning. We've got some investigating to do," he said.

"I can't just skip work like that." Why didn't he understand that?

"Yes you can. This is important. Remember that drifter the police talked with about Janet's murder? I found out that there were others in the park that night. There was a drug dealer with some new product and several of his customers were in the park about the time Janet got killed."

"How do you know? The police don't even seem to know that."

"I can do things they can't."

"Like what?" I asked.

"You don't want to know." He smiled.

I did, but it was clear that he wasn't going to tell me.

"So call in sick," he said. "And I'll pick you up in thirty minutes. Wear clothes you can hike in if necessary."

"Hike? I don't want to hike."

" Just do it. I'll explain on the way."

It turns out that we had lots of time for him to explain. The man we were looking for, Bob Spikes, had moved on to Bath county, about an hour and a half from Fort Madison. Dave knew from one of his informants that Spikes was in the Millboro area and was fond of a bar named Ray's Place.

"Why the hiking clothes?" I asked as I looked down at my jeans, sweatshirt, and hiking boots. "If he's in a bar that won't involve hiking . . . will it?"

"The bar is at the edge of the George Washington National Forest. If Spikes decides to make a run for it, he may well head into the woods. By the way have you ever been in that area?"

"No. Why?"

"I'll give you an overview. It's mostly woods with farms that have been in the same family for generations. Lots of mountains. Folks there are straightforward country people. They can be kind, generous, and loyal. But not at first. They won't be inclined to help us find someone who's been there for a while. So we'll be on our own. Be nice, friendly, and go slow."

"Okay. What makes you so sure that it's going to be a struggle to get Spikes to talk to us?"

"If he was inclined to talk, he'd have stayed in Fort Madison. Though he might be happier to talk to us than the police."

Bath County was just as Dave had described it. But he left out how beautiful it was. Being November, it was dark and gray out and most of the leaves had fallen. The stark gray branches of the trees overhanging the two-lane road looked eerie. Like an Ansel Adams photograph. I imagined it was like traveling through a green tunnel in the summer. The farms were well kept and loved. I began to imagine

Ray's Place as something similar — well maintained and clean, with a country gentleman sort of vibe.

Boy was I wrong. We pulled into a gravel parking lot filled with pot holes. Near the door with its peeling blue paint there were a couple of hay bales with rotting pumpkins on top. No one had raked the leaves that had fallen from the many trees surrounding the small graying wood building. Inside there was smoke-darkened pine paneling on the walls and dirty sawdust on the floor. Three or four mismatched tables and chairs were across from the long bar. A few small windows provided dim light. Already at ten in the morning, there were five men hunched over the sticky bar top. Everybody turned and looked at us as we entered.

Dave smiled and said, " Hey, y'all. How's everybody?"

Nobody answered. We took two stools at the end of the bar.

"What do you want?" I wasn't sure whether the bartender was asking about what we wanted to drink or was being more philosophical.

Dave didn't seem to have that problem. "We'll have two Buds. Thanks."

Everybody went back to their drinks.

When the bartender brought us two bottles of beer, Dave began. "Hey do you know a guy named Bob Spikes?"

"Why do you want to know?"

"We hope he has some information we need."

"You cops?" He eyed my outfit. *Do I look like a cop? Ugh.*

"Naw. We're just trying to find out what happened when a girl died in Fort Madison."

"You sound like cops." His sneer said loud and clear that cops weren't liked in this bar.

"We're private investigators working for the mother of the girl who died. Cops don't like us and we don't like them."

"Right" He didn't look convinced. Neither did the audience at the bar.

"Do I really look like a cop to you?" I asked the bartender. Dave was off his game today. Usually he could get anybody to talk to him. Guess it was time for me to use my therapist skills. Many people are reluctant to talk when they first come to therapy. I'd found that talking about something that wasn't important often made it easier for them to talk to me.

"Yeah" He looked at me curiously. My guess was that girlfriends didn't often talk when their men were talking with him.

"How come?" I was really interested. Maybe he sensed that, because he smiled at me.

"You're too dressed up. Looks like those hiking boots are new. You don't look like you've ever taken a hike in your life."

"You're right. My boyfriend here," I patted Daves shoulder, "he said to dress for a hike 'cause we might take time to do one. I didn't know what to wear. So this is what I came up with. Guess I got it wrong." I smiled an apologetic smile.

"Not your thing?" He seemed to have softened.

"No. I'm more likely to sit in front of a nice warm fire on a cold day like today. I really don't want to hike."

"So is he a cop?" He nodded at Dave.

"Naw. He's just what he said. A private investigator trying to find out what happened to that woman that got killed."

"He's not very good at talking to folks is he?"

I laughed. "Not today."

He grinned at Dave and said, "Bob Spikes is likely to come in any time now. This is when he's here most days."

"Thanks. I appreciate it," I said.

We smiled at each other as Dave's face grew red. He got very interested in his beer.

About that time the door opened. The bartender looked up and said, "Hey, Spikes. Here's some people who'd like to talk with you."

Spikes stopped, looked at us, and ran. I guess we looked like cops to him, too. By the time we got out the door, he was roaring out of the parking lot in his beat-up red truck. We jumped in our car and screeched after him.

The roads in Bath County are narrow, two-lane, and curvy. Spikes was going at least seventy, fishtailing around the sharp curves, accelerating on the few straight stretches. We followed as best as we could, but he was lengthening the distance between us. We were going to lose him.

Then it happened.

Coming out of a particularly sharp curve Spikes lost control and crashed into a big oak tree. As we pulled up to the crash site, Spikes ran into the woods. I was amazed that he survived, let alone was able to run. Dave jumped out of our car and ran after Spikes. I followed both of them.

It began to rain. We were surrounded by trees and a fine mist. I couldn't see the men, but I could hear them crashing through the underbrush. It was cold, wet, and scary. As I approached them there was a loud noise and the tree beside me seemed to explode, spraying bark and splinters on my face. I dropped to the ground and tried to hide. I couldn't hear anything but my pulse pounding in my ears. The rain soaked into my sweatshirt and jeans. I couldn't tell if I was so cold from the rain or fear.

There was another shot and then a lot of crashing in the underbrush and yelling. I couldn't just hide. I had to do something to help Dave.

"Alice! Are you there?" It was Dave *Thank God.*

"I'm here!" I yelled back. "I'm coming."

When I reached them, they were in a small clearing. They were rolling around on the ground hitting each other. It was hard to see who was who since they were both covered in mud. I did see that there was a gun on the ground about ten feet from them and each man was trying to get closer to it while keeping the other away from it. Neither was having any success.

It was obvious to me that it was up to me to end it. So I ran over and scooped up the gun. They were so busy fighting that neither noticed. So I backed up, pointed the gun at the sky and pulled the trigger. There was a huge recoil and I ended up on my butt sitting in the mud. I jumped up and pointed the gun at the men. They had stopped fighting and were staring at me with identical expressions of horror.

Dave spoke first. "Alice be careful with the gun. Don't point it at me, please." He pulled away from Spikes and stood up with his hand extended toward me. ""Give me the gun."

"Don't shoot, lady!" Spikes yelled.

Both men were pale despite the mud streaking their faces.

"Okay. Okay. Come over here, Dave, and I'll give you the gun."

"It's my gun! Give it back," Spikes said. Dave and I ignored that.

Dave held Spikes at gunpoint. Both had bruises and cuts. Dave looked over at me and said, "Good job, Alice. Are you okay?"

"I'm fine." Except for being cold and wet. "What happened?"

"He attacked me!" Spikes yelled.

"You were shooting at us," Dave said.

Spikes wasn't finished. "I'm going to sue you for police brutality."

"We're not cops."

"Ray said you were."

"He did not," I said. "He said we wanted to talk with you."

"Then why were you chasing me?"

"We're private investigators, working for the mother of a woman that was killed in Fort Madison. We were told that you were in the park near where she was killed. We wanted to talk with you to see if you might have seen something that would help us find out what happened to our client's daughter."

"Why didn't you say so?"

"You didn't give us a chance," I said.

"Why should I help you? You almost got me killed. Then you attacked me."

"I was defending myself when you started shooting at me." Dave's face was red.

"I was defending myself from you," Spikes said.

The two men stared at each other. Spikes began to laugh.

Dave frowned, then his laugh exploded into the silence. Soon both men were laughing so hard they had tears in their eyes. I didn't understand it, but I was glad the mood had lightened.

Eventually, Dave spoke. " It was the night of October 3. In the big city park near the bandstand. Do you remember about that night?"

"Not much. I got pretty high when I was in Fort Madison. No. Wait! There was something. I was in the park .Uh . . . I was getting ready to get high." He stopped.

"You mean you were in the park to buy drugs?" Dave asked.

"Well … yeah. My dealer was near the bandstand. That's where I saw him."

"Who?" I asked.

"There was a black man all dressed in black skulking around

behind some big bushes watching some people. A white woman and an older black man wearing a big brown sweater. He was kneeling on the ground holding her. She looked passed out. I couldn't see much. I was too far away, but the black guy wearing black was closer and watching them. I got bad vibes from that and left. None of them saw me… I don't think. When I heard that a woman was killed in the park that night, I wondered if I'd almost walked into that.

"Why didn't you tell the police?" I asked.

"Me? Talk to the police? I've had enough times of being arrested because I was a stranger and high. I figured that the local police would just love to pin that killing on me. So I left town. People in Bath don't ask a lot of questions. That's why I came here."

"Okay. Did you see or hear anything else? Anything you can remember would be helpful." Dave's voice was gentle.

"That's all I remember. Is that it? I need to get going"

"Yeah." Dave smiled. "But we'd appreciate it if you'd help us find our way out of these woods. Then we'll drive you back to the bar so you can see about getting your truck towed to a garage. Our client will pay to get it fixed since you've been so helpful."

I laughed and we all made our way back to the car.

On the long ride home, I thought about our adventure. I felt good that I'd been able to get the bartender to help us and help Dave when he and Spikes had been fighting. Guess I wasn't the passive wimp that I'd always been. I wonder how that happened?

CHAPTER 32

THURSDAY, NOVEMBER 7
AFTERNOON

almost called Rita two or three times that week, but I didn't know if she'd even take my call. I felt hurt that what had seemed to be a growing friendship just stopped so suddenly. It was confusing.

Thursday afternoon I received a message from Georgia to call Rita's number. I could hardly wait until my session was over so I could make the call.

This time she answered. But it wasn't what I'd hoped for.

"Alice, I am officially requesting that you come down to the station. We need to talk about a few things."

"Like what? Did Detective Gibbs tell you about the threatening phone call?" I asked.

"He told me," she replied, "but we're not going to talk about that. We're going to talk about Janet Ford."

I told Rita I'd need an hour to cancel patients, but she wasn't in the mood to wait. If I wasn't there in forty-five minutes, she'd come and get me.

I called Dave McGinty. We hadn't talked since we'd been to Bath county. He'd said then that I shouldn't go anywhere alone. I was hearing that a lot lately. Today, he was more worried about Rita's request than I was.

"Sounds like an official interview. What do they have on you?"

"Nothing. I haven't done anything wrong."

"Mrs. Whitmire found Janet's journal. She's furious at you. According to her, Janet wrote that you were trying to seduce her. Were you?"

"Of course not! I would never cross that line with a client. And besides, you know I'm heterosexual." I hoped he did, because I thought it was obvious.

"Be prepared. Call me afterwards. Oh, and call your lawyer before you go."

"I don't have a lawyer."

"I thought Collier was your lawyer."

"Not anymore."

"Get one before you go talk to the police."

I gnawed at the corner of my thumbnail. "Okay, but all I have to do is to explain why Janet wrote that. I have a clear idea of why she did. Then what could happen?"

Those words sounded familiar.

*   *   *

When I came out of our building, there was a squad car waiting to escort me. I was sure that Ron would make a note of it. I'd left Sweetie with Georgia, another black mark for Ron to put in his Alice-the-Troublemaker ledger. My head was pounding and my stomach was clenched into a solid knot of percolating anxiety by the time I walked into the detectives' office.

On the way to the station, I worried about my choice of lawyer. Collier'd been my lawyer for years. That's how we met. But his allegiance was to Mrs. Whitmire, not me. Was he the best lawyer for me now that the outcome could be serious?

When I'd called Collier, he didn't seem to have a problem with representing both Mrs. Whitmire and me.

"Of course I'll meet you at the station," he said. "I'm your lawyer."

"I wasn't sure we should continue to work together after what happened with Mrs. Whitmire.

. un.n.?.....?My worrying was abruptly interrupted by the policeman opening the door and motioning me out of his car. I hadn't even realized that we'd stopped.

I walked with him to the detective's office in the basement in a daze. The patrolman left as soon as I walked into the room.

They were all there again—the tall man, Jay Manson, and Rita. I felt awkward as I said, "Hi. I'm here."

Rita gave me a grim-faced nod and took me by the arm. "Come with me, please."

I wanted to say something appropriate to the situation that would show how surprised I was to be there, and how hurt I was at her attitude. Before I could say anything, I was in the small interrogation room where Rita and I had talked to Russ. I wished I could sit on the floor this time. Instead, we both sat in chairs across the table from each other. I wondered why Collier wasn't here yet.

"Why are you so unfriendly?" I asked, hoping that if I laid it right out we could get this weirdness cleared up.

"Unfriendly?" she repeated, staring at me.

"Yes. Unfriendly. I thought we were friends ... or friendly acquaintances or something like that." I tried to look as unhappy as I felt.

"We are here to discuss your relationship with Janet Ford. Not to be friends." Somehow Rita looked more mistreated than I did.

"She was my patient. That was the extent of our relationship." *What's wrong with her? She already knows this.*

"Just your patient, or something more?" Either Rita had no use for the tactic, or if she did had not yet learned, but being sweet to the suspect was not in her playbook. And I was very much beginning to feel like a suspect. I just wasn't sure for what.

"What do you mean 'something more'? She was a patient. Every Friday at three o'clock," I stated.

"Did you know she was keeping a journal?" Rita asked.

"Yes, I asked her to. It often helps patients get in touch with their feelings." I was about to suggest that Rita might benefit from a little journaling herself, but somehow resisted. I imagined we were being watched.

Rita smiled a death-head's smile. "Do you know what was in that journal?"

"Not really. Mr. McGinty told me she wrote that I was trying to seduce her, but I've never seen the journal."

"Are you a lesbian, Dr. Brenner?" Now Rita looked angry.

I could feel a blush creep across my face. "No, I am not a lesbian."

"Why did Janet think you were trying to seduce her?" Rita scowled.

"I don't know how she got that idea. I do have gay clients who are distressed about it, but Janet wasn't seeing me for that. If she thought I was sexually interested in her, she was wrong." Had I misread Janet somehow?

"She thought you wanted her to be a lesbian." Now Rita had a smug expression.

"That's ridiculous." I felt like the floor was falling away from me. I began to feel short of air. The room was tiny—probably poorly ventilated. Maybe I was going to pass out.

"Dr. Brenner, are you listening to me?" Now Rita sounded really angry. "Why did Janet Ford think you were a homosexual?"

I needed a moment to refocus. "I don't know, Detective. I never said anything to make her think that. I don't know." I had a vague feeling I was forgetting something important, but my brain seemed to be frozen.

"Janet wrote in her journal that you were in love with her, that you were trying to turn her into a lesbian. What happened, Doctor Brenner? Did your patient reject you, or did she string you along and then reject you?" Rita's voice was soft now. Seductive. "You couldn't stand that, could you? You couldn't let her treat you like that."

"No! I'm not gay. I never gave Janet any reason to believe I had those sorts of feelings for her. She was a patient. That's all—just a patient." *What am I forgetting?* More and more I felt its urgency, but I couldn't remember.

"You don't have a boyfriend, do you?"

"Yes. Well not anymore, but I did. Besides, why do I have to have a boyfriend to be innocent?" I could feel the anger flushing my face. "You have nothing but the writing of a disturbed woman. Patients can project all kinds of things on their therapists; it's one of the things we're trained to deal with."

Then in a rush my brain unfroze. I remembered.

"I don't want to talk anymore until my lawyer gets here," I stated. "I believe you two have already spoken on the phone."

This was a nightmare. One day I was feeling good about making a new friend in Rita Butler, then the next she's accusing me of murder. And of trying to seduce a patient no less. I couldn't think of anything worse. Well, I could, but this was actually happening to me.

Asking for a lawyer stopped the interview and I was put in a holding cell with a very drunk woman who was propped up on the one bench.

This was turning out to be a disturbing day.

CHAPTER 33

FRIDAY, NOVEMBER 8 MORNING

I was certain I'd be released at any moment, but it was the next morning before that happened. Collier was there when I was sprung. He was a total jerk, but he knew his stuff. In fact, he got the cops to admit that they didn't have enough evidence to arrest me. The only reason I was kept in jail overnight was that Rita "lost" my release authorization. How lame was that?

"It's harassment and intimidation," Collier grumbled as we walked quickly toward a side exit. "Alice, what did you do to piss off the police? You're at the top of their shit list."

I was shocked.

"I didn't do anything. I helped them." But if they thought I was trouble, it would explain all the attitude I'd been getting.

"That must be it, then." Suddenly he stopped and grabbed my arms. "I almost forgot, I am really angry with you, too."

"What are you talking about?" .

"You're a grown-ass woman, Alice. You should know better than to talk to the police without a lawyer present. What on earth were you thinking?" Collier was acting like nothing had happened between us.

Now it was my turn to be angry.

I placed my hands on my hips. "I know I shouldn't have talked to her before you got here, but Rita tricked me. And besides, if I'm innocent, why shouldn't I talk to the cops?"

"Especially if you're innocent.. I hope that night in jail taught you a lesson. Now let's get out of here."

At the door, we paused. Putting his hands on my shoulders, Collier began speaking to me like a coach explaining the next play.

"Here's how it goes. The press is out there and they expect a statement. It's better to play along than antagonize them."

"I just want to go home." I was tired and I smelled like jail. Ugh!

"Fine. You do that. I'll handle the press. I have a statement all prepared. Standard stuff, sound bite friendly."

"What?"

"Alice, don't worry, but try to keep up, okay? I'm giving a statement, as your lawyer, understand? You just stand next me. It's not a press conference, you won't answer questions. In fact, don't look directly at anyone, but don't look down either. That makes you look guilty. Remember, you're the wronged party here, mistreated and maligned by an uncaring system, so be strong and resolute. Can you do resolute? It's like fierce mixed with humble."

"I can do mistreated." I already had plenty of anger-fueled resolution.

Then Collier turned his back on me and opened the door.

CHAPTER 34

FRIDAY, NOVEMBER 8 MORNING

I was dismayed to see how many reporters and television cameras surrounded the police department as Collier and I left. *Fort Madison is a small town, where did all these people come from?*

"Dr. Brenner, did you kill Janet Ford?" one blonde yelled out. "Dr. Brenner."

Maria Escobar from the Harrisonburg television station slid in beside me. "Tell us how you feel about being in jail. Did you do it?"

Despite my anger, I was impressed as Collier quickly took control and gave the assembled fifth estate their sound bites. My anger fought my nervousness to a draw, but really, how good could I look on camera after a night in jail? I knew this wasn't going to play well at work. If I even had any work to go back to.

Without speaking, Collier escorted me to a silver car I didn't recognize, reporters tagging along, tossing questions like smelt to a seal, except I wasn't biting. I got in the car without speaking, sure my red face would be all over the TV screen within the hour. As we drove off I could see Collier distracting the reporters with an additional statement. Where had he learned all this media stuff? It was a side of him I'd never seen before. Looking at the driver, a young black man wearing a suit, I asked, "Who are you? Do you work for Collier?"

He grimaced and answered, "I'm William Acker. I work *with* Collier. I'm a tax attorney, and Collier and I play poker together. I lost last night so I got volunteered for car duty this morning."

"Oh! I'm sorry Mr. Acker. I didn't mean to insult you." I wasn't doing too well with anyone this morning.

Mr. Acker just smiled and nodded as if this had happened before. Maybe he wasn't a very good poker player.

On the ride home I thought about Collier having skills I hadn't known about. Could that also mean he could be a criminal? Could the weird mix of feelings I felt for him be disrupting my ability to read him? How much of my being able to imagine him being the killer be my anger and how much could be reality? I felt even more confused.

Lucy and Sweetie were waiting on the porch when I got home. "I've already called the office," she said as we dashed upstairs. "Told them you were dealing with a personal emergency and to cancel your patients for the day. We're going to think this out." Lucy had that "all business" look she gets with resistant patients. I told her my "personal emergency" would soon be on the local news.

"That just proves you're not lying. We can deal with it later."

She was wearing work clothes. The tan pantsuit with red pumps looked intimidating. Especially the heels. Lucy always wears heels. She goes clacking around in her high heels, seeming even taller than she is. I feel dumpy every time I think about it. Lucy says to get myself some heels, but after years of sandals and moccasins, I'd fall flat on my face if I tried to walk in heels. I've accepted that I'm not meant to be elegant.

"What about your patients? Don't you have to go to work?"

She smiled. "I'm sick, too. But not too sick for coffee and biscuits."

"I need a shower first," I complained.

"I know you feel cruddy, but you need food first. It'll be quick," she said, leading me back downstairs. I was helpless to resist.

We drove through Hardee's, loading up on Hardy Man boxes of biscuits and gravy and large coffees. I couldn't believe how hungry I was; I'd started salivating even before Lucy ordered.

"Alice, have you forgotten that you always eat when you're upset?" Lucy laughed.

By the time we got home my Harty Man was warming my stomach and there was spilled gravy on my shirt.

"Go get that shower and then we'll talk," Lucy commanded, using her warm social worker smile that I'd hadn't quite been able to master yet.

I showered quickly, but the overwhelming feelings wouldn't go away. Murder! Incompetence! How could people think such things about me? I was a very good therapist who never killed anyone.

I hadn't felt like this since I was ten. Tommy Edwards had just asked me to go steady. Not that we'd ever had any dates. But we'd heard of going steady and thought it was a good grown-up thing to do. After school that day he'd stopped me before I'd gone into our apartment building. He asked me officially if I'd go steady with him and I said yes. Then he kissed me right on the mouth and ran home. My mother saw it from our living room window.

When I got upstairs, she grabbed my arm. I could smell the whiskey on her breath as she yelled for the rest of the family to come into the living room. Everybody was there that day: Grandma, Aunt Hazel, my brother, and my cousins.

"Here," my mother shrieked. "Here is my little girl. The little girl we all thought was a good girl, pure and obedient."

"Mamma, please don't." I was still trying to reason with her back then.

"Don't!" She shook me with one arm while she pointed her finger in my face with the other. "You are not the daughter I thought you were. God help me, I've been betrayed by this whore!"

Everyone gasped. Nobody would look me in the eyes and nobody was going to help me. It was clear that, if I was going to get out of this without getting hurt, I'd have to save myself.

"What do you have to say for yourself, you Jezebel?" she screamed in my face. Before I could answer, she grabbed my dress and tore it off of me. I stood there shaking in her vice-like grip, naked except for my panties and my shoes. My cousin Nicky ogled me. I was crying and humiliated.

Grandma said, "Louise, what has the child done?"

"What she did is fornicate with that red-headed boy down the road. That's what. And she deserves a spanking for this. Nicky, give me your belt."

While everyone watched Nicky unbuckle his belt, her grip softened. I pulled loose, kicked her in the shin, and ran. When I got to my room, I scrambled up onto the shelf in the closet and shook, waiting for her to come after me.

But my running and Mamma's crying over her hurt leg must have broken the spell she had over the others. I could hear Grandma say to Mamma, "Come on, Louise, just calm down. Let's sit on the sofa and have a drink. It'll make you feel better." Soon there was happy chatter coming from the living room and later from the kitchen as they ate. No one checked on me. I didn't come out of the closet until the next morning.

When I left for school, Mamma was still passed out on the sofa. At school I told Tommy I couldn't go steady, that it was too dangerous.

Nobody ever talked about what had happened, except that cousin Nicky's looks from then on made me squirm.

That's when I learned not to trust. My training therapist said that it's also when I began to fear closeness and commitments. Who'd a thought.

Remembering that I was a survivor, I felt more in control. I shuffled out to curl up on my sofa. I did feel better. I even began to relax. Behind me, I could hear Sweetie moving in her sleep.

Sweetie …

"What happened to Sweetie last night?"

"When you failed to return from you chat with the police I took her off Georgia's hands," Lucy said. "I took her out and gave her some butter pecan ice cream afterwards. She seemed happy. She was probably more comfortable than you were. The whole office knew you'd been carted off to the slammer."

"I was not carted off. More like tricked into coming voluntarily, but yeah, I didn't sleep much." The drunk woman's snores rattled the high window above the bench; the floor was slick with her vomit. Pushing myself into a dry corner, I tried not to think. It didn't work. I'd imagined in great detail what it would be like to be executed five times by morning.

About then Dave McGinty called. "What happened? Did they accuse you of murder? Did they have Janet's journal? Why did you have to spend the night in jail?"

By the time I'd answered his questions I was exhausted. He wanted to come over, and ordinarily I'd have jumped at it, but not today. I sat on the living room floor, leaning back against the sofa. Sweetie sat beside me and eventually collapsed into a big pile of sleeping dog. I stroked her absently, amazed at how relaxing the simple action was. I could feel my emotions begin to surface again.

What am I going to do? What do I tell my patients about problem solving? I tell them to think about what they can do about the problem. Then I tell them to do that and not waste time with what they can't do. Concentrate on what actions they can take. So I'll do that.

I turned to Lucy. "I suggested to Janet that she keep a journal, record her feelings as a way to help make our sessions more effective. Except she wrote about how I was in love with her and was making advances, trying to lure her into a lesbian relationship."

"Wow!" Lucy laughed. "That's an extreme form of Borderline behavior—your treatment threatened her, so she was trying to discredit you."

"I wonder if she was going to let her mother 'find' the journal entry." I managed a smile.

"That would have put an end to the therapy. There's a logic to it," Lucy agreed, nodding her head.

"Yeah and if it had gotten out, it would have damaged my practice—maybe even put me out of business."

Lucy grimaced. "So that does look bad. It gives you a motive. What else do we know?"

I sighed. "We know that someone is trying to hurt or kill me. And that I'm scared."

"Why don't you leave town until this is over? Take an extended vacation. You haven't had one in years."

"You know I can't do that. My practice would be dead. My patients wouldn't wait until this is all over. Besides, I have to work to feel okay about myself. You know that."

"We've got better security here at the house now. Spotlights and cameras. But, Alice, you have to remember to turn it on at night."

"I do ... most of the time."

She shook her head at me. "It only takes once."

"I'll do better. But there is something else we can do."

"What? "Lucy looked at me with a smile.

I reached over to the end table and pulled a brown paper bag out of the drawer. "Here, last week I got this for us."

I removed two small spray cans, labeled Lady Pepper, out of the bag. "It's pepper spray. Just point at their face and spray. Now, we've got this covered."

"Cool. That's a good idea."

"Also, I'm going to ask Dave to teach me some self-defense moves."

"Okay. That's another good idea."

We sat and enjoyed the quiet for a few minutes, until Sweetie snored, bringing us back to the matter at hand.

"What else do we know?" Lucy asked, her expression grim.

"Janet said that she was having an affair with someone she met in the park, and that her ex-husband didn't know."

"Maybe he actually did," she remarked.

"Whether he did or didn't doesn't matter. Rita said he was out of town when Janet was killed. I still think there's a motive there that 'being out of town' doesn't negate." I took a bite of biscuit and washed it down with coffee. Things felt brighter, thanks to the instant mood-elevating properties of carefully prepared caffeine.

"How?" asked Lucy. "He was her ex. Saying he was still jealous?"

"That's one theory. The other is that if Janet married again, the ex couldn't intimidate her into giving him money now and then, and in the event of her death he wouldn't get control of their daughter's trust."

"So if he was going to kill her to get control of the trust, he'd have to do it before she married?"

"Yes. And with the amount of money at stake, we're talking a life-changing amount, I don't see why the ex couldn't have hired someone to take care of Janet while he was conveniently out of town. Rita says that stuff only happens in the movies, but we've seen enough true crime shows to know that's not strictly true."

Lucy was nodding her head. "I like that theory. What's the ex doing now?"

"Acting upset," I replied. "McGinty is keeping an eye on him while Mrs. Whitmire meets with Collier and her accountants concerning Janet's will."

"Okay," Lucy murmured. "Now let's look at the other side of the coin. If Janet did have a lover, maybe he was involved somehow. Though from what you say, I don't see a motive, at least not until Janet remarried. Did she say who it was?"

Pursing my lips, I shook my head. "No."

"Any hints?"

"Only that they were both runners and about the same age. And that he didn't like kids," I said.

"That would have been a problem."

"We see that, but I don't think she did," I said. "Maybe they argued over kids. Maybe she just wanted a discreet affair and Janet wanted to take it further. But she knew if she married someone who wasn't 'suitable' to her mother, it would be a big scandal. Huge drama there. You got a taste of it."

Lucy laughed. "Yes, I did. Seemed like Mrs. Whitmire takes all that 'ladies who lunch' stuff pretty seriously."

"I could be wrong … I don't think Mrs. Whitmire would kill her own daughter over some imagined scandal. Instead perhaps Janet wanting to marry her running buddy threatened *her*. We don't know anything about her. She could be more scandal-adverse than Mother Whitmire. Janet loved drama. Maybe she overplayed her hand with this woman."

"Maybe. If so, why didn't the police think of this? Why haven't they found her?" she asked.

"Janet didn't sound like she'd told anybody else. The only other evidence was the security camera footage from the emergency room. It had to show something, or Stan wouldn't have been killed. Yet Rita implied that it wasn't usable for some reason. Which left Stan as the only witness. That's what makes me think the mystery girlfriend either killed Janet and Stan or knows who did."

"The police will think you made it up unless she told someone else. Who would she have confided in, besides her therapist?"

"Janet had two close friends: Mary Lou Jenkins and Sally Lambert."

"Mary Lou?" She smiled. "That's a very southern sounding name."

I couldn't contain the grin that spread across my face at her tone. "Yeah, we live in the South, Lucy."

Lucy smiled again. "I guess my Chicago roots are showing."

I stood and extended my hand toward her. "Let's go talk to Mary Lou."

CHAPTER 35

FRIDAY, NOVEMBER 8 AFTERNOON

Mary Lou Jenkins lived in one of the old houses on Church Street. Hers was the house with the immaculate garden out front and the freshly-painted blue shutters. A sweet-faced, blonde woman came to the door at our knock. She was dressed in a lime green blouse and pink plaid pants. Garden Club all the way. The interior of the house was just as you'd expect: quiet, shining, and antique. There were no plants, pets, or children. Only the frilly pink sweater hanging from the cast iron coat tree seemed to have any life.

"Oh, I saw you on the news when they were talking about poor Janet. You were her therapist, isn't that right?" She nodded at me. "Come in. Both of you." She seemed satisfied with me, but glanced questioningly at Lucy.

"I'm a social worker at Alice's practice. I knew Janet from the waiting room."

That seemed to satisfy Mary Lou about Lucy, too.

After Mary Lou sat us down on the hard seat of her Chippendale sofa and offered us tea, there wasn't much to do other than jump right in.

"We're here," I began, "because we want help in finding out what happened to Janet. The Medical Examiner can't determine whether she killed herself or if there was foul play. The police think it might be a homicide. We're trying to find out. For ourselves, and Janet's friends, of course." My voice rang in the silent house.

I felt the walls closing in.

"Yes. Poor Janet. " Mary Lou took a moment to note her friend's passing. We nodded in a "we are all grieving together" manner. "She wouldn't have done that to herself. And I'm sure I don't know who would have." Mary Lou shifted gracefully in her chair. Her eyes were dilated, and I wondered if she was on drugs.

"Actually," Lucy offered, "you may very well know something. You're just unaware that you do. It could be something quite trivial to you, but in the right context, it could be very useful."

"Oh, I hadn't thought of that." She seemed confused. "What kind of things?"

"Well," I said, "it might be that Janet had a secret friend. Somebody new. Someone she wasn't ready to 'go public' with."

"You mean a *man?*" Mary Lou didn't seem very surprised by this theory.

"Yes. A romantic friend. Did she ever mention anything about that?"

"I told the police I didn't know anything. Why don't we leave it at that?"

"Yes, of course. But we're not the police. They have their own agenda, and are being pressured by City Hall, the media, the community at large. We aren't like that, we're friends. You can share with us."

Lucy broke out her best "just us gals" smile. I joined in.

Mary Lou thought for a moment, then giggled and averted her gaze. "It's so tasteless," she said, wrinkling her face as if a bad odor had just entered the room.

"What is?" Lucy asked.

"Getting murdered like that. In the park, I mean. With the blood and the awful news coverage. It's not something Janet would have wanted."

I hid behind my smile. Did this woman really think that Janet would have wanted to get murdered in some other more sophisticated manner? Clearly her thinking didn't go that far, but it was hard not to make a comment.

"Or her mother," I noted, still smiling.

"Oh, heavens no!" Mary Lou responded, a sliver of self-consciousness piercing her politeness. "Doris, I mean Mrs. Whitmire, nearly died from embarrassment. Janet was always good at that."

"At what?" I asked.

"Embarrassing her mother. We both were brought up to be ladies. Janet often resented it."

"How? In what way?" I asked

"Janet didn't join Spinsters when we were young, and she'd go to DAR and say outrageous things. Whenever that happened her mother wouldn't make her go for a while. No mystery how Janet worked that."

"That was the pattern, then. If Janet didn't want to do something she'd find a way to embarrass her mother in order to get out of it …" I remarked; a statement that could almost pass for a question.

Mary Lou nodded. "Sort of a game between them. Except not."

"Why would Janet's having an affair upset her mother?" I pressed. "I mean, she'd already been married and divorced, what's one more fling?"

Mary Lou laughed. "Oh yes! That was part of the thrill—the naughtiness of an illicit romance. Mister Wrong was always just right for Janet. And she knew it. Lived for it, I think. Love is the drug, and she was addicted to it, as the songs go."

"So she did talk about it," said Lucy.

Mary Lou blushed, looking down at her exquisitely manicured nails. "Well, yes. She did."

"Who was it? This mystery man. Do you know?" If this woman had information . . .

"She wouldn't tell me, which was unusual. Said I'd be surprised, but that she wasn't ready to reveal who it was." Mary Lou looked up at me. "She often played games like that. This time felt different. Do you know who it was?"

"Not the faintest clue," I replied. "That's why we're asking you."

"Oh yes, of course. Too bad. I've been wracking my brain. I haven't the faintest clue either."

"Do you think that you could tell this to the police? About Janet's secret lover," I asked. "I know you want to help find your friend's killer. And it would give Mrs. Whitmire some measure of peace." At the time, I didn't think that the information might validate Rita's idea that I was the killer.

Mary Lou agreed with these sentiments and promised to call the police with the information, even though it was embarrassing. She even thanked us for coming, so I guess we made her feel better. Mary Lou told us she had a busy day ahead and needed to get ready. Before we could say anything else, we were out the door.

"Wow," Lucy said on the way back to her car. "What was … something."

"Wow is right," I agreed.

"We didn't learn anything new, but at least she confirmed our suspicions." Lucy laughed as she grabbed the passenger seat. She knew I didn't like to drive her car.

"Come on, Lady Columbo." I slid behind the wheel. "Let's brace Sally Lambert before *her* day gets too busy."

Lucy cringed as I roared down Church Street on our way to Lucy Avenue and Sally Lambert.

CHAPTER 36

FRIDAY, NOVEMBER 8
EVENING

Sally Lambert, Janet's other good friend, lived in a Craftsman bungalow on Forth Avenue. I recalled Janet saying that she was the Assistant Director of the women's military program at Fort Madison's Martin College. She sounded like a formidable combination of brains and brawn. I wasn't looking forward to trying to get her to tell us something useful.

When we arrived at her house, Sally was on her front porch doing stretching exercises. Her olive green running shorts molded hard muscle, and the matching halter top showed her perfect abs. I felt like a day-old dumpling.

After Lucy explained why we were there, Sally said, "Can't talk to you now. Gotta run. Literally."

"We won't take long," I assured her, as she eyed my extra twenty pounds. She was probably thinking about how she would shape me up.

Lucy didn't seem intimidated at all. If anything, Lucy would have been proud of some extra weight, like it was proof of a life well-lived. Easy to do when you have a long, slender frame like Lucy.

Sally shrugged, then crossed her arms over her chest. "Make it quick."

"We're here," I began, "because we believe that Janet's friends might know more than they think they do."

"I suppose that could be true," Sally admitted. "We often talked while on a run. She might have revealed information that I forgot. What are you looking for, exactly?"

"Trouble she was having with other people," I answered.

"That's too broad a category. Janet was always having trouble with other people … especially her mother. Either in trouble or causing it."

"I understand, but do you remember anyone recently? Besides her mother, of course," I inquired.

"No. I'm sorry. Janet's recent conflicts seemed to be about little things and there wasn't anyone she talked about more than the others."

"Janet told me that she was in love, but didn't tell me who her boyfriend was. Do you know anything about her new lover?"

"No, but it's really unlike her to refuse to talk about a new boyfriend. Maybe she just made one up. She was capable of that."

I smiled. 'Oh, I think this one was real."

"Well." She smiled, a "we're done here, honey" number that was Hall of Fame caliber. "Now I have to run or I'll have to stretch all over again."

As we watched her jog down the hill toward the park, Lucy shook her head. "She's not telling us all she knows, but I'm not sure what to do about it."

"Me either," I muttered. Truth be told, I was kind of scared of Sally. I wondered if an ultra-fit woman like Sally would have the strength—and I didn't mean that just in the physical sense—to slice Janet's throat. It seemed a given.

* * *

Sweetie was on the sofa when we got home, the remains of biscuits scattered around her. She burped as we walked into the room, and then she wouldn't look at me.

"Sweetie, you pig. You'd eat anything. Now she'll throw it up or have to go out over and over." I sighed, suddenly sad and tired.

Sweetie wagged her tail, scattering crumbs across the red rug. I had to fight my urge to run for the vacuum. My latest dog training book said not to let them see you cleaning up after them, because that put them in the dominant position. I wanted to be the top dog, but crumbs on my prized Persian rug made me cringe. Maybe I was too neat. If so, living with Sweetie would surely cure me.

"I can't deal with this now!" I grabbed Lucy's hand and pulled her down the stairs and onto the porch. "I've got too much going on to handle crumbs on my rug. Or to train that damn dog."

"Alice! Focus." Lucy shook my arm.

"Okay," I replied, "but first I have to tell you something."

Lucy was suddenly very alert, like when you tell a boyfriend "we need to talk."

"Dave McGinty and I aren't actually dating," I told her, unable to meet her gaze. "That's just our cover. We're really working together. For Mrs. Whitmire."

"*What?*" she exclaimed. "I don't believe it."

Now that I was committed to the truth, I rushed to finish my shameful confession.

"Dave isn't an antiques dealer appraising Mrs. Whitmire's furniture and art. He's a private investigator looking into Janet's death because the police are chasing their tails or covering their asses. I'm helping him."

"And you're not a couple? But this is right out of Nick and Nora Charles, chasing after the Thin Man while swimming in Sidecars and Champagne cocktails."

"Now that would be cool. Unfortunately, McGinty and I are just fellow players on Team Whitmire. Dave is being paid and I was basically shamed into it."

"You can fool yourself, Doctor Alice Brenner, but you can't fool me. You two are a couple. All my social worker instincts say you're a good match for each other. And solving a murder together? It doesn't get any better, dating-wise."

"Stop kidding around. I kinda wish it was like you say, but it isn't, and we aren't."

"Crime solving aside, the best way to get over an old boyfriend is with a new one. More importantly, I want to know why you lied to me. That's not like you, keeping secrets."

"I promised I wouldn't tell. My hands and tongue were tied."

She shook her head, her expression sad. "But I'm your best friend. We tell each other everything."

"I know, but I couldn't do it. Mrs. Whitmire wanted it that way. And like I said, I promised Dave."

"So you chose McGinty over me? Now I know you're a couple."

CHAPTER 37

TUESDAY, NOVEMBER 12 MORNING

Tuesday morning the first person I saw was Ron Margolis. I groaned inwardly. The only time he went out of his way like this was when he had something to tell me that he knew I wouldn't like.

"Oh, Alice," he began, smiling, "so glad I caught you this morning. I wanted to tell you in person that we've called a staff meeting for this evening at seven. We need to talk about what you're doing to this practice."

I smiled back. "Thank you for telling me, Ron. I'm always happy to talk with the practice about anything." I wasn't surprised. Being involved in a murder, I really did owe the practice a formal account.

His smile became a little tighter. "Alice, you're such a sweetheart."

"Thank you, Ron." Swiveling on my heel, I walked to my office as fast as I could and still maintain my dignity. Inside, I slumped against the closed door. How could this group let a little jerk like Ron destroy the good relationships I'd had with some of these people for seven years? How could they doubt me? They must, or they wouldn't have agreed to the meeting. Maybe they were with Ron in wanting me gone. This was my home and my family. What would I do if I had to leave? I couldn't imagine it.

It was time to call Lucy.

I didn't waste any time. "Have you heard about the staff meeting tonight? Ron must have really pushed hard to get it done that quickly.

"Are you all right?"

"No. Do you have time to talk? I'm … sort of upset. I'll come to your office if you like." I blew my nose again.

"Of course we can talk. I'll be right down."

A few minutes later, Lucy came in my office with two cups of coffee and a determinedly cheerful face. "Boy, you do need to talk. You look like hell. What's going on?"

"Ron told me about the staff meeting tonight. Ron's been out to get me for months. Maybe this is it. He'll get the others to vote me out. The Murder Girl. "

"I won't."

"I know, and I'm grateful. But what about the others?"

"Alice, you're a good therapist and they know that. And …" She waved her arm to the side, almost knocking the brass lamp off the end table by her chair. "You send us all referrals when you get more referrals than you can handle."

"That won't happen again," I said, wiping at my eyes. "I'm damaged goods now."

"Yes it will. The family doctors who send you referrals won't care about what's in the paper. They want to refer their patients to a therapist who will help them and they know that's you. And didn't you get a new referral last Friday?"

"Yes, I guess," I answered. "A fluke."

"No way. It means that this publicity hasn't shaken their trust in you." She smiled again. "And didn't your patients start rescheduling those missed appointments?"

"Yeah." I sniffled. "I'm full this week."

"See. They know you're good. Once the initial shock wore off, they knew you couldn't have killed anyone who didn't deserve it."

"Thank you." I always felt better when I talked things over with Lucy.

We drank some coffee, and by ten I was good to go for my first patient. The rest of the day I listened to my patients' hurts, fears, and doubts. By lunch, I had things back in perspective. My problems were relatively small compared to theirs. My problems right now were big, but they were short-term. I hadn't had to deal with them my whole life like most of my patients had. And I had the skills to deal with them. My patients had yet to learn those skills. When they did, I felt joy at their increased happiness. Once again, I felt deep gratitude to have been granted such a wonderful job. Not even Ron could ruin that.

* * *

My last patient of the day was Ben Asher. And once again, he seemed a little depressed. His coming out as a gay man so far had been a hard journey for him. We'd talked about it for the last four sessions. He looked like things hadn't improved.

"This is so hard, Alice," he whispered, wringing his hands in his lap.

"Tell me what's happened. You don't look so good," I said.

"I know you told me to tell family next, but I went ahead and told someone at work, Joe Harris, a guy I often eat lunch with. We're usually on the same side in office politics and we follow the basketball playoffs together. I didn't get together with him after work, but thought of him as a friend."

Crossing my legs, I leaned back in my chair. "What happened?"

"One day at work Joe brought up the gay marriage thing and said he didn't think it was fair. He asked what I thought about it, and I told him I thought it was terrible … and then told him I was gay."

I sighed inwardly as I asked, "How did he react?"

"At first he seemed okay with it and said we were still friends, but then he told other people at work."

"Did you want him to keep it a secret?"

"Yeah. I asked him not to say anything. That I would be telling people individually. But I guess he just had to talk about it. Several people made comments."

"What kind of comments?" I bet I could guess.

"Snide, homophobic remarks … like, 'This is a bank. We can't be having you cry during business hours.'"

"Ouch." Yeah, that was pretty homophobic.

"I know, right? And the head of my department called me in and said that it might upset some of the bank's customers to be served by a homosexual, that I shouldn't 'act gay' at work. Only one person said she thought I was brave for coming out and that she was okay with it. And she's not even in my department." He sighed.

"I was afraid work would be tough," I said, then paused. "Are there people who haven't commented?"

Frowning, he nodded. "Yeah. Most people haven't said anything, but it feels like they're all talking about me."

"Yes, but they might be saying good things," I pointed out.

Ben seemed surprised. "You think so?"

"Yeah. The woman who said she was okay with it is probably not the only one." No way to tell how many supporters he had, but he needed to realize that he had supporters as well as detractors.

He appeared to contemplate this for a moment. "I guess you're right. Miles over in Estates smiled at me yesterday, and so did two of the tellers."

"See."

"Yeah, I guess it's not all bad."

I smiled. "And soon there will be another bit of gossip to talk about and you won't be the hot topic."

"You're right," he admitted. "I might even get through this okay."

"Yes, you will. You haven't been fired and nobody has done anything more than talk about you and say some ignorant things. All in all, you got through this pretty well."

"I've been lucky."

"Yes, you have."

He didn't realize how lucky. Homophobia can be virulent in small, Southern towns. It could have been much worse for Ben. I felt relieved.

CHAPTER 38

TUESDAY, NOVEMBER 12
EVENING

At seven, I walked into our staff break room. I reminded myself of my feelings of gratitude for my work and added gratitude for being able to practice in such a great building.

And what a great building it was. The practice owned a beautiful, two-story craftsman house near downtown. It had wonderful woodwork, high ceilings, and big windows. The break room was, like most of our offices, decorated with sofas and chairs and a big Persian rug. It had a small table on one wall, which held the coffee maker and cups. Along another wall there were our mailboxes. And a chandelier sparkling with cut glass hung in the center. Warm and comfortable, the area was for relaxing between patients and business meetings—not thinly-disguised inquisitions.

I sank into the down cushions of the green velvet sofa, next to Lucy. The other partners were scattered about on the two blue denim sofas and three floral patterned easy chairs. It had turned warm in the afternoon and someone had opened the big windows that overlooked our parking lot in the back. The white lace curtains waved softly in the evening breeze. Ordinarily I would have enjoyed being in the well-lived-in room. Not that evening.

Marvin Lane, our only psychiatrist and the practice's director, began to speak. "Everyone is here now, so let's call this meeting to order. Ron has some concerns about Alice's recent bad publicity. Ron, will you elaborate for us?"

"Gladly, Marvin. As you all know there have been a series of events concerning Doctor Brenner here that may effect all of us. First there were the newspaper articles about her dead patient. Or I should say 'murdered patient'?"

"No, you shouldn't," I said.. "The coroner couldn't make a definitive determination."

Ron glared at me, but didn't argue the point. "Then there was the publicity around the deceased patient's mother complaining to the licensing board, accusing Doctor Brenner of incompetence, of indirectly causing her daughter's death. That, by the way, has triggered an investigation by the licensing board."

I knew Lucy was about to point out that such investigations are not unusual, so I put my hand on her arm to stop her. *Let Ron have his say so I can have mine.*

"Then," Ron was saying, "there was the media uproar about Doctor Brenner being a 'person of interest' in the police's investigation of her patient's death, even spending the night in jail. And I understand that her patients have been canceling appointments at an unusually high rate. They don't trust her. How long will it be before *our* referral sources dry up and our *own* patients begin canceling? Like it or not, Fort Madison is a small town, with small town sensibilities. We need to react accordingly. To some of our clients, we are, after all, in practice with the killer therapist."

"That's way over the line, Ron!" I shouted. I could feel Lucy's hand on my arm, but it didn't matter. "How dare you call me that! It's an unfair smear. We're both better than that. Aren't we?"

The room exploded into conversation and comments, with Marvin trying to restore order. "Doctor Brenner, please." Belatedly, he turned to Ron. "You too, Doctor Margolis."

When the room quieted, Marvin said, "Would you like to respond to Ron's statement, Alice? In a professional manner."

Lucy whispered in my ear, "Take a deep breath, then tell them the way it really is."

I did as she instructed. "Some of you have known me for seven years. You know I'm a good therapist. That's why I was asked to join this practice. I have a large base of referring family doctors. Over the years, if I had referrals that I was too busy to see, I've sent patients to most of you. We all at times get bogus complaints from family members of patients. If we didn't we wouldn't be doing our jobs. I've talked to the licensing board's investigator and she said not to worry about it. And those canceling patients have calmed down and are now rescheduling appointments. And I got a new referral just last Friday." I moved on to my big closer. "And at the end of the day, all we have is our reputations. They're easy to loose and hard to rebuild. So, if anyone here thinks that I am a 'killer therapist,' then I will immediately drop out of the practice. The partnership agreement covers partner misconduct; I'm sure the killing of patients is discouraged."

There were chuckles around the room. "Thank you, Alice," said Marvin. "Does anyone else have anything to say?"

"I do." Lucy stood up. "What are we doing here? We all know Alice. We all know she's a good therapist. The kind that we're proud to have in this practice. She refers us patients; she does a good job. We should be supporting her in this hard time, not criticizing her."

Judith Byrne, one of our newer Licensed Professional Counselors, stood as Lucy sat. "Lucy's right. I thought part of being in a group practice was that you help each other through those hard times everybody has."

"But," Todd Owens, one of our psychologists, began, "isn't one of the main reasons for a group practice to make money? This is a business, run for mutual benefit. Doctor Brenner is right when she says it's hard to rebuild one's reputation. I sympathize with any partner losing a patient, no one can control that, but becoming part of a media circus regarding a patient's tragic death, that is a choice, not a natural disaster or simple bad luck. Isn't it a form of malpractice to have anyone in the practice that might hurt our reputation and thus compromise the level of care our patients receive? Yes, what we do is a calling, not just a trade, but if we don't care for the health of the business, we won't be able to practice that calling for very long."

Mary Sanger, another psychologist, spoke next. "I agree that many of us think of being a therapist as a type of calling. Alice is one of those. I'm proud to be in practice with her and don't want that to change. So far no one has really explained how the rough patch she's going through is effecting our bottom line. I think something else might be going on here and I don't like it."

Ron stood again. "Don't let your admiration of Dr. Brenner make you paranoid. There is nothing going on here but our attempt to keep this practice running and profitable for all of us."

Mike Ecke, a social worker hired just two years ago, clapped and said, "I'm all for profit. My wife, Louise, is pregnant with our second baby. I can't afford to lose patients."

"None of us can, Mike." Lucy replied. "But isn't supporting each other through good times and bad just as important?"

There were murmurs from both sides.

Marvin stood and declared, " I don't think we have enough evidence of Alice hurting this practice in any way. I'm beginning to wonder why I let myself be talked into calling this meeting."

All but Todd, Mike, and Ron clapped.

Smiling, Lucy stood again. "Let's just go home. There's nothing to do here."

Then everybody but Ron, Todd, and Mike got up and went home. On the way out, most of the others gave me a hug. It was all I could do not to cry.

CHAPTER 39

WEDNESDAY, NOVEMBER 13
MORNING

The next morning Russ was sitting on the front porch when I left for work. He seemed to be upset.

"Dr. Brenner! Oh, Dr. Brenner. I'm so glad you're okay," he said.

"Of course I'm okay, Russ. Why wouldn't I be?" I asked.

"Because you're in great danger, remember? The Company agents are watching you all the time. They're going to hurt you. There was even one by your car last night. I looked underneath, but didn't see anything. Be careful!"

"Russ," I glanced at my watch, "I appreciate your concern. But I'll be fine. There's not going to be a problem with Company agents. I'm going to work now and everything will be fine."

"No it won't," he replied.

Since I'd been attacked the other night, I'd be lying if I said I wasn't nervous. And the men who'd chased Dave and me the other day. Where were they? Delusional or not, Russ wasn't wrong.

"Can I give you a ride somewhere?" I asked.

Russ looked alarmed. "Uh, don't take this wrong. I like you, but it's dangerous being around you. Especially trapped in a car. So I'll just walk to the park on my own."

I smiled. "Okay. It's up to you."

We walked down the porch steps and onto the sidewalk next to my car. *Russ is right*, I thought. *It would be easy to do something to my car since I have to park on the street.* Not everybody had driveways when our house was built.

Russ waved to me from down the sidewalk. "Remember. Be careful!"

I got in the car and sat there for a while. I wasn't really in danger, was I? *Of course not.* I sat there some more feeling silly, but spooked. Eventually I took a deep breath and turned the key. The car started. I felt stupid.

I continued feeling stupid on the short drive to work. I shouldn't pay so much attention to Russ. I knew he was psychotic. What was wrong with me that I let him spook me? Because mental illness was highly contagious. Bad thoughts travel fast.

* * *

At work, I got thumbs up from the secretaries and smiles from Judith and Marvin. I felt great. I may have troubles, but the practice was going to support me.

Everyone except Ron, of course. Today he was wearing a carefully arranged navy sweater over gray slacks. I always wondered how he could look so pulled together and pressed while working with kids. Child therapy usually involved a certain amount of play and hugging. Why wasn't Ron rumpled? I knew he did the hugging part. I'd seen him give kids with runny noses big bear hugs and I'd seen him shuffle out to the waiting room to talk to a parent with their child wrapped around his leg. So why didn't he rumple?

As we passed he asked, "May I speak with you? When you have time, that is."

I smiled. It was a good thing to be gracious after winning. "Sure. I have some time. Do you want to talk now?"

"Thanks," he said. "This is a good time."

We walked silently to my office. He sat in the blue denim chair that Janet Ford always chose. I sat in my red leather easy chair opposite him. The silence continued. I had my therapist face on.

After a moment, he spoke. "I know that the two of us have not gotten along lately, but I have always admired your skill and dedication as a therapist. During the meeting, Mary said that something else was going on, namely a power grab on my part. I will admit that I am concerned about the effect your bad press is having on the practice. Good will is a vital asset to our partnership, and I guess I've been too focused on the business side of the equation. I will concede to the knowledge and experience of those of you who have been here longer than me. But I wanted to let you know that I don't want us to feel like adversaries. Alice, if I may call you that, I would like to start over."

"Thank you, Ron. Of course you may call me Alice. Everyone does. I'd like to start over, too."

We stood, shook hands, and he left. The defeated paying homage to the victor. I felt great. The rest of the morning was good. So good, in fact, that I decided to stay with the practice. When the issues came up about the negative effect I was having on the practice, I'd thought about quitting my career as a therapist or just leaving the practice and going out on my own. But today I decided that I'd continue being a therapist right where I was. It felt good.

CHAPTER 40

THURSDAY, NOVEMBER 14
AFTERNOON

The next day, I was so wrapped in thought, that it wasn't until I got to work that I realized I'd left Sweetie at home. I tried to put it out of my mind, but it's practically impossible to will yourself *not* to think about something. Before I knew it, it was time for lunch. I always ate at Kathy's on Tuesdays. Today was no exception.

As I drove the short distance across town, I tried not to think about Stan's accident. I'd agreed to keep Sweetie with me after that. And now I'd forgotten to bring her. Instead, I 'd been thinking that today after work, I might go to the Co-Art Gallery downtown and buy the watercolor of Fort Madison in the rain that I'd been admiring. I had a bare spot on the wall opposite my chair in the office where it would be just perfect. How could I have been so careless?

Coming down Statler Boulevard toward the railroad tracks, I noticed a black SUV with tinted windows pull up beside me on the left. As it got even, the side window rolled down and I saw a flash of metal. *A gun?*

Without thinking, I ducked to the opposite side of the car, my hand on the steering wheel pulling the car along with me. As the right wheel hit the side of the road, there was a thunderous explosion of glass to my left, and I couldn't hear. I was lying on my right side, so I felt rather than saw my windshield shatter. The next thing I remember, the car was in the small parking lot next to the road. There was another car tangled with mine.

I was vibrating all over. I still couldn't hear. My head hurt. I was lying on my right side stretched across the arm rest and cup holder in the center. My ribs hurt every time I took a breath. They hurt almost as much as my face. I was covered with small pieces of glass. The driver's side airbag had blown out and partially covered me.

But there wasn't any blood. I was going to be okay if I could get my mind to focus. I lay there trying to remember how to get up.

There were people around the car. Someone opened the driver's side door. It was a young cop who looked as scared as I felt. He was speaking, but I couldn't hear him.

"I can't hear you!" I shouted. "Something happened."

He felt along my arms and side.

"Stop!" I yelled. "My side hurts!"

He said something that sounded like "Lub … touch … hep … out."

"What?"

"You're okay. The EMTs are just pulling in," he shouted.

"Oh! I can hear you." I was so relieved that I almost forgot I was twisted up like a pretzel.

The young cop patted my unhurt left arm. "You're going to be real sore, but it looks like you've been lucky."

I tried to sit up. My muscles screamed and I gasped in pain.

He pressed on my arm. "Don't move. Wait for the EMTs to get here. You seem okay, but you need to go to the emergency room."

At that point, I noticed that the car was lying on its side. It looked pretty smashed up.

"Oh no!" I wailed. "My car."

I might have been lucky, but my car wasn't. It was as dead as I could have been.

*   *   *

Sirens were screaming all around us. In fact, it felt like the whole world was screaming. I went from not being able to hear anything to hearing everything ten times louder than it probably was. My head throbbed.

The EMTs came and loaded me on to a gurney without hurting anything but my head and side. Loading me and the gurney into the ambulance was a comparative breeze. There were lots of police. It wasn't often that someone got shot at in my small town. I saw four police cars before the sides of the ambulance cut off my view. One of the officers rode to the hospital with me.

The hospital was a confusion of white and noise and being rolled around. I remember that they took me to get CTs of my head, ribs, and shoulder. The machine scared me. Not that I wasn't scared already. I jumped at every sound and I couldn't stop shaking.

Eventually, a young doctor, Doctor Winter or maybe Wonder, came in and said, "You're a very lucky woman, Doctor Brenner. You could have been killed in a wreck like that. Instead, you have a sprained shoulder, two broken ribs, and you'll have black eyes from the air bag hitting your face. The CT showed that your brain is all right … no concussion this time."

"I don't feel good," I said, sounding like a whiny five year old.

He smiled. "You won't for a few days, but there's no permanent damage. Go home. Don't do anything that makes it hurt worse, and take ibuprofen. I'll write you script for the industrial strength ones. You'll be okay in about a week."

"Thanks." I tried to sit up, but he stopped me.

"No. We're not finished, Doctor Brenner. You've had two concussion scares in the last month." He glanced at the chart he held. "It looks like the first was from a fall in a parking lot and now this. Are you having dizzy spells? Are you unusually clumsy? What's causing all of this?"

"Just lucky, I guess." I smiled up at him. It wouldn't do any good to say someone was trying to kill me if the police wouldn't back me up. And I didn't want to spend the next few days on the psych ward while they tried to decide if I was crazy or just peculiar. I'd had enough incarceration lately.

"Just be more careful. You seem to have had a number of visits to this ER lately for suspected head trauma," he said. "Brain damage is cumulative. You could be looking at some noticeable impairment if you continue like this."

Is he saying I need a helmet?

"I'll be careful, Doctor." I tried to look as responsible as possible. Being a dog owner, I knew I could pull it off.

He left me again and I remembered the last time I sat in the emergency room—the day I met Stan. I had no doubt that Stan would still be working here if he hadn't met me that day. If he hadn't decided to help me investigate Janet's death. It wasn't fair that he died and I was still alive. The little piece of information he had—that Janet's running friend was a woman—cost him his life. It wasn't right. I knew I'd carry guilt about Stan's death for the rest of my life.

When the doctor came back and discharged me, I called Lucy. She was at work, but I told Georgia this was an emergency, and I had to speak with her immediately.

"Are you okay?" Georgia asked. "The police told us about your accident." She sounded worried and tense.

"Yes. I'm okay, but I'll be out a few days. You'd better cancel my patients through the rest of the week. And what about this afternoon's patients?"

"We've already called them. Don't worry. We'll take care of everything. Now hold for Lucy."

I was really lucky in lots of ways.

Lucy came on the line. "What's happened now? There's a policeman in the office talking to the secretaries. I knew it had to be about you."

"I think Janet's killer tried to get me again. I totaled my car attempting to avoid getting shot. Right now, I'm at the hospital waiting for you to come and get me."

"Oh, my God! Don't move. I'll be right there.." She hung up.

While I waited for Lucy, the policeman that had been hanging around interviewed me. I told him what I remembered, which wasn't much.

He asked, "How did you know it was a gun? You only saw a flash of metal."

"I knew it was a gun. A friend talked to me this morning about being careful. He believed me when I thought somebody has been stalking me." I didn't tell the nice policeman that my friend was psychotic. It wouldn't have helped. "I saw the flash and reacted automatically. He shot the window out. I've been to the police about getting threatening phone calls and being threatened in the park."

"The witnesses and bullet holes in your car corroborate your story. Someone tried to shoot you, all right. You're lucky to be alive." He smiled. "As to why someone would do this, that's for the detectives to answer. We've been in touch and they'll be talking with you soon."

His validation of what I already knew—that someone was trying to kill me or scare me to death—didn't help. I was doing my best to be calm and adult on the outside, but on the inside I was quivering and wailing like a terrified baby. He stood and led me through the ER to the waiting room. Lucy was already there.

"Come on, girlfriend. Let's get you home." She loaded me tenderly into her car. It smelled of lemons.

Once in my apartment, she ushered me toward the sofa. "Lie down and don't move. I'll bring you some dinner later."

I did as instructed.

Sweetie seemed to understand that I was injured. She licked my hand and then lay on the floor beside the sofa in her version of protecting me. Occasionally she'd sit up and lick my face to make it all better. Surprisingly, it worked. Doctor Sweetie, in the house.

I didn't talk to the reporter, Sue Thompson from the television station, who kept calling. Eventually I unplugged my phone. Lucy brought me two bowls of soup. I spent the rest of the day lying there with Sweetie watching the sun dance dapples across the red and blue of my oriental rug. That always brought me peace. It didn't today.

Later that day the detectives came to interview me. Sweetie didn't approve. She growled at them. I was embarrassed. She was usually way too friendly with strangers. Eventually I had to lock her in the bedroom.

"I'm sorry about that. I don't know what got into her," I said.

"That's all right. My dogs sometimes surprise me, too," said Captain Bob Pearson. He was a sandy-haired man in his mid-forties, and Rita Butler's boss. I counted that as progress.

Rita was with him, clearly irritated. She didn't meet my eyes or say much more than introduce me to Capt. Pearson. We sat in my living room, me talking with Pearson, Rita pointedly ignoring me, save for a glare now and then. I didn't mind that this was difficult for her, but the vibe was definitely … weird.

Captain Pearson was saying, "It looks like you might have been right about someone stalking you. Certainly someone tried to shoot you yesterday. Witnesses confirmed it. Your car has five bullet holes. One of the witnesses got a picture of the SUV on their phone and we were able to get the license plate. It was reported stolen that morning. We eventually found it last night. It was clean, no fingerprints or anything to lead us to your attacker."

"I hope this means that you no longer think I killed Janet Ford," I said.

Now Rita spoke. "There is no proven connection. They could be two different things. We haven't ruled you out."

Wow, she just couldn't let it go.

Pearson gave her a look that would have made me faint, but didn't seem to bother Rita in the slightest. "They could be unrelated, but the simplest answer is usually the correct one. To my mind, the two things are indeed related, which makes it unlikely that you are Janet Ford's killer. However, the investigation into that case is still ongoing and I'm not going to rule anyone out totally."

My "incident" was on the evening news. Sue Thompson made do with interviewing the police and talking about how frightened everyone else was that such a thing could happen in our little town. *No shit.* My insides were still quivering. Dave called and offered to keep me company, but I felt too bad to have to make the effort to be polite. I was too scared to be polite. Which is why I yelled at Collier when he showed up at my door. Even though I wouldn't let him in, I did enjoy both the flowers and the chocolates he brought. Later in the night I almost called Dave and asked him to come over after all. As I reached for the phone I saw my alarm clock. It was 3:00 a.m. I hung up.

I couldn't go back to sleep. Behind the pain in my face and shoulder there were questions. *Who's doing this? Will they eventually kill me?* I wasn't optimistic.

FRIDAY, NOVEMBER 15 MORNING

The next day my shoulder and ribs still hurt, but I didn't feel quite so fuzzy headed. And I was able to focus on how lucky I was, rather than on when my mystery assailant would get me. Sweetie approved.

When I told Lucy about my meeting with the detectives, she said, "It sounds like you're not their number one suspect anymore, girl. So something good came from this." She always did have an overly positive outlook. What she didn't say was that someone was still trying to kill me.

"I guess. They don't seem too concerned about my safety. They didn't even mention trying to keep me alive."

"Perhaps we should go over what you remember about Janet again. I can't do it until tomorrow. We could sit on the porch in the morning and see if there's anything we missed," she suggested.

I lay on my sofa the rest of the day, thinking about how this might end. Maybe Janet and Stan's murders were related. There weren't that many murders in our town. It would be quite a coincidence that Stan knew something about Janet's case and then was killed by a totally unrelated person. Would whoever killed them eventually kill me? Probably.

I wasn't trained to protect myself from a determined killer. So far, my survival had been a function of pure dumb luck. That wouldn't last forever. I needed to ask Dave to teach me some self-defense moves. Or maybe get him to teach me to shoot. Reaching down, I stroked Sweetie, who whined up at me. She was right. I had to remember that I had a family now. I had to make sure someone would take care of Sweetie when they finally killed me. I wasn't feeling very optimistic about my chances of survival right then. Maybe I'd feel better about it when my ribs stopped hurting.

CHAPTER 42

SATURDAY, NOVEMBER 16 MORNING

The next morning, I woke up with humongous pain in my shoulder and aching ribs. And that was just the beginning. When I managed to crawl out of bed and pull myself upright, every muscle and every tendon hurt. A loud clang of pain. I wondered if I'd ever be able to move normally again. I'd called Dr. Crosby, my family doctor, yesterday afternoon and told her what happened. She wanted me to go to see the physical therapist next to her office as soon as I could. Just the thought of it made me hurt.

After brewing a pot of coffee, I lowered myself onto the sofa with my first cup. Even drinking it hurt. But after the third cup it wasn't as bad. Now that my head was clearer, I began to remember that I had more to worry about than the fact I was in pain. Like who tried to shoot me. And what was I going to do for a car.

I couldn't do anything about the who-was-trying-to-kill-me question. Lucy and I had planned to go over what we knew that morning, but she called before I'd even gotten out of bed to say that she had a patient who was in crisis and she had to go into work to see them. She wouldn't be back for a while. As engaging as thinking about who wanted to kill me was, there was a more pressing concern. What the hell was I going to do about my twisted and totaled car? I didn't have enough money to pay for a new one without a payment from my auto insurance, so I guessed that was the first step.

Luckily, the cops had brought my purse from the wreck when they came to interview me the day before. After some lumbering and protests from my ribs and head, I pulled my insurance cards from the wet purse. Somebody must have thought the car was a fire hazard and hosed it down. After falling back onto the sofa with the card and my phone, I took a deep breath and dialed.

The call was not pleasant. The agent who answered was appalled at how much damage had been done to my car in the last month and implied that at the very least my payments would increase as a result. However, her attitude improved when she said, "You invested in a policy big enough to cover replacing your vehicle and a rental car for one month." She sounded proud of my foresight.

I felt better. At least until we were finished and I realized that I didn't have a way to even go look for a new car. At that point I gave up and took a nap.

Later, after a shower and changing into car renting clothes, I felt better. Jeans and my favorite green sweater always made me feel better. Or at least good enough to call Lucy. Since she wasn't answering, I left a message for her to call me. Maybe she'd have time to take me to get a rental car.

Instead of calling, Lucy showed up at lunch.

"Come on, girl. We have to get you a car," she said.

"I have insurance coverage for a rental car for a month, so let's go there first." I was standing before I remembered that I hurt all over.

My muscles, ribs, and head all punished me for that. *Maybe I can get a car with heated seats and therapeutic massage.*

As it turned out, there was a new red Cadillac in the rental lot which looked like it would have heated leather seats that would do anything you wanted.

"I want that red Caddie," I told the rental guy.

He shook his head. "That's a luxury car. It's not covered by your insurance."

I had to have it. My ribs told me so. "How much extra?"

"Twenty dollars a day," he answered.

"Only twenty?" I exclaimed.

I drove off the lot, cuddled by tan leather seats that made me feel like a queen.

CHAPTER 43

SATURDAY, NOVEMBER 16 AFTERNOON

The wonderful Cadillac seats hadn't cured my aches and pains by the time we got home. We sat out on the porch since it was another unusually warm day.

"You know what? I think we should do some yoga," Lucy said. "Let's go get our mats and do it out here in the fresh air. It might make you feel better."

I groaned, obviously she'd forgotten about my broken ribs. "Do what you want, but I have two broken ribs and I'm going to go take some aspirin. Then I'm not moving." I'd just finished when my cell phone rang.

It was that almost familiar voice again. This time I realized that I really couldn't put a gender or a race to it. It sounded mechanical and brassy, not at all human.

"I see you got a nice car," it said. "Too bad you don't have long to enjoy it."

"Who are you?" I shouted. But I was talking to a silent line.

"Lucy, it was him again! On the phone. He knows I have a red car and he threatened me," I cried.

"Oh, honey. Could you tell who it was?" she asked.

"No. It was a neutral voice, like they used a machine to modify it."

"That's a clue and I bet not everybody can get equipment like that."

I nodded, relaxing a little. "Let's look it up."

We went into her place, straight to her very Chippendale office, and booted up the computer. "I'll do a search," she said.

My hopes fell as we stared open-mouthed at the number of places selling spyware. Just to be sure we opened one at random. There it was. One hundred and twenty dollars for a voice modifying device. With free shipping.

"Anyone can buy one. It's not a clue at all." I sighed.

"Try to think of who it could be. Does it remind you of anyone you know?" Lucy had that determined look she gets.

"It's too mechanical sounding - like a robot or computer voice in a 1960's movie."

"Is there anything about the way they phrase things? Do they use unusual wording?

"No. Nothing. I'm not sure whether the voice is familiar or not. It's useless to try to place the voice. Maybe a high-tech place like an FBI lab could do it, but we can't."

"You should tell the police," Lucy said.

My shoulders slumped. "They won't care. They didn't the last time."

"Now they know you're not guilty," she replied. "Call them."

"No." I was too stubborn to involve them.

"If you don't, I will," Lucy threatened.

"I'm taking Sweetie for a walk," I said—and did, if you could call my slow shuffle a walk.

* * *

When we got back, I called Dave and talked with him about what had happened.

"You can't stay out of trouble, can you? Do you know something that might get you killed?"

"Not that I can think of, but that's not the point. Whoever's after me believes that I do. Or that I'm a danger to them in some way. I'm thinking of putting a full page ad in the paper: 'You Win! I Quit!' "

"I know you're joking but there's something to that idea," Dave replied. "Why not give an interview to one of those reporters? Pick your favorite. Admit on the record that yes, you were looking into Janet's death on your own, you felt you owed it to her, and since then you've become convinced that the poor woman did commit suicide. The police's inability to reach the same conclusion is just making a tragic situation worse."

"But I don't believe that," I complained.

"I'm not asking you to believe it, just to say it," he said. "The point is to convince whoever is targeting you that you're no longer a threat. Isn't that worth lying for?"

I had to admit he had a point. "Do you really think that would work?" I asked.

"It's just dumb luck that you haven't died."

"Don't I know it." I could feel my stomach clench. "I'm so scared."

"I tell you, Alice. Do the interview, make the statement, then leave town. Take a vacation. I'll call you when it's safe to come back."

"I can't. My therapy practice would die."

"Better it die than you. Don't you want to feel safe again? You must be halfway to an ulcer by now."

"I just can't go. My patients need me."

"That's crazy. You'll wind up getting killed if these attacks continue much longer. Don't be a martyr."

"That's why I called you. I want you to teach me some self-defense moves. Ones that would work in a life and death situation. Like gouging-eyes-out things. Or teach me to shoot."

"And why do you think I know any of that?"

"I just do. You're that kind of guy."

"Ha!" he laughed.

"Please."

"Nothing I can teach will stop a bullet. You need to get off the gun range. There's a target on you."

I knew he was right, but I just couldn't turn tail and run. I'm not a brave or foolish person, but here I was being both. Maybe just foolish, in a brave way. "I'm sorry, Dave. Right now I can't leave, but that could change. Can't you help me out, defense-wise?"

"Okay, okay," he relented. "Maybe I do know a few things you could try. Let's meet on tomorrow afternoon at your place. Meanwhile, I could come over and protect you."

"No thanks. I'll be all right until then."

"It's your choice. But I am guaranteed. Trust me."

I laughed and hung up, then wondered why I didn't let him come over. I didn't want him to think of me as helpless, though he probably did already. I wanted him here, but I didn't. It was all too confusing—maybe Dr. Wonderful was right about the concussions.

CHAPTER 44

SUNDAY, NOVEMBER 17
MORNING

On Sunday morning, Lucy and I reviewed the memories I had of Janet. Again. We were sitting on the front porch. Lucy had the swing so I was sitting in the big, white wicker chair with the blue cushions. People must have thought we were crazy, because it was a chilly day, but we seemed to think better there.

We made the process more pleasant by drinking wine. The bottle sat on the coffee table between us. Sweetie lay across my feet, sleeping soundly.

"Before we get started, I just want to say that I'm happy for you." Lucy's eyes twinkled above her wine glass.

"Why are you happy for me?"

She smiled her therapist smile. "Because, girl, I think you really care about Dave McGinty. You seem to glow whenever you talk about him. You're spending more and more time with him. And you're checking your phone a lot, like you're hoping for a call from him. Maybe you can get past your fears and develop a real relationship with him."

"Thanks. I think," I answered.

After sitting in silence for a few moments, Lucy picked up the notepad she had next to her. "Now let's review what we know about

Janet." She leaned back into the swing. It creaked softly as it began to move.

"Okay," I said. "Janet was very unhappy. She was dramatic, impulsive, manipulative, with quickly changing moods. She enjoyed shocking others, especially her mother. But she was also bright, generous, and loved her daughter. I'd diagnosed her as having Borderline Personality Disorder."

And," Lucy added, "Janet had a lover— a female lover. Powerful, according to Janet. They ran together in the park. Do we know how often?"

"No we don't," I said, "but it sounded like a regular thing. At least a few times a week. And don't forget, Janet wanted to marry her lover."

"Yes, and I wonder if her lover felt the same. Didn't Janet's condition pretty much make long-term relationships impossible, or at least improbable?" asked Lucy.

"That's why I know she didn't commit suicide," I replied. "Janet was getting better. She was taking medication, controlling her symptoms. Taking her therapy seriously."

"I wonder what Janet's ex-husband would have done if she got married to this mystery woman..." Lucy pulled her feet up onto the swing. "Would he have demanded more money or custody of the kid?"

"Janet said he wouldn't be able to intimidate her for money once she was remarried," I answered.

"What about the daughter?" she asked.

I shook my head. "Janet wouldn't let anyone take her child."

"She didn't do much mothering. I bet the nanny saw more of that poor girl than Janet did."

"Yeah, that's probably true. I imagine that Mrs. Whitmire has the girl now. I hope she pays more attention to her than she did to Janet."

We both sighed.

Sweetie barked in her sleep, gave a high-pitched whine, and rolled over onto my feet.

We sat in silence for about fifteen minutes. I tried to move my toes, but they were asleep.

Lucy stared when I pulled my feet from under Sweetie and started stomping them on the porch. "What are you doing? About to have a seizure or something?"

"No. It's just that my feet are asleep from having an elephant lie on them." I laughed.

She grinned. "That's a happy elephant."

"Yeah. Isn't she cute?" I felt my insides get warm and soft.

I shook my feet again.

"Stop that!" she barked. "You're making me nervous."

"I can't help it," I said. "There are pins and needles in my feet. I can't think about anything else now."

"Yes, you can. Your feet will be fine. Just don't think about it." She paused to gulp some wine while eyeing my feet.

I tried not to think of the dagger-like pains in them. At least there was some feeling coming back.

"The girlfriend is involved," I stated, trying to focus on something else.

Sweetie barked again and began to scrabble her legs on the porch floor. Her eyes were rolled back in her head and there was a small amount of drool on the floor by her mouth. She was so cute.

"*She's* not having a seizure, is she?" Lucy looked alarmed.

"No, she's dreaming, you dope. What's with the seizures?"

"Last week one of my patients had a seizure while he was riding the trolley. It sounded awful, so I'm all worried about sudden seizures now," Lucy answered.

"Seems reasonable." I smiled and took a sip of wine. "You dope."

Lucy sighed and drank the rest of her wine. While she poured a new glass, she said, "We really do need to do this."

"Okay." I smiled. "Why would the lover kill Janet?"

Lucy pushed the swing back and let it go. "Crime of passion, maybe?"

"You mean an 'I loved her, so I killed her' thing, like a country song? I guess it's possible," I mused. "Love sure can make you crazy."

"My point exactly." She grinned.

Shrugging, I said, "Perhaps the girlfriend just couldn't stand the psycho-drama behavior anymore and wanted out, but Janet wouldn't let her go."

"That sounds pretty good in the passion department," she agreed. "Now we just have to figure out who the girlfriend was."

"I think it's obvious. Sally the soldier, right? She's a runner and powerful. It's got to be her."

Lucy nodded. "You're spot on. The girlfriend's got to be Sally."

"So now what do we do?" I asked. "The police know about her, and I told Rita Butler."

"Who doesn't seem to think much of your ideas. Maybe we should talk to Rita's boss instead," Lucy suggested.

"Captain Pearson. He did seem nice," I said.

"Who's Captain Pearson?" It was Russ. We'd been so involved that we hadn't noticed him until he was on the porch. Sweetie woke, went over to where Russ sat near the railing, and plopped down in his lap.

"He's one of the people investigating the death of the lady you found," I told him.

"Ugh!" He shuddered. "Her blood got all over me. And then they took my coat and wouldn't give it back. They're bad people. Especially the orange-haired lady. She's an agent."

"She was kind of mean to you when we interviewed you," I said. "But she's not an agent. The agents aren't real, Russ."

"You always say that, but I know you're wrong," he answered with a stubborn expression.

"Alice," Lucy said, "are you calling Captain Pearson or not?"

"Okay. Hand me the phone."

Moments later Captain Pearson was on the phone, all friendly and courteous. Lucky me. When I told him about Sally, he seemed confused. "Why would you ask me to look into Sally Lambert? Not that I'd tell you what I found anyway. This is an ongoing investigation and I can't talk to the public about it. Even if you were a consultant for five minutes."

"I don't expect you to talk about your investigation," I replied. "But I told Detective Butler last week about our belief that Sally might be the woman Janet Ford was having the affair with. We were wondering what the progress on that was."

"I can't tell you any details," he answered. "But I don't remember hearing about Sally Lambert. Detective Butler must have neglected to tell me. Thanks for letting me know."

When I told Lucy and Russ what the detective said, Russ became very serious. "That detective woman is out to get you, like I've been saying. She won't even take information from you. What did you do to her?"

"I don't know. I thought we were friends, but then she turned all cold and tried to arrest me. I'm beginning to wonder if she's a Borderline too," I said.

"Could be," Lucy remarked. "Her behavior has been all over the map."

Russ seemed confused. "Borderline what?"

"A Borderline with the power to arrest people," I laughed. "Now that's a scary thought."

Lucy laughed with me. "It's probably just you. You and your terrific social skills."

"I don't know what a Borderline is and I don't want to know," Russ said. "But you two need to be careful. I just heard about your accident, Dr. Brenner. Now, didn't I tell you to be careful? That the agents were going to get you if you wasn't careful? Why don't you listen to me?"

"You were right about being careful, Russ. And thanks for warning me. I was being careful because of what you said and that's why they didn't get me."

"Well, you keep being careful. 'Cause that agent is still around." He pushed Sweetie off his lap, jumped down the porch stairs, and turned to give me a serious look. The kind you give misbehaving children. "Don't go out after dark. It's not safe for you."

Lucy smiled indulgently. "Thank you for looking after her, Russ."

"I appreciate it," I said.

"Like babies," Russ mumbled and walked away down the street. "Just like babies."

Lucy and I sat silently for a while sipping our drinks. I patted Sweetie on the head and pulled her ears. She liked that almost as much as a full body rub. Her tail thumped.

Lucy was looking like she felt the wine. She sat in the swing and swung back and forth, watching the floor move beneath her.

"I have great social skills," I said into the silence.

"What?" She glanced up, laughing. "You do not. I've seen it."

"Well," I was the serious one now, "Stan liked me."

"I'm so glad you found someone besides Collier. And I'm truly sorry Stan died. It was cruel, what happened. He might have been a good match for you."

"I miss Stan. I didn't know him well, but I really liked him, Lucy." I sat in silence feeling the sadness of lost possibilities. It could have been good between Stan and me. If we'd had a chance.

Lucy leaned back in the swing and let me be.

"I'm sorry to be such a downer."

"You're not." Lucy smiled, but I could tell that Sweetie was worried. I patted her head and told her it was okay.

"I didn't want to believe I still had issues about relationships."

Lucy laughed. "Oh, honey, I'm sorry. But it's so obvious to everybody else. How could you think we didn't know?"

"You knew?" I felt naked.

"Of course."

"Stan wasn't the only possibility."

"Yeah I know." She smiled again. "Dave may be even a better fit for you than Stan would have been."

I could feel my cheeks burn. Lucy could be too observant.

"Lucy, you've got to help me." I looked her straight in the eyes. "I always seem to mess up relationships. I don't want mess things up with Dave. He's nice and smart and sexy. I don't want to chase him off."

"Don't worry, honey. I won't let you chase him off. He's the kind of catch your mamma would have approved of."

"I don't want to talk about either of my parents."

"I know, honey. You didn't have a good childhood. But you know that helps you understand your patients' pain." She paused. "And it also left you with scars. If you're going to change how you sabotage relationships then you'll have to poke at those scars. You know this, right?"

"Yes. But it'll hurt and I don't want to," I whined. I wanted to say that repression and denial were still mostly working. Except I knew that was a lie.

CHAPTER 45

SUNDAY, NOVEMBER 17
EVENING

That evening, Lucy and I went out to eat. Taco salads at the Baja Bean. Heaven. Of course we had sangria with our salads. The dark interior and happy chatter from other patrons made sangria the logical choice. The smell of grilled meat and wine underscored the mariachi music playing in the background. Add thick cigarette smoke and it would be just like a real Mexican cantina.

Midway through the meal we were both feeling mellow.

"I've been so tense lately," I said.

Lucy laughed. "Of course you have. Most people wouldn't have survived it as well as you have."

"Yeah. You're right. But I'm beginning to believe that the police aren't out to get me anymore."

"You never know, but it does look like you're off their list of suspects," she remarked.

"Maybe I'm going to be okay." *Please, God, let it be so.*

"That's a change of attitude, honey. Did anything happen to make you feel better?" Lucy asked.

"I got a letter from the state licensing board today. They ruled that I was not at fault in Janet's death. That my treatment had been usual and customary," I answered.

"Great! That's worth celebrating."

For a little bit, we both drank more sangria, enjoying the surrounding chatter and tossing silly smiles at each other.

Relaxing back into my seat, I took a deep breath and briefly closed my eyes. "I just believe this police thing will turn out okay, too."

"Me, too. Of course we know you're innocent," she said.

As we finished our salads, Lucy gave me a serious look. "Alice, honey, does this mean you're not as invested in finding the real killer?"

"Yeah, I guess it does," I answered. "I'm tired of being so tense. And Russ's warnings are beginning to scare me."

"You and me both." she said, giggling. It looked like the sangria was getting the best of her.

"Maybe," I began, "we should think about relaxing and letting the police catch the killer. I want to know who did it, but if I'm not in danger of being arrested, perhaps we should give it a rest." Of course my inner Negative Nellie had to remind me that I was being stalked. But she shut up after a couple more sips of sangria.

"Good," Lucy nodded, "because I'm ready to quit. We're therapists, not the police."

We toasted each other and continued drinking the ruby-colored wine until we were both very relaxed. It was late - much later than we'd intended. And I was definitely drunk. As soon as I got home I walked Sweetie, though it was more like Sweetie walking me. When we got back inside I sat down on the sofa and fell asleep.

I dreamt of my office again. Janet was there as usual. This time she was smiling. "At last you're starting to show some sense. We're more alike than you know."

I was smiling when I woke.

CHAPTER 46

SUNDAY, NOVEMBER 17 NIGHT

Much later that night I was lying on the sofa watching reruns on TV when there was a loud knocking on my door. Sweetie barked and practically fell down the stairs to the front door. It was Russ.

"Can you come out and talk?" he asked.

It was chilly and I didn't want to leave the warmth of my living room.

"Why don't you come on up where it's warm?" I said.

"You sure? Usually people don't want me in their houses."

"I'm not most people. Come on up."

"Is it okay, Sweetie?" He looked intently at the wiggling dog.

She answered with a soft woof and a pant.

"Okay then." He chuckled and followed me up the stairs and back into the living room. "Oh! What a pretty rug." He sighed. "I wish I had me such a pretty rug."

I patted his shoulder. "Maybe someday you'll get a room somewhere and then you could get yourself a pretty rug."

"Can I sit on it?"

"Of course. You can even sit on the furniture."

He stiffened. "Dr. Brenner! Do you want me killed? You know that furniture will eat me."

"No. I don't want you killed, Russ. You know I don't think the furniture will eat you. But go ahead and sit on the rug if it makes you more comfortable."

"Whew! I thought you'd turned against me." He sat cross-legged on the corner of the rug. Sweetie crawled on his lap. They both appeared to be happy.

"So, Russ, why are you here?" I knew that Russ didn't come just to hang out. He had a message for me.

"It's important," he said.

"Okay." I tried to look encouraging. I felt like pacing around while he made up his mind to tell me whatever it was he'd come to say, but I knew that would scare him."

Russ sat up straighter and sighed. "It's just that you've had all kinds of warnings. From me and from the agent that's after you. I don't know how you've survived so far. Sooner or later she'll get you, then you'll be dead and I won't be able to come over and visit you and Sweetie."

"She? You said, 'She'll get me.' Who do you mean?" This was the first time Russ had identified the agent as a woman.

"Yes. She will get you if you don't pay attention. Then I won't get to come over here. And what would happen to Sweetie?" His speech was rapid and tense. "You've got to be careful."

"Who is she? You didn't tell me the agent was a woman. Why didn't you tell me?"

"I did." He looked hurt.

I shook my head emphatically. "No, you didn't. How do you know it's a woman?"

Seeming insulted, he sat up straighter. "I can tell the difference between boys and girls."

"Okay. What does this girl look like?"

"She's tall and thin. And she has long orange hair. Lots of the time she's in a black SUV."

I almost choked. He was describing Rita Butler!

"That sounds like Detective Butler. You know, the lady who interviewed you at the police station," I said.

"Yeah. I told you she was an agent, but you didn't listen."

"How do you know she's an agent?"

"She was following you in the park when you and Sweetie went out, and I saw her leaning against your car the other morning. Whenever anyone would come by she'd walk away and then when the other person was gone, she'd come back." He looked at me very intensely while he scratched his nose. "She's very tense and shifty-eyed, too." Russ actually had tears in his eyes. "Now that you know what she is, you just keep away from her. Okay?"

Russ hugged Sweetie, slunk down the stairs, and out the front door to disappear into the dark-shrouded sidewalk. I don't think he even heard me call ,"Thanks, Russ."

I threw myself into my rocking chair and rocked. Had he really seen Rita Butler stalking me? Was she just watching me as part of her investigation of Janet's death? Or was Rita trying to kill me? As I rocked I wondered who else it could be. Collier hadn't been the sweetheart I used to think he was. And Dave came to town about the same time that bad things started to happen to me. Eventually, I wondered if everybody was after me. Everybody but Sweetie.

CHAPTER 47

SUNDAY, NOVEMBER 17
LATE NIGHT

By the time I'd finished rocking I almost believed that Rita could have been behind the threats, the accident in the park, and the shooting. As a cop, she had a lot of opportunity to slip away and do something, and then appear at the aftermath claiming she'd heard it on the police band. Her position also gave her an excellent opportunity to frame me for Janet Ford's murder. Of course the attacks against me and Janet's murder were connected. The attempts to harm me became more violent as I talked to more people and tried to clear myself. But what would Janet and Rita have in common? They didn't move in the same circles. They probably didn't even shop in the same part of town. They had me in common, but what else?

All the same things that made it so easy for her to hide what she was doing made it especially difficult to catch her. She'd left no hard evidence at the scene and she had Janet's journal to twist into a motive for me. The only thing that would get her convicted would be a confession and she'd be able to resist interrogation. I felt my anger build as I realized that she'd probably get away with it. I had almost no chance of getting her arrested.

I called Lucy to tell her. The first thing she said was, "Do you know what time it is?" The second was, "Does Rita look like a lesbian?"

I frowned. *What's wrong with her?* Lucy knew lesbians looked like everybody else. She was a licensed social worker! She must be in a contrary mood tonight.

"Did she have a masculine air? Wear men's clothing or have real short hair?" Lucy was sounding mischievous.

"Damn it! Don't joke about this, you dope. She looks like every other woman. You know that. She's tall and thin and has long, curly red hair. And her clothing is casual, but feminine."

"Did she do or say anything to make you think she was a lesbian?"

"Of course not. Why would we have talked about her sexual orientation? I don't know one way or another. Maybe she was the running partner and lover and maybe she killed Janet, because she was going to out her. Or maybe she killed Janet for another reason." I frowned.

"Like what?" Lucy asked.

"I don't know." I frowned. "And the jogging partner may not be the lesbian lover or the killer. We've been assuming that."

"We need help."

"Yeah."

"Why don't you call your gay friend?"

"You mean Hank Shifflett?"

"Yes. Call him. He might even be able to inform us whether Rita is a lesbian. In a small town, the gay community is bound to be even smaller. Maybe small enough that they all know each other."

"I doubt it," I said. "Being gay isn't a club with Friday night parties, like the VFW."

"Even so, I think you should get his ideas about this."

"Okay. Why don't we invite him to lunch tomorrow?" I smiled over the phone at her.

Sweetie wiggled at the idea.

CHAPTER 48

MONDAY, NOVEMBER 18
AFTERNOON

Hank was in my kitchen devouring Lucy's fried chicken when we first mentioned the case to him.

"Hank," I said, "I think I need your help with something."

"Okay," he mumbled with a mouth full of chicken.

"I'm involved in that murder case. Janet Ford. It's been in the paper."

He swallowed quickly. "Yeah. You sure have been, too. I didn't think I should mention it. Bound to be painful, what with being accused of incompetence and suspected of murder. So … how's that whole thing going for you?"

"Wow! You don't mince words, do you?" Lucy seemed shocked.

"No, not usually. That's why I didn't mention it." Shrugging, he took a big bite out of his chicken leg.

I shook my head. "I don't mind, Lucy. Hank and I are old friends. I'm used to it."

"Okay then." She smiled. "Hank, we're trying to find out if a specific woman is a lesbian and if she'd been seeing Janet Ford."

Hank laughed. "And I'm your token gay friend."

"You are my friend who happens to be gay. If my pipes were clogged, I'd be serving fried chicken to my friend who happens to be a plumber. See how it works?"

Hank grinned. "Yeah, I see. The newspaper never said anything about Janet Ford being gay. Is that a cover-up by the press?"

I smiled again. "She was gay this month. Just how gay, I don't know. Who knows if it would have lasted. She was impulsive and mercurial. We think she might have been seeing a police detective named Rita Butler, who Lucy and I believe was probably involved in Janet's death, or knows more than she's admitting. Does she sound familiar to you? Rita Butler."

"Just from the newspaper," he replied. "Seems like you've got yourself in a mess. Can't you get yourself off the hook without accusing a police detective?"

"Not right now. And I admit to being less than certain, but when the facts we have are viewed in one perspective, it really does look like Rita Butler is involved somehow with Janet's death. We have evidence from a psychotic man and a dead man, which is hardly proof that will stand up in court. The police won't even consider one of their own without strong evidence. And like I said, this is one perspective. One that Lucy and I feel is compelling, but there could be other explanations as well."

"Well, that sounds kinda flakey, if you ask me," he said. "But if you want to play out that particular string, and if I was in your position, I'd ask around at a lesbian bar. You gotta hunt where the game is, know what I'm saying?"

I laughed. "Yes, I do. And does Fort Madison even have one of those?"

Hank shook his head. "No. People don't hardly come here for the thriving gay scene," he said. "Charlottesville has two such establishments, but one's only for bikers."

"So you know how to get there? Would you show us?"

"Yeah. If you want to go, I can take you," he said. "But it might be better if you went with a card-carrying lesbian rather than a gay man. And Lucy should go with you."

Smiling, Lucy nodded.

"I have a friend, Lynn Shapiro, who's usually up for anything. I think I can talk her into taking you. I'll go call her now." He wiped his hands and went into the living room with his cell phone.

When he returned he was all smiles. "Lynn thinks it would be a hoot to take a couple of straight shrinks to the Oasis Girl. Says you should get there on Saturday night, about eleven. Should be your best chance for finding someone who might have seen who you're looking for. It's late enough for lots of people to be there, but not so late that they've gone on to other parties."

"Okay. But I need to tell you that it might be a little dangerous."

"With you, how dangerous can it get?"

"A little." I smiled. I didn't know how much I wanted to tell Hank. If he thought it was really dangerous, he might not want his friend to go, and I needed her to. But I really should tell him how dangerous. That I'd been attacked. I felt frozen. Maybe, if I was with other people, witnesses, then whoever was bringing me grief wouldn't be foolish enough to cause trouble. I doubted they would.

Hank was smiling back at me. "Lynn will be up for a little danger. It'll make the trip more exciting."

"Okay! Let's do that. Lucy, are you sure you want to come?" My conscience was poking me again. Lucy was important to me. I didn't want anything bad to happen to her, but there I was putting her in potential danger. In the end, I didn't pay any attention to my conscience. Safety in numbers.

"Yes, of course," she answered. "I wouldn't let you have all that adventure without me."

"Okay," Hank said, grinning. "Now, can I have some of that cherry pie on the counter?"

CHAPTER 49

SATURDAY, NOVEMBER 21 NIGHT

Hank was with Lynn when she arrived to get us. "I just wanted to introduce my girls," he said. "Now play nice and have a good adventure. I'm going to visit some friends a few blocks from here."

"Thanks, Hank." I waved to him as we drove off. Lynn was kind of quiet, but seemed nice, and her car was a roomy blue SUV. She looked a little mannish in her black leather jacket and jeans, in contrast to Lucy's feminine blue cashmere sweater and gray pants. I was in my usual folk tunic and jeans. We made an odd looking bunch.

"Thanks for driving, Lynn. I'll pay for gas, of course." I put a couple of folded twenties in the cup holder. Hardly enough to cover the valuable information we might get tonight.

She turned briefly to smile at me. I was dazzled at the difference it made in her appearance. She transformed into a sexy, warm woman. Who would have known?

The night was clear with a full moon. A beautiful night for a drive. As we climbed Afton Mountain on our way to Charlottesville, the forest on either side of the interstate was dense with leafless trees. Occasionally there were open spots where you could see for miles. I was surprised there was so much traffic on I-64 at this time of night. When I shared this with Lynn, she laughed.

"You don't get out much, do you?"

"Not at this hour. I'm usually where I'm going by ten. When I was young, I was told that nothing good ever happens to a girl after 10:30. Scarred for life, I guess."

Lynn laughed. I was relieved. Hopefully she was beginning to loosen up. "That's a very sensible outlook. Hank said that Collier isn't a late-night guy, so I'm guessing that works out well for you."

"No, he's not," I replied, "but I'm not exactly with Collier now. We're still friendly though."

Lucy gave me a meaningful look.

"Oh," Lynn glanced at me, "I thought Hank saw you guys at Madison Grill the other night."

"Yes, we were there, but you see, Collier is the lawyer for the mother of my client who died recently. So it's complicated and now we're both dating other people."

"Really?" Lynn turned to look at me and the car swerved. She smiled that smile again and I wondered if she was flirting with me. Whatever it was, it felt awkward.

"Watch it, Lynn," warned Lucy. "We don't need to have an accident before we even get there."

"Okay. Alice, tell me about these other men. I didn't know you were such a social girl."

"I'm not that social. I met a doctor at the hospital and we dated a couple of times. It might have gone somewhere, but he was killed."

"Part of this case?" Lynn asked.

"I believe so," I answered. "He was run off the road coming back from Charlottesville."

Lynn glanced at the curving road. "You mean this road? Off this mountain?"

"Yeah. We should be extra careful coming back." I tried to sound unconcerned.

"You could have told me, Alice," Lynn replied. She sounded irritated. "This is more excitement than I usually care to have."

"Would you have come? Hank said you liked adventure when I warned him," I countered. *You did it again, Alice. You should have been straight with her about the possibility of danger. Dishonesty doesn't pay.*

"Probably." She paused. "Well, maybe. What do you think happened? To your friend."

"What I *know* is that last weekend, Stan, my friend, died in a bad wreck here on I-64 coming back from Charlottesville. I have an uneasy feeling about what happened."

"I'm getting the feeling that you don't believe that Stan's death was an accident."

"Right, I don't. I think I know who ran him off the road and killed him. We're trying to prove it." My voice was getting thick with emotion. I didn't want to lose it in front of Lynn, at least not until I knew her better.

"You are creeping me out, big time. Hank said it might be a little dangerous, but I didn't think he meant it."

"I don't think it will be, actually. Stan was alone, we're a group. We haven't given that person any reason to follow us, and she doesn't know you or this car." I decided things would go better if Lynn didn't know about the attempts on my life.

We drove along in silence for a while. Lynn turned on some music to fill the silence. I thought about what I'd told her, and what

I hadn't. I still felt we were fairly safe, but I couldn't be sure, and that was beginning to bother me.

"Lynn, would you mind slowing down here, please?" I asked as we rounded a steep curve.

Perhaps lulled by her music, Lynn didn't ask why, just slowed to a crawl with her hazard lights blinking. Her face seemed blank, maybe she had decided that all of this was okay with her.

She turned to me and asked, "Why are we doing this?" Her voice was tight. I guess she was still angry … or scared.

"This is where Stan died." I pointed to the broken guard rail across the highway. "Over there. I-I want to say a prayer for him. I need to do that."

"Okay, but don't get us run over," Lucy said.

"And don't take long," Lynn added. Her expression now revealed that she thought I was out of my mind.

I bowed my head and whispered, "Forgive me, Stan. I didn't mean to get you killed. I'm so sorry." I felt a little lighter inside.

Wiping the tears in my eyes, I said, "Thanks, Lynn. That was important to me."

"You miss him a lot?" She was looking a little sympathetic. Maybe she wasn't as angry with me.

"Yeah," I sniffled. "A whole lot. I'm sorry I didn't tell you this might be dangerous. I was so wrapped up in getting justice for Stan and my patient that I wasn't thinking about what I was doing to you. I'm very sorry. We can turn around after we get off the mountain and go home. I've had enough for tonight. It's past 10:30."

"No," Lynn shrugged, "I'm in. This woman you suspect really did bad things. I'd like to help catch her. But you should've told me the truth. I don't like being … kept in the dark like that."

"I know. I'm sorry."

The rest of the trip was in silence, with Lynn watching the rearview mirror as much as the road in front. I think she was still a little mad at me. I didn't blame her.

CHAPTER 50

SATURDAY, NOVEMBER 21 NIGHT

The Oasis Girl bar looked like any small-town dive. The windowless concrete block building sat at the far end of an enormous parking lot. Its only identification was a big sign over the door that read OASIS GIRL. The lot was filled with cars, trucks, and motorcycles. Here and there groups of women stood talking. Some couples were kissing or hugging.

The bar was crowded and hot. The interior was dim. Artificial candles flickered at the tables. Between the tables and the bar there was a medium-sized dance floor where about a dozen couples were shuffling around to an old ballad. Scattered about, couples or small groups stood talking, drinking, or kissing. This was probably tame compared to San Francisco bars, but all that public affection was enough to embarrass me.

Lynn waved at a couple of people as we pushed our way up to the bar, but otherwise was still silent. I guess I really did scare her.

Before we made it to the bar, a group of women yelled for us to come over. The main yeller was a big woman with long gray hair. She wore black jeans, a white tee, and a black leather vest. She looked scary to me, but Lynn seemed to know her.

"Hey, Willis," Lynn said. "Haven't seen you in a while."

"You haven't been here in months, baby," the scary woman answered. "We missed you."

"Well, I'm back." Lynn grinned.

"With girls, too. When did you get a harem?"

There were frowns at the table and someone laughed and said, "Oh. No."

"Not likely, you idiot," Lynn said, putting her arm around my shoulders. "This is Alice Brenner, one of my token straight friends. Don't worry about her. She's gay-friendly. So's her friend Lucy over there."

Willis puckered up. "How gay friendly are you, Alice?"

"Not that friendly," I answered with a smile. "We're here on a mission."

"What kind of mission?" a pretty blonde woman asked.

Lynn answered. "Alice is being framed for murder by someone. We think the victim was in a lesbian relationship, but the cops haven't talked to her lover yet and Alice thinks she might know something. We're trying to see if we can put the two of them together."

"Together in a lesbian bar might imply they were lovers?" Willis asked.

"Yeah," I answered. "It could look that way in court. I have pictures of the two of them. Not too clear, 'cause they're from the newspaper. Can you see if you recognize either of them?" The picture of Janet was a headshot maybe a publicity photo for her business. The picture of Rita was from the newspaper of her recent press conference about the investigation.

The group became considerably less friendly. One of the women looked at Lynn and said, "Lynn, what do you think you're doing." The others glared at us.

"We don't want to upset you." I coughed. My throat was dry and scratchy. "All we want is to see if they've been here." I was confused about why the mood had abruptly turned hostile.

Willis seemed to be their spokesperson. "We don't out people. If they haven't outed themselves, we won't do it for them.

"Oh. Okay." Lynn spoke. "This isn't what you think. Alice is a therapist. She is being falsely accused of murdering one of her patients. This woman is the victim." She pointed to Janet's picture. "And the other is possibly her lover who has the power to get Alice arrested. If we can show that they may have been lovers, that at the very least suggests a conflict of interest for Alice's accuser. We think that it's more. It's likely that this person either killed Alice's patient or knows who did."

Lucy leaned toward Willis. "We desperately need your help. . .just to know if they'd been here together."

The group whispered amongst themselves. Then Willis took the pictures from me and said, "Under the circumstances, it's okay to say if we've seen them." Willis looked, shook her head, and passed the pictures around the group. But after all of that, no one had seen them. They all shook their heads. "Naw. Haven't seen them. Sorry."

Shrugging, I cast my gaze down at the picture. "Thanks for looking."

"You come back and play with us when you're through," Willis said.

"Don't worry, we'll be back," Lynn said, laughing.

We stopped a couple coming off the dance floor and had them look at the pictures. One of them thought she had seen Janet somewhere, but they didn't remember Rita.

When we got up to the bar, the crush of people pushed me into the rail. Lynn waved at the cute blonde mixing drinks. "Hey, Jody. How's it going?"

"Good night so far, Lynn. How come we haven't seen you lately?" She wiped the bar as she talked. At a wave from a black-haired woman several feet down the bar from us, she began preparing some kind of drink that turned blue as she mixed it.

"Oh, you know," Lynn said. "My last ended badly. It hurt too much to come back to where I met her. The scene of the crime, right?" She gave me a sly wink.

"Maybe you'll meet someone even better." Jody slid the drink down to the black-haired woman and turned to eye me. "You aren't trying to play straight, are you?"

"No," Lynne laughed. "She's not my type. This," she nodded at me, "is a new friend of mine. Alice. She's a murder suspect looking to find out if someone is gay."

"Murder suspect, huh? That's hot, but I don't out people. What happens here stays here. Maybe your 'friend' should go home and contemplate her sins." Jody's voice had taken on a steely edge, apparently a special frequency because some big women wearing wife-beaters over lots of muscles and tattoos were moving toward us.

"Hold up, Jody," Lynn interrupted. "That's not what this is." Jody gave the scary women a nod, but they stayed close. The noise level resumed its normal roar. "Do you have a break coming up?" asked Lynn. "We should talk. Privately. You won't regret it."

Jody regarded Lynn for a moment, gave me a brief look, then waved the muscles off.

"Yeah, I guess I can. Only because you're such a sweetie, Lynn." She signaled to the other bartender, a curly-haired brunette, and led us to a small room behind the bar.

It was obviously used as both storage and a break room. A faint odor of cigarettes hung in the air. A coffee pot gurgled on a small table in the corner. Jody sat down at a beat-up dinette set and invited us to join her. "You really accused of murder?" she asked. "Most of those girls are over at the Gorilla Lounge."

I didn't know whether to be flattered or insulted, and didn't have time to decide which. "Yes, it's true, but I don't like being defined by my alleged crimes." Lucy snorted at my attempt to lighten the mood. "I work as a therapist. Lucy here is one my colleagues. One of my patients recently died under mysterious circumstances and I'm being accused of her murder."

Jody took this information with a calm expression, but I got a sense she was getting interested in my situation.

"Alice and Lucy asked me to help them find some answers, so here we are," said Lynn.

"Isn't that the police's job? Finding answers," Lynn asked, her eyes right on me.

I nodded. "I think a cop is framing me. One of the detectives on the case. If I can prove she was seen with the victim, it's pretty likely that she's the one who killed her, or knows who did. Please help me."

"Well, you *are* more interesting than I thought," Jody remarked, winking at me. Suddenly, she became more relaxed. "What you just said about the cop doesn't make sense. See if you can explain it better."

"Witnesses have seen the victim with a woman, who we have come to believe is gay, but not out. The victim was in love with her and was planning to tell everybody."

She shook her head. "That's such a passé reason for murder, even in Virginia."

"I would tend to agree, but in small town police culture I don't think it's that much of a reach. Given what we know, it looks like that's what happened."

"Alice has been threatened and harassed as well," added Lucy. "Someone doesn't want her to find justice for her client."

Jody nodded. "So how can I help?"

I handed her the pictures. "We believe they may have come here in the last few months."

Jody examined the two photos. "Yeah. I've seen both of them. Together. They came in a few times. Didn't stay too long. The one in the headshot was more excited about being here than the redhead. Last time was about three weeks ago. They had an argument and left."

I inhaled deeply, exhaling loudly. "Thanks, Jody. That's a huge help."

"Anytime." She hurried back the bar and a spike-haired girl who had been waving at the other bartender who was busy mixing drinks.

As we went back to Willis and her group, we showed the picture to some of the women customers. One couple had seen them, but the others hadn't. Apparently, Janet and Rita weren't regulars.

Now that the ice had been broken, I discovered that Willis and her gang were as much fun as a pile of puppies. They all thought I was cute, and after one of them recognized me from my television debut at the city jail, I didn't have to buy any more drinks. Lucy wasn't drinking or saying much. In fact, her face seemed tight. But I didn't care. I was having too much fun.

As I talked with the women, relief washed over me. At last some real evidence against Rita. Maybe now the police would listen to me.

We ordered more drinks. After all, I'd dragged Lynn and Lucy all the way over here, it wouldn't hurt to party for a bit. Besides, I'd always wondered what a gay bar was like. I'd discovered that this one was a fun place. Wouldn't hurt to have a drink or two, maybe do some dancing. It had been too long since I'd been on a dance floor in the middle of a happy crowd.

I totally lost count of how much I was drinking. I found out later that Lucy was too uncomfortable to say anything.

Now I wish she had.

CHAPTER 51

SUNDAY, NOVEMBER 22 VERY EARLY MORNING

It was two in the morning before we left and the bar was closing. Jody waved good-bye as Lynn and Lucy guided me through the throngs of last-call survivors.

Once outside, I looked around trying to get accustomed to the cold morning air. Off to our right there was a person in a dark hoodie watching us. I couldn't tell if it was a tall woman or a man. My mind didn't seem to be working well, but I thought I probably should point the watcher out to the others. Then Lynn gave me a push towards the car and I forgot all about being watched.

Getting to the car wasn't as easy as I thought it would be. The paving had developed mysterious hills and valleys that weren't there when we came in. Lynn's car door handle didn't want to cooperate and the seat was much lower than it had been. It didn't bother me, though. It all seemed hilariously funny. Even when Lynn had to buckle me into the backseat.

"I told you those drinks were powerful, Alice. You should have listened." She looked at me with cold eyes.

"Oh!" I tried to laugh it off. "They were so good. I'd never had blue drinks before." I felt happy and *floaty*. Life was good, except that

Lynn and Lucy seemed to be angry. I couldn't figure it out. If truth be told, I didn't want to know why.

"You're not much of a drinker, missy," Lynn muttered.

"I am so too. How dare you say that? I only had three or four. Take it back." She was spoiling my good mood.

"You're drunk." She was not nearly as happy as I was. A mystery.

"I am not. Take that back, too," I giggled, "or we'll have to have a gunfight." Why'd she have to try to bring me down? For once I was having fun.

Lynn sneered. "You couldn't stand up long enough to have a gunfight."

"Could, too. Take that back, also." I sat tall in my seat, nodded my head at Lucy, and fell asleep.

*   *   *

I woke to Lucy yelling my name, "Alice. Wake up, Alice!" There was a dull impact, tires screeching, and Lynn yelling obscenities.

"Wow. Where are we? Aren't we home yet?"

"No!" Lucy screamed at me. "We're in trouble. Pay attention!" Her eyes were wide and her face pale.

Lucy was scared. I paused to congratulate myself on being so astute while drunk. This was hard, because I just realized that we were hurtling down the interstate.

"Why are you speeding? It's so bright in here."

"Look behind you, idiot." Lynn barked, white knuckles gripping the wheel.

I turned to look and was promptly blinded by the glare of headlights. Some maniac was right on our bumper.

"Yikes! What's that?" I yelled.

"A big, black SUV," Lynn snapped. "Must've followed us from the Oasis. Been harassing us for five minutes, Sleeping Beauty."

"Don't do what they want. Slow down." I was scared now. And not so drunk.

"When I do the SUV bumps us. If they bump us too hard, we'll go off the road."

This scenario was all too familiar. I tried to get oriented, see where we were on the mountain, but there weren't any other headlights on the road. It was too dark and the SUV's headlights too bright to see what the terrain was like. Then a cold shock hit me and I knew where we were. *Dead Ladies Curve*. The same stretch of road we'd taken earlier, where Stan had gone hurtling through the guardrail. Suddenly I was sober and thoughts of Sweetie flashed through my mind.

Although I was sober,, I doubt my reflexes were normal. I was confident Lynn hadn't drank as much as me, though I couldn't really remember.

"Lynn! What are we going to do?" I felt like crying. Or screaming. I could hear Lucy crying in the front seat, which was unlike her. "Call 911."

"We did that. They won't get here in time…but I know the road here. We'll be off the mountain soon and on the flat road in the valley. We'll just hang on until then."

"What if they have guns?" I remembered the flash of metal just before bullets shot up my car the last time I had a close encounter with a dark SUV. At that point the SUV backed off, then accelerated.

Lynn yelled, "Brace yourself!" The SUV hit with a thunderous crash. We swerved toward the guardrail. Lynn steered away from it, just like you'd do on an ice patch. There was a screeching howl and we tore through the steel guardrail.

I smashed against the seatbelt and came to a sudden stop. Maybe it was the alcohol or maybe it was the crash, but I couldn't help it. Watery vomit splashed down the front of my blouse and onto the floor. The car reeked of it. Lucy was crying while Lynn fought her way out of her deflating airbag. My stomach and shoulder burned where the seat belt had hit me. I looked out of the car and saw a blurry vision of trees all around us.

Instead of plummeting off the shear bank as Stan had done, we'd hit the forested side of a hill. The SUV had waited too late to make its move, hitting us as the interstate passed over the beginning of the foothills, just after the steep drop to our side. We were safe by a few yards.

Headlights from oncoming cars lit up the interior of the car. Both Lynn and Lucy had blood on their faces, but seemed okay otherwise. I couldn't see the SUV. *Would they come back and shoot us? Best not share that thought, Alice.*

Lynn pulled off her seatbelt and turned toward me. "Alice. You all right back there?"

I was sore all over and probably had bruises from the seatbelt. But I was okay. I opened my mouth to say this to Lynn, but instead I howled, "I want to go home!"

"Was that Rita?" Lucy asked. She looked shaken, bruised. The airbag hadn't been kind to her.

"It could have been," I said. "She has a black SUV. Thank God those cars came. She couldn't do anything else with witnesses here. She might have gotten out and shot us if they hadn't been here." Still being a bit drunk despite the adrenaline rush, my ability to shut the hell up was still severely compromised.

"Oh, God," Lynn said. "You're just too dangerous to be around."

*   *   *

Three hours later the police had come, the car had been towed, and we'd been checked for hidden damage at the University of Virginia Hospital in Charlottesville. I called Dave McGinty and asked him to take us home. He yelled at me, but agreed to come and get us. By then it was five-thirty.

As Dave pulled out of the hospital parking lot, Lucy said, "It'll be after six when we get home. Do we want to get breakfast?"

I grimaced, even though it hurt the big bruise on my face. "No, Lucy, I couldn't eat anything now. Maybe just some coffee."

"Coffee. I could go for some coffee and an explanation of what you all were doing out there tonight," Dave said. He turned to glare at me. "Alice, sometimes I think you're too dumb to live."

CHAPTER 52

SUNDAY, NOVEMBER 22
EARLY MORNING

As soon as we got home I ran upstairs to check on Sweetie. I was greeted by her running at full force at me. I was afraid she'd knock me back downstairs, but she screeched to a full sit right in front of me. I couldn't tell if she was so happy because she missed me or because she had to go out to relieve herself. Either way, I liked her wiggles.

Finally, we were gathered around my kitchen table. The room felt warm and cozy. It was filled with early morning sunlight and smelled of coffee. We'd all had three cups already. I was wide awake despite the pull of fatigue.

"We need to decide what to do about this," Dave said. "Somebody almost killed you last night. The next time they won't miscalculate."

"We need help," Lucy replied.

"Guys, I don't know about the 'we'." Lynn was still pale and her coffee cup shook as she tried to drink. " I don't think I'm cut out to be a member of your squad. Bad things happen around Alice. I'm going home."

Dave looked irritated. I wasn't sure if it was at Lynn or me.

"That's okay, Lynn. You're probably right." I said. "You've been a big help already. I'll let you know what happens,"

After Lynn left, Lucy looked at me. "Are you okay?"

"Maybe. It's not like similar things haven't been said. I do get into trouble." I paused. "And I pull my friends into trouble with me. I'm . . . not good to be around. What's worse is that I usually don't think about what's going to happen to any of you until something bad happens. Maybe I'm not the woman I thought I was. Can you . . .could you forgive me for being such a self-centered shit?"

" Oh, honey, you're my best friend. I know the good and the bad of you. And I love you just as you are." Lucy smiled at me. "Even if you are sometimes self-centered."

"I don't know you as well as Lucy does, but what I do know I like very much. You're okay in my book." Dave smiled .

"I'll try to be more thoughtful . . . this is all new to me." I promised.

"That would be good." They both responded.

We all laughed and Dave squeezed my hand. His touch made my stomach drop. What did that mean?

Lucy brought my attention back by stating, "We need to get back to this morning's incident. Alice, I think you should call the other detective on the case, Jay Manson."

"The problem is that he's Rita Butler's partner," I reminded her.

"But you have some hard evidence that Rita was dating Janet. Surely he'll believe you." Lucy stared at me. "Also, it was a dark-colored SUV that tried to kill us on the mountain. It's always a dark SUV. Rita drives a black SUV."

"I know, but he works with her every day. He likes her. Says she's a good cop. And lots of people drive dark SUVs. Why would he change his mind based on that?"

"You can make a logical case for Rita being involved. If she's such a good cop, why didn't she reveal that she was dating the victim when she took the case? And since he's her partner, he probably knows more about her than we do."

Shrugging, I shook my head sadly. "He won't believe us."

"Maybe not, but perhaps we can convince him. So call him now." Lucy's expression was determined.

Dave glared at me as he said, "Yes, *Alice*, call Jay."

I couldn't deal with his sarcastic tone right then so I ignored it.

I felt like I was on a driverless train careening out of control. So I called Detective Manson.

He was in my kitchen within fifteen minutes. I made more coffee and brought out some brownies with walnuts on them. I greeted him with a brownie in one hand and chocolate icing on my lips. "I have something serious to talk to you about," I said.

Detective Manson smiled a sexy smile at me. Lucy handed me a napkin. Dave looked like he'd like to kill somebody.

Detective Manson waited for me to clean my face, and then glared at the three of us. "All right, what's so serious? Even under all that chocolate, you look as if your closest friend died. And where did those bruises come from?"

I began. "We think we know who killed Janet Ford and who has been trying to kill me."

"That's a good thing," he said.

"Yeah. It is. But we don't know if you'll think it is."

"Dr. Brenner, stop playing games. Tell me who you think it is and why."

Lucy and I both sighed. Everyone looked at me. Guess I was it.

"It's Rita Butler," I said. I could see surprise and then anger wash across his face.

"Rita! That's ridiculous. I've worked with her for five years. We've been partners for two. She wouldn't murder anyone. How could you think that?"

"I didn't want to believe it either. I like Rita. I thought we might become friends. At least until the two of you decided I was the killer. By the way, it's really nice that you were ready to believe that I'm a killer, but can't imagine Rita is one." By then I was angry, too.

"Guys," Dave interrupted, "let's look at this logically." He turned to stare at me. "And don't let our hurt feelings get in the way."

"You're right," Jay muttered. "The only way this will work is to leave emotion out of it."

"Yeah." I sighed. "You're right, Dave. I'll try to do that."

Detective Manson turned to me with an intense expression. He seemed to be thinking things through. "Why do you think it's Rita? Do you have any evidence?"

"Russ saw her following me and hanging around my house early in the morning. The car that shot at me was a black SUV. Rita drives a black SUV. Rita had opportunity to crash in to me and to shoot at me. She had opportunity to frame me for Janet's murder."

"That's not conclusive. Even if Russ saw her, which I'm not sure of, she could have been investigating you for Janet's murder. You don't have any evidence that she was involved in Janet's murder."

"Russ said he saw her running in the park with Janet. Stan Wilson told me that he saw Janet's running mate, and that he thought he knew her from somewhere. He could have seen Rita on the TV news. We know from what Janet told me that her running partner was the person she was in love with. Janet's mother told us that Janet was in love with a woman. So the woman Stan saw was probably her lover. It's likely that her lover is involved in her murder."

"Not necessarily," he said. "Didn't she have another friend who was a runner? The woman who's part of the women's military program at the college."

"Then why hasn't she come forward?" Lucy asked.

"Maybe she's reluctant to be identified as another woman's lover."

"That could be a motive for killing Janet. She was a diva-level drama queen, and Janet told several people that she was going to tell everybody who her lover was. That could easily have led to a violent quarrel."

"So how do we know Rita was this lover?" he asked.

"Russ and Stan saw them together."

"Russ is crazy and Stan's dead." He scowled.

"Yeah. Stan's accident happened just hours after he called Rita to tell her that he could identify the lover."

"We don't know that Stan called her," he countered. "Rita said he didn't."

"Russ saw Stan making a phone call just after he left me. Just after he promised to call her."

"That's still not proof, but we can check Stan's phone records to find out if he called the department."

"We have other witnesses, ones who aren't delusional or dead. Last night, Lucy and I went with a lesbian acquaintance to a bar in Charlottesville and got positive IDs on both Rita and Janet. They'd been there together several times, and quarreled the last time they were there. Then on our way home a black SUV ran us off the interstate coming down the mountain. If she'd been a little quicker, Rita would have killed us."

"So that's where the bruises came from." His voice was soft.

Dave shifted in his chair. I stared at him. Could he care more for me than he's letting on?

Lucy gave me a stern look and said, "Doesn't it seem like Rita was the other woman and that she was involved in Janet's death? Can't you see that she was probably involved in the attacks against Alice? I'm sure going over the security camera footage for the date Stan said he treated Janet would show Rita there also."

"Even if Rita was the lover, why would she kill Janet? Being outed as gay isn't a motive."

"It is if you work in a homophobic police department. If you were ambitious and wanted promotions."

"We aren't homophobic." Detective Manson frowned.

"You aren't comfortable with straight female officers … let alone lesbian ones."

"That's not true." He appeared to be insulted.

"Don't be willfully naïve. Who do you all expect to answer the phone?"

Jay paused. "Well, Rita always does it. She wants to."

"Bullshit. You expect her to and she does it because of that." I looked him in the eye. "Think how her life would change if everybody knew she was homosexual."

"No. She's a respected detective. Nothing would change." He was tense and his chin had a stubborn cast.

"Please think about it. Yes. She's respected now, but wouldn't that change if your buddies thought of her as gay?"

He paused, then sighed. "She'd end up doing traffic and missing dogs." His shoulders drooped. "I just have a hard time believing this. And we don't have any hard proof. There's nothing that puts her at the murder scene or at the attacks on you."

"What about the black SUV?"

"Did you get the license number?"

I shook my head.

"Didn't think so."

"Can you get us any evidence?" Lucy looked at the two of us.

"Russ's prints are the only ones on the knife." He frowned. "There's no evidence that Stan's death was anything but a bad accident on a dangerous road. Any involvement with you, Alice, could be explained away as part of an investigation into Janet's death. Even if Rita lied about Stan calling her, we don't have enough evidence to convict her of anything but doing her job. At the most - *if* you could prove Rita and Janet were dating - it would be a conflict of interest. Her investigating her girlfriend's death. And might get her written up by our supervisor. But that's all.

"I'll go check the phone records and the hospital security footage. But even if she did this, I don't see a way to arrest her, let alone convict her. And," he paused, "I don't believe she's guilty of anything. I'm not going to help you ruin the career of a good cop."

After Dave, Lucy, and Detective Manson left, I sat at thee brownies. It see med so clear to me th Rita was the killer, but with no real evidence, the detective was right. Rita would h it. Unless she confessed. What would make her do that? Could I provoke her a confession? Or would she kill me? I wasn't betting on my chances.

CHAPTER 53

SUNDAY, NOVEMBER 22
AFTERNOON

That afternoon, I took a nap to make up for all the sleep I'd lost and woke with a start when my doorbell rang. Sweetie barked and ran down the stairs. I followed slowly. It was Dave at my door.

"Dave. Why are you back? I mean, I wasn't expecting you. What's up?"

"I have something to show you."

"Come in." We sat on the sofa together. I felt his presence far more than I should. Maybe I liked him more than I thought I did.

"Here." He handed me a grainy black and white picture. "I got a picture of Craig Fletcher, our crime boss. My FBI friend finally came through."

My heart beat through my chest. I couldn't breathe. There were black spots in my field of vision.

"Dave! I know this guy," I said. I felt myself gasping for air.

"What?"

"He's one of my patients. Only he's not using the name Craig Fletcher."

His eyebrows rose, his eyes widening with the action. "You're saying that the valley's most wanted and dangerous criminal is one of your patients?"

"Yes." I felt like I was about to pass out. Why couldn't Dave hear my heart beating? I sure could.

"How long have you been seeing him?"

Leaning over, I placed my elbows on my knees and my head in my hands. "About four weeks."

"He might be using the therapy to keep tabs on you. But why?"

"I don't know."

"Maybe some of my research on Janet's family wasn't as discrete as I thought," Dave said, running his hands through his hair.

"What should I do? I can't call the police on a patient." I couldn't seem to stop wringing my hands together.

"Yes, you can, and you should. Criminal activity breaks privilege. Stop seeing him. He's dangerous."

"About that. I did get a call from an old graduate school buddy. His practice in Boston is looking for a temporary replacement for one of their therapists that's about to go out on a six-month maternity leave. I told him I was interested. I may just leave after all.""Thank God!" He looked relieved "Even after I explained about all of my troubles here, he said I was perfect. He's going to clear it with his colleagues today. I could be gone in two weeks."

"That's great. You need to stay safe. I'd…I'll miss you, but it's for the best." His face was slightly pink. Maybe he did like me. As more than a friend. Wow.

"Yeah." I could feel myself begin to blush. "I'll miss you, too. But maybe we can call each other. You know. To keep each other informed about the case." My cheeks were really burning now.

"I'd like that."

"Me, too." I smiled, but I couldn't look him in the eyes.

After an awkward silence, I looked at Dave and said, "But Louis seems to be invested in the therapy. I can't just drop him, he'd be injured. I can't injure a patient."

"Can you even hear what you're saying right now? Craig Fletcher is a killer. The product he sells kills, and he kills whoever gets in the way of selling it. So he might kill you, too, you idiot! He could be the one behind the attacks, not Rita. Think about that. Don't be alone in a room with him again."

"I can't promise that," I said, "but I will call the police."

"When do you see Fletcher next?"

"Wednesday. At two."

"I'll be in your secretarial area. I'll install a wireless alarm button next to your chair. If he starts to get out of control, you push that button and a light will go on near me. I'll come in and restrain him while the secretaries call the police."

"I don't think that'll be necessary."

"Please! If you insist on seeing Fletcher again, please let me protect you."

"Oh. Okay. If it makes you happy." I smiled shyly.

"Yes." He smiled back. "It makes me happy to keep you alive."

After Dave left, I called Detective Manson.

"What do you want now, Alice?" His tone wasn't friendly.

"This isn't about Rita."

"What then?"

"Jay, I just found out that one of my new clients is a major criminal. A Craig Fletcher."

"Craig Fletcher! The White Powder King? You're kidding. 'Major criminal' is an understatement. Are you sure it's him, and why's he seeing you?"

"Dave McGinty just showed me a picture of him. He's using a different name, of course. Came in saying he was depressed, but I don't believe he is. McGinty thinks he's keeping track of me. Because I was Janet's therapist and was becoming friends with Rita."

"That doesn't make sense. Are you saying Fletcher had something to do with Janet Ford's death?"

"I don't know. That's the only reason we could think of for him to put himself in a fake therapy situation. That kind of man wouldn't want to share about himself or to have a therapist know things about him that others didn't know. And there's something else."

"What else, Alice." He sounded distinctly unfriendly.

"We found out that he and Janet were cousins."

"Impossible."

"No, possible." I took a deep breath and explained about Craig Fletcher being adopted by Janet's relatives and about the check.

"Then he decided to become one of your patients to keep track of you." There was a sarcastic tone to this.

"Yes."

"He probably lied to you."

"About some things, not everything."

"Are you going to specialize in master career criminals from now on?" He laughed, but it didn't sound friendly.

"That's not funny."

"Okay. Here's what's going to happen. You're going to act like you don't know who he is. I'll put a microphone in your office. A very small one. He'll never know it's there. When you can, steer the conversation to heroin or meth. I want to see what he says. Or try to find out where he's staying. I'd rather arrest him at home than at your office."

"Wait just a minute! I'm not going to let you to bug my office. That's unethical, not to mention illegal … no matter who the patient is."

"Yes, you are. I'll get a court order."

"If you can."

"Yes."

"No."

"We'll see."

"Never."

CHAPTER 54

MONDAY, NOVEMBER 23
AFTERNOON

I saw Louis the next day. He came into my office in his usual aloof style.

"So how was your week?" I asked.

"Pretty good. Pretty good," he replied, nodding his head.

"Glad to hear that. Any feelings of depression?"

He smiled a small smile. "Just a little. My dog is getting old and I've begun to think about having to put him down."

I gulped. Here we were in the first minutes of his session, and he's talking about killing something. Was this "dog" really a person?

"That is a sad thought. Will you have to do it soon?"

"Probably not. He has a good quality of life, even if he can't run much anymore."

"Have a good vet?"

"Of course I do." His tone indicated irritation, but his smile belied that. I eyed the emergency button that Dave had installed for me.

"Aside from that, how are you feeling? Any anger?"

"No." He continued smiling, but his eyes glared. It was disconcerting, especially now that I knew he was a violent criminal.

"What do you want to talk about today?" This was a statement I used when my patients seemed stuck. I'd used it with Louis often.

"I think I'd like to talk about my relationships with my employees."

"Okay. What about them?"

"As we've discussed, I own a small trucking business. Sometimes my employees don't seem to care about getting their deliveries made as quickly as I think they ought to. I have trouble motivating them without getting angry or making threats. It upsets me when I get angry with them. I lose several a year after I've yelled at them. I tell you, that 'what the hell' attitude about doing your job, it triggers something in me. I feel myself getting angry the way you feel a fever come on when you get the flu. Except it's much faster. Understand?"

"Yes I do. And this anger, it makes workers quit?" More than likely he killed them for messing up.

"Eh, yes they quit." He looked sad. "I take it personally. It's like I commit to them, but then they betray me with poor performance."

"Have you tried retraining them?"

"No." Now he seemed disdainful. "I'm a busy man. I don't have the time or the money to waste on subpar employees. It's probably better that they quit. It's the trucking business, not brain surgery."

"What about feeling bad when you yell at them?"

"Now that I think about it in logical terms, my feelings don't matter. It's better to save time and money. Better business. Not to get so emotionally involved."

"Your feelings always matter." Maybe I shouldn't have said that, but I couldn't help it.

"Not in my business." Now he was definitely glaring at me. It wasn't the best timing, but I had to talk with him about ending.

"We need to switch subjects for a while."

"Okay. Why?"

"We've just started our work together, and normally we'd be having sessions for quite a while. But something has happened that will impact that. I've made a decision to move out of state and will be closing down my practice here. This will be our last time together."

"What? Couldn't you have given me some notice so I could get used to the idea? That's not very professional of you." He looked out and out angry now.

"Normally I would, of course, but I have an opportunity to join the practice I was originally aiming for, and if I leave this week, then it's a done deal. So unfortunately, there is no time to give anyone notice." Even though I knew I had to do it, I felt guilt over ending so abruptly with a patient—even if he was dangerous.

"I don't know what to say," he muttered. "I don't like this. It's too sudden and abrupt. Kind of cruel." His voice was soft, but his eyes were like rocks.

"It's not meant to be cruel. And I am sorry."

"No you're not." The soft voice had a menacing quality now.

I moved my hand toward the emergency button.

"We have to end now. It's been good working with you. I can refer you to another therapist if you like." I held out my hand as I stood.

Ignoring my hand, he snapped, "Don't bother."

Before I could reply he was gone.

At least he didn't kill me . . .

But what about later?

CHAPTER 55

MONDAY, NOVEMBER 23 EVENING

That evening I was still consumed by guilt over kicking Louis out of therapy. Drug-dealing killer or not, he was still a patient and I had a duty of care. But I was also obsessed by what Russ shared a few days before. The agent who he thought was trying to kill me was Rita Butler. He'd tried to tell me, but I just didn't hear it … until he mentioned her orange hair. There weren't many women like that in Fort Madison. I was restless all evening and had trouble sleeping that night.

I was still tired by the next morning, and just as regretful about Louis, but I had a plan for Rita. Sort of. Rita was too good at covering her tracks. Even our proof that she was Janet's lover wasn't going to be enough. If she was ever interrogated she'd already know all the angles, could probably even beat a lie detector. If Rita didn't admit to it, she was literally going to get away with murder. I believe in justice and this thought, Rita skating on Janet's murder, shook me to the core.

I was certain the only way we'd get Rita to confess was if she was provoked enough that her emotions took over. Emotions don't lie, which is why most people go to great lengths to control them. Rita had to be under a huge amount of stress since the murder, having to investigate a crime she'd actually committed. Last night she tried to run us off the road just where she'd done the same with Stan. But she'd miscalculated, made her move a few seconds too late, an error that was probably due to strain and anxiety. Hopefully, that meant if I provoked her enough, she'd snap like dry spaghetti.

I still didn't know why Rita was a bad cop. Was it money? Or was Louis/Craig blackmailing her? Maybe I should ask Dave to trace Rita's finances. Anyway, getting Rita so agitated that she confessed also had a high probability of her trying to kill me again. That was indeed a big flaw in my plan, but if someone were hiding somewhere close by then they might be able to save me and confirm her confession. It was risky, and Jay wouldn't help. Maybe Dave would. I called him and invited him to lunch.

*   *   *

When Dave met me for lunch at Kathy's, I told him my plan. I ended by saying that I had to put my scheme into action quickly, before my luck ran out, which could be any day now.

"That's the dumbest idea I've ever heard," Dave pronounced. "You'll get yourself killed and still not prove anything a good lawyer couldn't fix. How do you come up with these things? I sure hope you're an excellent therapist." He didn't have to complete that last thought.

"Well, thank you for your sensitivity," I muttered. I was feeling hurt and exasperated. "I don't hear any other plans for catching Rita. I'm a sitting duck here."

"There aren't any plans for Rita right now because I just got on board with you about that particular theory and haven't had time to formulate something approaching viability."

"Is there any way to convict her other than a confession?" I asked.

"There might be some evidence we don't know about, something Rita forgot or couldn't get to, but that seems unlikely," Dave replied. "Especially without hard evidence from the scene. But provoking Rita to kill you on the hope that she might reveal something about Janet's murder is … well, it's ridiculous."

I had really hoped that Dave would have a better solution than mine. But without the cooperation of the police - even if we found evidence, like damage to her car, we couldn't do anything. I looked into his eyes and said, "It's the only way,"

"No, it's not," countered Dave. "Call Rita's boss and tell him your suspicions. Then leave it to the cops."

I picked up my burger. "He wouldn't believe me any more than Jay did."

"You're probably right there."

"I'm going to do this whether or not you help me."

He ran his fingers through his hair in frustration. "Alice, don't talk crazy. I should have you committed for being a danger to yourself."

I gulped down the bite of hamburger I had in my mouth. We wouldn't be in this mess if I'd had Janet committed for observation. "You wouldn't do that, would you?"

"Only if provoked," he groaned. "Okay, I'll help, but let me think of a few angles first. And don't go near Rita unless you know I'm close by. Okay?"

"Okay." And I meant it. At the time.

*   *   *

I had agreed to put any Rita-trapping schemes on hold until I heard back from Dave. He said he'd call me later that evening. I hoped he'd be more on board once he'd thought about it.

281

Instead, Rita called me that afternoon. She sounded friendly for once. "How well do you know Mrs. Grimes at the Mission?" she asked.

"In some ways fairly well, but in others not much," I told her. "I've been doing volunteer work there for the last three years and we always talk while I'm there. Always pleasant, but more about the problems at the Mission or its residents than anything else. I don't really know much about her personal life."

"Do you think she's honest?" asked Rita.

That seemed like an odd question. My brow furrowed. "Yes, I think so. Never known her to be dishonest. Why?"

"I have reason to believe that Mrs. Grimes lied about Russ Logan having an alibi for the time of Janet Ford's death."

"Really?" This was a cold shock, if it was true. "What reason?

"Can't reveal that, sorry. Shouldn't have said what I did." She paused. "Do you know anyone who might know Mrs. Grimes better?"

"Like I said, we never socialized outside of the Mission. The only people I know are staff or other volunteers. Nodding acquaintances, really."

"Already talked with them," said Rita. "I know Grimes is a widow. Is there a man in her life that you know of?"

"I didn't get that impression, but everyone has secrets, right?" I replied, attempting wry humor.

There was an uncomfortable pause, common with my humor attempts. "If you remember anything that might be relevant about Mrs. Grimes, or about Russ Logan, you let me know." Not quite a command, but leaning there.

I promised that I would, and for a moment wondered if I should mention that Russ thought she was the one trying to kill me. Then the moment passed. I didn't want to get Russ in any trouble; he was troubled enough.

I wondered if I should discuss Rita's call with Dave. He was supposed to be improving or replacing my confession plan, but would he use Rita's call as an excuse to postpone any action? If Rita was focused on Russ again, then she was less likely to be after me; and after all, she did call me. Despite that, I was sure Rita was hiding something. I decided to sleep on it and call Dave in the morning. Or not. Maybe I'd call Rita tomorrow.

*   *   *

I woke to the cell phone ringing in the living room. The bedroom was dark except for the glow of the street light flowing through the window. I could feel Sweetie sit up and lean against my legs. My cell phone clicked off, but immediately started buzzing again.

That jerked me awake, a cold stone blooming in the pit of my stomach at the thought of some new tragedy. I threw on my bathrobe while the phone clicked off again. Leaving the lights off, I went into the living room and checked my phone. A missed call from "Unlisted." My anonymous stalker, maybe? The last thing I needed was another threatening call. Maybe I should get a new cell and only give the number to Lucy and Dave.

Then the phone began chirping in hand. I almost dropped it before instinctively answering. I was about to hang up when I heard Rita's voice.

"I'm glad I got you, Alice," she was saying. "We've found something in the park. I don't know what to make of it. Can you come and take a look? Maybe you can explain it."

"Rita, it's the middle of the night. Can't this wait?" This sounded even fishier than my confession plan. Had she really found something or was she luring me to my doom? Maybe this was fate telling me to take matters into my own hands, stop depending on others to solve my problems. Did fate even work that way? In any case, I'd have to be crazy to meet with Rita in the middle of the night. Well, call me crazy.

I didn't want to go. I'd felt such relief when Lucy and I had decided to stop with the investigating thing. But that didn't last, and then Lucy, Lynn, and I were almost killed. Thanks to Rita, I was sure. Now here I was again—neck deep in an investigation, with Rita on the phone asking to meet up like a spider to a fly. Frightened, sleep deprived, and confused, I wasn't sure which end was up. When I'd been sharing my confession plans with Dave I had felt so clever, brave, and adventurous. Now my head hurt and I was getting queasy, along with tired and scared. But this was the only way I knew to get Rita to confess, so I was going.

I heard myself say, "Of course. Where do I meet you?"

"Dolly Madison Park. You know the far side, back where those big rocks are?" Rita asked.

"Yes, I know it," I said.

"Meet me beside the biggest rock."

Sweetie followed me around as I got dressed. I wondered if this would be the last time I'd get dressed. It was easy to identify the clothes I wouldn't want to be caught dead in, but what were the ones I wouldn't mind so much? Instead of catching Rita, would Rita get me? There was an urgency in her voice - a deeply human need to see me. I felt like I had to respond to it. I knew my going was stupid, but I was going. Reluctantly. I wasn't cut out to be a hero.

CHAPTER 56

TUESDAY, NOVEMBER 24
VERY EARLY MORNING

I drove slowly to Dolly Madison Park. On the way, I called Dave, expecting him to say that he'd be right there, ready to stop Rita from hurting me. I was betting that she couldn't resist telling me what she'd done when she thought I wouldn't be able to turn her in, on account of her killing me right after confessing. Would Rita act like a James Bond villain, explaining her evil plan before abandoning me to my fate? If Dave wasn't around, I'd have to improvise and hope he would come up with a better idea later, something that didn't involve me being live bait.

But instead of Dave, all I got was his voicemail. Maybe his phone was off. I left him a message that I should have practiced beforehand. "Dave, this is Alice," I managed. "Rita just called and asked me to meet her at Dolly Madison Park by the big rocks. I know you must think I have a death wish or something, but I'm going to meet her. There was something in her voice. I just don't think she means me any harm, at least not tonight. I hope you get this message and will come. Bye." God that sounded lame, but there had been something unusual about Rita's manner, I just didn't know how to describe it. Not consciously, anyway.

I know. I know. It was totally stupid. What if Dave didn't get the message in time? What if Rita confessed and then killed me before I could get rescued? What if she kidnapped me? Stupid me. But I'm like that sometimes and this was one of those times. I promised myself I'd be better in the future … if there was one.

I wanted to turn around and go back home, but I was determined to be brave. I'd let others take care of me too long. It was time I took the lead. It was my life at stake, not anyone else's. Just me. So it had to be me checking this out. I hoped I'd feel braver the more I acted brave. It often works that way. Acting "as if" turns into reality.

I knew where the big rocks were at Dolly Madison Park, in general. They were in an isolated and kind of creepy area of Fort Madison's biggest park.

I glanced at the large trees beside the narrow park road. It was dark with streetlights widely spaced. The rocks should start soon. They were scattered throughout this area, with the most noteworthy ones being a particular cluster that included an enormous square rock the size of an average outbuilding. It was beautiful during the day, especially in summer, with thick woods behind and grass dotted with large trees between it and the tree-lined road. At night in November, it was post-Halloween scary. Sweetie whimpered from her place in the backseat.

As we crept along searching for the big rock, I remembered Russ's warning, "Don't go out after dark." I wished I hadn't. I glanced at Sweetie; she didn't look at all happy to be here. Her ears were back and her tail was tight to her body. Soft shivers sent the hair up on her back. No, Sweetie wasn't happy.

I probably shouldn't have brought her, but having Sweetie with me was automatic by now, and I knew I couldn't do this alone anyway. "You may not be happy, but I'm glad you're here, Sweetie pup."

When I turned back I saw Rita's SUV parked to my left, some way off. I pulled over and parked, then let Sweetie out on her leash. It took a while to get to the SUV. Sweetie wasn't being cooperative.

Rita was nowhere in sight. I called out to her several times. No response. This was not good. Had I misread her and right now she was about to attack me with a cleaver?

I reached the SUV. Silence. No sounds of movement, no radio. Sweetie sniffed the air and whimpered. That wasn't good. What was she smelling that I couldn't? My own fear, maybe.

Holding my breath, I peered in the passenger side window, expecting the worse. I got it.

At first it was dark as pitch inside the SUV, but I could make out a manila envelope on the passenger seat with my name on it written in large black letters. I tried the door, expecting it to be locked. It wasn't. I cracked the door open, surprised that the interior light didn't come on. "Rita?" Sweetie whimpered again, getting very agitated. And now I knew why. A distinctive odor was coming from the van. "Rita?"

As my eyes adjusted to the gloom, I saw her. She was slumped behind the steering wheel, held up by the seatbelt. Dead weight. The front of Rita's shirt was dark and wet, so were her pants and legs. Gasping, I jerked back. "Rita!" Then I saw the kitchen knife on the floor between her feet. It was also wet with fresh blood. "Oh Rita, no. This can't be happening …"

Rita Butler, my first dead body. Was it somehow my fault?

For several minutes, I stood there staring at Rita until the immediate shock wore off. Memories of a gruesome google search at a Halloween party last year reminded me that you can bleed to death very quickly if the right artery is cut, and it was obvious that Rita had known how to do that. It took me twenty minutes to get to the park;

with a severed jugular vein, Rita would have been dead in under five.

Sweetie's mewling and tugging brought me back to reality. She desperately wanted to get away from the smell of death. I was glad to have someone, even a dog, tell me what to do, and it wasn't until I let Sweetie jump into my car that I realized the envelope Rita had left for me was in my hand. I knew I had to call the cops, but did I have to turn over this letter as well? A private communication? But found at a possible crime scene. Sweetie was no help with this one.

"Gawk!" I cried in shock, my cell buzzing loudly in my pocket. "Dave," I gasped into the phone.

"Alice, where are you? You haven't gone—"

"Rita's dead. I just found her at the park. Dolly Madison. By the big rocks. She …"

Dave was yelling questions at me, too fast for me to follow, so I kept talking.

"… she cut her own throat, Dave. With a kitchen knife. There's a note. What do I do?"

"Are you alone? Stay in your car. Lock the doors. I'll call the cops and come right over. Don't touch anything. Just because it looks like suicide doesn't mean it is." I hadn't thought of that. The parallels between Rita and Janet's deaths couldn't be coincidence.

I did as Dave said and locked myself in my car. Sweetie was happy I wasn't leaving her alone, but seemed to expect me to start the car and head home. I was beginning to tremble.

All I could do now was wait. And read Rita's letter.

Dear Alice,

I'm sorry you had to find me like you did, but better you than some stranger. Somehow it feels right that an almost friend who's already involved with my life should participate in my death.

I want you to know that I didn't kill Janet, but I feel like I did, even if it was suicide. Jay told me you thought I did kill her, which I can understand because it was almost the literal truth.

Yes, I was there just before Janet died, but I didn't take a knife to her like I will soon do to myself. I want to die like she did, by my own hand, alone in the night.

Janet didn't do anything to cause her own death. Not really. She was just being Janet. But I had let her know things about me. Things that needed to be kept secret. That was before I discovered Janet couldn't keep a secret. She had to tell. Why didn't you fix that? It was a secret, damn it!

The hard truth of it is that I've been corrupted by a well-connected drug supplier. At first I simply passed along information about department investigations. It paid well, was low risk, and no one got hurt. That was in the beginning. Things escalated. Evidence had to go missing, which was trickier. Next was the names and addresses of witnesses. And when those witnesses began to go missing, I knew I was lost.

Janet found out. She thought it was hilarious. That should've tipped me off. She didn't understand how important it was to keep it a secret. Or how it tortured me.

We had a fight at her house. In the kitchen. Her mother had the daughter overnight. I came over to party and relax. Only Janet wanted to talk about commitment, a public commitment that would shock her mother and all her friends. I told her that was impossible for me. I wasn't going to ruin my career because of some soap opera psycho-drama of hers.

Janet was screaming that she hated me, that she didn't want to live. She grabbed up a big kitchen knife and ran out of the house toward the park. I ran after her. I couldn't let her do something really stupid. In the state she was in, I knew she was more than capable of it.

I found Janet near the bandstand, holding the knife at her stomach. Like she was going to commit hara-kiri. I tried to calm her down, get the knife away from her, but she was totally out of control. She cut her stomach and the knife became slippery with blood. I got it away from her and she dropped to the ground.

She lay there moaning and crying for me to help her. It seemed like such an act, total teenage theatrics. I just stared at her and watched. I was so angry that I didn't care if Janet lived or died. I didn't think her wounds were that bad. Then she passed out, which I assumed was from shock and exhaustion.

"Oh no," I said aloud. I felt sick. Janet could have been saved, if only Rita had called for help.

Yes, I was afraid of the man I sold information to … he had involved me in murder, I had betrayed my own values and hadn't realized it until too late. I knew Janet would tell all eventually, one way or another. I had gotten involved with her much too quickly. We were both exploring our sexuality in new ways and it was like a drug for both of us.

When Janet tried to hurt herself that night in the park, I couldn't pass up the opportunity. I cleaned up any trace of my being there. I had no thoughts, no feelings. Just calm, like I was another person. Janet was lying there with her eyes closed, but breathing steadily when I left.

The moment I got into my car remorse hit me so hard I shook. I used one of my burner phones and a voice changer to call the police, report a body in the park. Then I went home, took a shower, and burned my clothes. The next day I was sickened to find out that Janet had died after all, and I was assigned the case. It was almost too much to bear. I knew I was being punished for what I'd done.

Later I got a message from the drug dealer saying he'd taken care of my mess. So you see, Janet's death was my fault after all. I'm sorry.

I am trapped in a mess of my own making. My own crimes condemn me. And now there's only one way out.

Good-bye, Alice. Best of luck to you.

Rita.

PS: I did not run your doctor friend off the road. I'm not a killer. Not like that, anyway.

Tears were sliding down my face as I finished reading. My phone rang again; it was Dave. He was on his way after having called the police. He told me not to talk, just say that Rita called to meet and this is how I found her.

"Did you read the note?" Dave asked. "Does she admit to killing Janet?"

"No … I mean, yes. I read it but Rita says Janet was alive when she left her."

"Damn," Dave muttered. "I was hoping it would tie everything up."

"I'm going to give the note to the cops when they get here. I can't obstruct the investigation by withholding evidence, they'd lock me up again."

"Agreed," said Dave. "But take photos of the letter before you do. And don't let the cops know you did. Hide your phone in your car … they can't search without a warrant, but they can pat you down."

"Yes, okay." I started crying again. Sweetie licked my face and whimpered.

"I'll be right there, kiddo. Hold tight."

I was never so glad to hear anything.

* * *

It took a couple of hours for the police to take my statement, do the forensic work on the SUV, and take away the body. I didn't feel I could leave until Rita's remains had been properly dealt with. Dave understood.

In fact, he spent the rest of the day with me. I called and left a message for Georgia at the office, asking her to cancel my patients for the day due to a personal emergency. I was too shaken to be of any use to anyone, and didn't want it known that I was involved in another death. Maybe Lynn was right, I was too dangerous to be around.

Lucy stayed home as well. Dave had texted her while the police were questioning me, which I thought was nice.

I didn't talk to anybody. Dave was good at keeping the reporters away. He called Collier and gave him an update for Mrs. Whitmire, so that was one chore taken care of.

Meanwhile, I just rocked in my rocking chair, sipped Lucy's tea, and wondered how responsible I was for Rita's death. *Was* I too dangerous to be around? Maybe so.

CHAPTER 57

TUESDAY, NOVEMBER 24 NIGHT

Late that night, I was in a deep sleep when Sweetie's growls woke me. The only light came from my alarm clock. It was two in the morning. Sweetie sat up and I grabbed her collar. I kept my hold on her as I got up and slipped on my bedroom slippers. She pulled me toward the bedroom door.

"Stop it, Sweetie. You'll pull me down," I mumbled.

"That would be unfortunate," a man's voice said.

I froze, my breath caught in my throat.

"Who's there?"

A man stepped into the room. It was Louis/Craig, my patient and Rita's secret boss.

"Louis. How did you get in?"

He chuckled. "Security systems only work if you set the alarm."

"What are you doing?" .Sweetie growled again and tried to pull away. I held her collar tighter.

"I hear that Rita killed herself. It's time to take care of loose ends." He pointed a gun at me.

"I'm a loose end? Since when?"

"You know too much about me."

"That's therapy information and it's confidential. No one will know any of it."

"Don't treat me like I'm stupid." He glared at me. "I know there are certain circumstances that compel you to reveal what you know. A murder trial is one of them."

"For the witnesses you eliminated, of course. But why are *you* here? I thought being the boss meant you didn't have to do the dirty work."

"So you do know who I am. I thought so when you dropped me like a hot rock."

"Yes, I just found out," I admitted. "It upset me. Dropping you, I mean. I was pressured. They wanted to bug my office."

Now that I was facing death, I was surprised at how calm I was, no begging for my life or anything. Sweetie started growling and I pulled back on her collar.

"I wondered if that was the case," Louis replied. "Impressive … you didn't let them plant a wire. Protected me like that. And yes, I do have people for the wet work. But in your case, they weren't successful. Not as competent as they think they are, clearly. Didn't care enough about their work. I do—this is special to me. You are special to me. You got me to talk about myself in ways I never have before. Got me to care about you, too … the one person who seemed to understand me. And then you dumped me like I meant nothing to you. I knew I'd get hurt if I trusted you, but I did anyway. You seduced me into thinking I could trust you."

"Why did you begin therapy if you didn't want to talk about yourself? Do you think I seduced you into betraying yourself the same way you seduced Rita into being your mole in the department?" If I could keep him talking, perhaps I could come up with a plan, or maybe even get him to just go away without killing me.

"It was just business at first, the therapy," he stated. "Rita was keeping an eye on you, but it sounded like she was getting too close. That nut job, Janet, found out about Rita's involvement with me and she was your patient. I learned when I loaned her some money that she couldn't keep her mouth shut. You sounded like someone who might know too much, so I became your patient to find out. See if you needed to disappear maybe. I don't believe in … interfering with people without cause. Life is complicated enough."

He almost sounded like he cared about others, but I knew better. My intuition had been telling me that he wasn't depressed. I just didn't know how I knew that. He acted much more like someone with an antisocial personalty. Such people don't have empathy. They're incapable of caring about anyone but themselves. I should have trusted my intuition. Perhaps he didn't realize that I could see through his pretending to be a normal person. That might work to my advantage.

"You overestimate me," I said. "I never knew about Rita's involvement with you, just Janet's. Her check to pay off the loan from you."

"Then it sure sucks to be you, Doc. Besides, you betrayed me. Nobody gets away with that. Not you, not Janet. I never should have loaned her money."

"You betrayed me by lying about who you were."

"That was for your own protection. Then you had to turn detective and ruin everything." Louis shook his head. "I was three steps ahead of you all the way. You thought Rita was trying to scare you off the case, but she wasn't. She was watching you, trying to protect you. Even had you locked up for a night to get you off the streets. I'd have eliminated her if she hadn't done it for me herself. She was getting ready to flip on me."

The longer I engaged Louis, the better my chances were. But beyond that, things were hazy. I had no plan except to tire him out. I better step up my game.

He was clearly someone with an antisocial personality, a psychopath. That meant that he didn't feel emotions unless they related directly to him. He had no feelings toward other people. He would have no feelings about killing me, but he might feel sad that he'd lost a person who listened to him. I had to use that.

"I know you don't have anyone you can talk freely with about what you think and feel." I began.

"Don't start, Dr. Brenner," he snarled. "You left me. It's your fault that I don't have anybody. I don't want to hear about how sorry you are. I'll make you even more sorry."

"I'm not saying I'm sorry. I've already said that. I'm trying to help you find someone else to talk with. We both know you need that."

"No! Talking with you was a mistake I'll not make again."

He moved closer with the gun pointed at my head. I had to distract him.

"Rita left me a suicide note." I stammered. "She said she didn't kill Janet. Did you do it? Solve two problems at once?"

Louis smiled at this. I wasn't sure why, but I knew I didn't like it.

"I was keeping a watch on Janet. She was my cousin, you know, and I didn't trust her. Couldn't trust her, the drama queen chatterbox. I thought I could use her affair with Rita to my advantage, so that night I was watching them, saw the fight, and decided to kill Janet. Like you said, that way I solve the Janet problem and I'd have something on Rita."

"You're right. You are smarter than me." I was appealing to his narcissism. Maybe I could still sweet talk him out of killing me.

"You have a grasp of the obvious, Doctor Brenner, I'll give you that," snarked Louis. "But I didn't kill Janet. I followed Rita when she left the park; had to see what she'd do next. I saw her use a burner phone with a voice modifier, calling in Janet, I figured. I couldn't risk being picked up in the area so I bugged out. It was just my good luck that Janet turned up dead anyway. Everything was working out fine until you got involved."

I was stunned. "Janet was alive when you left the park?"

"Yes. Now follow me," Louis instructed as he backed down the hall toward the living room.

I followed. In the dark, I grabbed the dusty cylinder of pepper spray that I'd put on the hall table weeks ago. It felt right, but I couldn't be sure in the dark. My hands were shaking so much when I slid it across the table that my hand hit a ceramic vase. It crashed to the floor and broke into pieces.

Too bad. I liked that vase. But I guess it doesn't matter now if he kills me. Then I worried that Lucy would hear it, come upstairs to investigate, and get shot, too. The thought shot through me and I froze where I was, stopped me from breathing. Whimpering, Sweetie nudged me.

"Stop delaying!" Louis yelled. He was in the middle of the living room, motioning me to come closer.

Sweetie and I stopped right in front of him. "Don't do this, Louis. At least Rita knew when it was over."

"Shut up. And stop calling me Louis. My name is Craig."

"You'll always be Louis to me."

"Betrayer!" he shouted. The gun waved before me erratically.

I let go of Sweetie's collar and sent a stream of pepper spray into Louis's eyes. Not waiting to see if it worked, I turned and ran for all I was worth.

I heard Louis howling in pain, followed by a thunderous explosion and a sharp yelp. *Sweetie!* What had she done? Hadn't she run away? She hated loud noises.

I kept running. The wall next to me exploded around me. Two, three times. I was zigzagging toward the front door when Louis caught up with me, grabbing my arm, almost breaking it.

"You've caused me enough trouble, you meddling bitch." His gun was aimed at my forehead. I could feel its heat and smell the oily smoke from the muzzle. "This is when you get all the answers."

I froze. Dizzy with fear, I couldn't talk. I couldn't breathe.

There was a loud crash at the downstairs door and the sound of men running up the stairs. Louis bolted toward the kitchen and the fire escape where he'd entered.

Suddenly, he turned and said, "Good-bye, Alice."

There was another loud explosion and everything went black.

CHAPTER 58

THURSDAY, NOVEMBER 26 MORNING

It was all white when I opened my eyes. White and quiet. Peaceful. I wondered if this was heaven. Somehow, I thought there'd be more to heaven. Not gold paved streets, but at least some dead relatives to greet me. Children singing, that sort of thing.

"She opened her eyes," a woman's voice said.

"Mama?" I croaked.

"I'll get her some water," the voice answered.

"Am I dead?" I asked.

There was silence, then black.

"She'll be awake soon," a man's voice was saying. "She'll have significant pain and probably some confusion, but it should wear off fairly quickly. Your friend is in relatively good physical shape, aside from a few extra pounds."

"Oh good." The woman sounded relieved, but I couldn't let that crack about a few extra pounds go unanswered. What sort of bedside manner was that? Would God say that? What kind of place was heaven anyway?

I opened my eyes. I knew that I did because there was painful brightness. And noise all around me.

"Oh, Doctor, look! She's awake." It was the woman's voice.

Two faces swam into view. One looked almost like Lucy. Except she had mascara smeared down her face and her hair wasn't combed. It couldn't be Lucy. She'd never go out like that.

"Alice, I'm so glad to see you. I was afraid you wouldn't come back to us." It was Lucy. Who'd a thought.

"Alice, I'm Dr. Osborne, your surgeon. How are you feeling?" A white-haired male face was talking at me.

"I'm not dead?"

"No honey, just hurt," the woman said. She smiled.

"My shoulder hurts. Bad." It felt like it was being pounded with a sledge hammer, but from the inside.

"That's to be expected. You were shot. The bullet hit your clavicle. Pain meds don't always stop that kind of pain. But you're a very lucky young woman." It was the man speaking. A doctor, I guessed.

Someone moaned.

The doctor chuckled. I didn't think they could laugh at patients. I wanted to chide him about that, and the weight remark, of course, but I was just too tired. And besides, everything hurt worse when I talked.

"I'll give you something stronger for the pain," he said. "You'll sleep for a while, and when you wake it won't be so bad."

Somebody did something above my head and it got white and quiet again.

The next time I woke, it wasn't as bright or noisy. I could hear someone moving around near me.

"Hello," I said.

"Alice. Good morning." It was Lucy again. "You slept like a rock."

"What time is it?" I asked.

"Eight in the morning. The sun's up and it's going to be cold and sunny," she said.

"How long?" I asked.

"All day, I think. Oh, I see what you mean … It's been a day since you were shot."

I tried to sit up. It was a bad idea. The sledgehammer was back. "Ouch."

"The doctor said you should move slowly, but it's okay to sit up. The nurse showed me how to operate your bed. Here, is that better?"

The bed crawled to a sitting position. I didn't have to move at all. Now I could see that I was in a beige room with a big window. There was sunlight streaming across my legs. Lucy stood beside the bed, and on the window ledge were vases of flowers: daisies and deep red roses.

"Am I in the hospital?"

"Yes, silly," she answered. "You were shot, remember?"

"Shot?" So that's what the deafening noise had been. I felt okay, except for the weakness and the bad pain. And suddenly being very sad.

"You were lucky." Lucy smiled.

"Don't smile," I complained. "I hurt like a dinosaur stepped on me." I looked at Lucy. "I did tell you that it was Louis who shot me, didn't I? I'm surprised he missed. I mean, missed killing me."

"You didn't tell me, but the policemen who came in your apartment saw him do it. Detective Manson already had the police out looking for him."

"So they caught him?"

"Yesterday evening in Greensboro, North Carolina."

"Good." That was relief. But now I'd probably have to testify at his trial, which would be awkward. But maybe he'd confess, do me a favor to make up for shooting me in front on cops.

"How did the police know to rescue me? I couldn't get to a phone."

"But I could. I heard a commotion upstairs, the lamp breaking …then the shots. I called 911."

"They sure got there quick."

"That was Detective Manson. After you found Rita dead, he thought you might have been in greater danger than he had assumed. So he arranged for a couple of patrol cars to be in our neighborhood. They were practically outside when they got the call."

Sweetie. Oh my God. Where's Sweetie?

"Did anybody find Sweetie? I let her go. I thought she would run away. You know how she hates conflict, loud noises. But I heard a yelp."

"Um …" Lucy's expression was somber. "Sweetie didn't run. She saved you."

"Saved me?"

"Yes. She attacked Louis, knocked him back, and bit his hand pretty badly. Broke it. That's why he couldn't shoot straight. They said he was still ranting about you and 'that damn dog' when they arrested him."

But Lucy wasn't making eye contact. I knew something was up. I knew there was a reason for the sad feeling I had.

"Lucy, where's Sweetie?" I croaked "Is she dead?" *Dear God, please let her be okay.* Tears dripped across my cheeks.

"Sweetie is alive," Lucy assured me, "but Louis shot her to get her off him. She's still at the vet after a long surgery. It's going to be touch and go. The vet won't promise anything."

"Can I see her?" If Sweetie died before I could hold her again I'd never forgive myself. I simply had to touch her.

"I don't know. You'll probably be discharged tomorrow. I'll call the vet and try to arrange a visit on our way home or when we go to physical therapy."

"Physical therapy?"

"Yes. Your shoulder was really damaged. You'll have to go to PT to get it functioning again. In fact," she hesitated, "you may have some permanent disability."

My confused brain had trouble with that. Better not think about it yet.

CHAPTER 59

THURSDAY, NOVEMBER 26
EVENING

Imust have fallen asleep, because when I opened my eyes Collier was standing beside me holding daisies.

Blinking my eyes to clear my vision, I gave him a small smile. "Collier, I didn't hear you come in. It's nice to see you."

"It's nice to see that you're still alive. How could you have done something so stupid?"

"At the time, I felt I had to. That the risk was worth the potential result. It just didn't work out as planned." Collier could be so unimaginative sometimes.

"Why couldn't you let the police handle it?" Was this cross-examination really worth a handful of daisies?

"I couldn't trust the police. They thought I was a killer and had a mole in their office, maybe more than one. What happened at the park and Louis attacking me later are two separate events. If I had it to do over, I would have left town, as I had been urged to many times. But not by you." Even with the pain killers I was getting annoyed.

"Okay, you're right," Collier conceded. "It just freaks me out. What if that maniac had just shot you right off and hadn't bothered telling you the whys and wherefores?"

"I'm the psychologist here. I knew he couldn't resist showing me how smart he was." Stupid Collier never gave me credit for my professional skills. It was like you were nothing if you weren't a lawyer or worked in Washington.

I was getting really irritated with him now. This seemed to happen when we were together lately. Well, if Louis could clean house, why not me?

"Collier, look at us. We're at odds again. I'm feeling irritated. What're you feeling?"

He seemed confused. "I'm fine. Why are you irritated?"

"We always do this. You lecture me, question my behavior, my competence, and so I get angry. Then we break up, make up, and do it all over again. You don't see that? Or it's fine with you, maybe?"

"If you'd just act with a little more circumspection," he said, getting defensive.

"And how likely do you think that is, Collier? We've been having this same argument for over two years. I'm not going to change who I am. At least not for you. And I doubt you'll change for me either. I'm not asking you to because there's no point to it." Now he was looking scared, realizing he'd just wandered into the Girlfriend Minefield, the poor sap. I could see him trying to find a way out.

"I really care for you, Alice," he finally said, giving me that special look. "But your behavior is too … unpredictable."

For the first time in the two years of our on and off relationship, I felt certain I knew what was happening. "Do I scare you? Is that it?"

"Er … maybe."

"I care a lot for you, too, but I don't think this dynamic will change. My behavior scares you, and when you try to control it, I get mad. I don't see a solution for this, and I wonder if our caring is deep enough to get beyond it."

"What are you saying, Alice?"

I could feel tears begin to fill my eyes. "Collier, I value you as a friend, but it's just not working romantically. It hasn't for a while and I think you already know that." I watched him carefully. Was he going to accept this or get mad?

Collier sighed deeply as he squeezed my hand. Then he whispered, "I don't think we're a good match either."

"Why didn't you say something?" I asked.

"I was afraid of hurting you. And I didn't want to lose your friendship." His stare was intense.

"We don't have to give up the friendship. We don't have to be enemies. Let's stay friends." Smiling at him, I squeezed his hand.

Collier smiled back and stood taller. "We'll still be friends."

Later I stared at Collier's daisies in their vase in the window and wondered if I'd ever be lucky enough to have someone that was both a friend and a lover. Just before I fell asleep again, I thought of Dave McGinty and felt myself relax.

It was my day for being visited. After supper, Dave McGinty came into my room. No flowers this time.

"You just can't stay out of trouble." Grinning, he shook his head. "That's one of the things I like about you."

"Oh. So there are things you like about me?" I teased.

"Yeah, a few."

"Tell me more." I hoped he'd tell me more flattering things about me, but instead he changed the subject.

"Well, Mrs. Whitmire terminated my employment. And says not to expect a bonus or a reference."

My eyebrows rose in surprise. "*What?* Why?"

"Because she's still convinced Janet didn't commit suicide, but mainly because she found out that I'd looked into her background and found the family relationship to Craig Fletcher."

"I can understand her feelings. I find it hard to believe that Janet killed herself," I replied. "It wasn't like her."

"Your beliefs aside, she must have." He shrugged. "The cops thought Rita's call was a prank and didn't check it out until hours later. Probably, Janet came out of her swoon after Rita left her, and finding herself bleeding and abandoned, grabbed the knife from where Rita left it, slashed her throat, and bled out. Who knows what her state of mind was. Later your friend Russ stumbles upon her, messes up the forensics, takes the knife, and heads back to the Mission. Makes sense to me."

"Yes, it does," I agreed. "But it's not definitive proof, is it? Louis could have lied to me. Maybe he did go back and kill his cousin, or sent someone to do it, just to be sure."

"If he had done Janet, wouldn't he have bragged about it to you?" Dave questioned with an air of authority I found amusing. "Anyway, Mrs. Whitmire said she'd sue me if I told anyone about her and Craig being related. I told her that our employment agreement included a non-disclosure clause, but that's not good enough for her. You, on the other hand, are not bound by any such agreement, so I think you'll be hearing from Mister Collier about the dire consequences awaiting you should your lips get loose." He smiled at the prospect.

"You did all you could," I said. "Mrs. Whitmire is just acting out again. And I won't tell in any case. I'm not the only one with professional standards." I was grinning now. Why did this irritable man make me so happy?

"Good. I'd appreciate it. Though what's to stop Craig from airing their dirty laundry during the trial I don't know. I bet he'll try to use it as a bargaining chip somehow. That won't work out well for either of them." He was standing next to my bed holding my hand. When had that happened?

"I guess that means you'll go on to another job in another place."

He began gently stroking the top of my hand. "Not for a while. I have some personal business to take care of."

"Oh?" I replied shyly, casting my gaze downward. I hoped he was referring to me.

"Yeah."

Leaning down, he lifted my chin so that he could look into my eyes, then kissed me.

My insides went liquid. My head was spinning.

"Wow," I murmured.

He rested his forehead on mine. "Wow."

CHAPTER 60

SUNDAY, NOVEMBER 29 AFTERNOON

Three days later it was one of those unusually warm late fall days. Lucy and I sat on the front porch. I was curled up in the wicker chair wearing a turquoise sweatshirt, jeans, and a big white bandage on my shoulder.

My scuffed brown boots firmly planted on the floor, I declared, "Life is good, Lucy."

"Yeah it is, isn't it?

" The vet says Sweetie can come home Wednesday." She'd pulled through her surgery like a champion. Even with a bandage around her middle, she looked beautiful. Louis would have killed me first thing if Sweetie hadn't attacked him. She saved my life.

"That's great. I'll cook paprika chicken. It's her favorite." Lucy smiled.

"Mine, too."

"Speaking of cooking for someone … Russ came by yesterday morning before you were up. He says that he'll have to keep us safe, because we're no good at doing it ourselves. All he wants in return is a home-cooked meal once in a while."

I chuckled and said, "Mrs. Grimes from the Mission called yesterday afternoon to see how I was, and told me that Russ finally got approved for Social Security Disability."

"Wow! I didn't even know he'd applied. So will he be able to afford a room somewhere?"

"Yeah. She said the Community Services Board people were taking him around to look at places. I'm so happy for him." But I couldn't help thinking about what Rita had said about Mrs. Grimes's alibi for Russ. If it didn't hold up, then Russ could have been with Janet when she was still alive. I still didn't believe that he could have intentionally killed her, but what about unintentionally? When he wasn't taking his meds, Russ was not participating in the reality that society at large accepted. Would locking him up in a hospital for the rest of life really be justice, or merely revenge?

Did "the truth" of Janet's death really matter? In what way? I think truth always matters, but can mean different things for different people. It was hard for me to accept that I might never know what really happened, at least as far as Janet was concerned. I had been hoping that she would appear to me in a dream and tell me, but Janet hadn't seen fit to visit me again.

If Rita had shared her information about Russ's now-phony alibi, it never came out. The police were backing the suicide scenario in the wake of Rita's own suicide, the note she left me, and the capture of Craig Fletcher. It didn't look like the DA was interested in trying to pin Janet's death on the drug lord, since there were plenty of other bodies on his resume.

It finally dawned on me that Lucy had been talking and was now waiting for a response.

"Oh, sorry," I said. "You were saying?"

Lucy smiled indulgently. "I thought you were nodding your head for no reason. I was just agreeing that it's great news about Russ. And I'm also happy that you're here in one piece. Maybe not always present, but here physically at least."

"Yeah, sorry. My shoulder still hurts and I can't remember exactly how I got shot, but I'm alive. When I called Georgia at the office to thank them all for the fruit basket, she told me the phones were ringing off the hook with self-referrals. That convinced me that my decision to turn down the Boston job was the right one.. And Dr. Owens just sent me another Borderline with sexual identity issues. Looks like work is going to stay interesting."

"Yeah. I saw that piece they did on Channel Three about you being a 'Hero Therapist'."

I laughed even though it hurt. "That's me all right."

"You can't go back to work until your doctor clears you," Lucy reminded me.

"I know." I smiled. "Before I go back I've got some romancing to do. Did you see the get well card Lynn sent?"

"Yes, I did. Cute. And don't try to change the subject. Does this romancing you speak of have anything to do with Collier?" Lucy knew I was prone to backsliding, boyfriend-wise.

"Don't worry. That ship has sailed. We're going to try being friends … without benefits"

"Good luck with that," Lucy remarked, clearly not meaning it, but in a nice way.

"Did Dave McGinty have anything to do with that determination?" Her eyes twinkled.

"Yeah, I think he did. I've never met such an interesting man. He knows so much. He's irritating, but fascinating. And he's also a really good kisser."

Her eyebrows practically flew off her head she raised them so fast. "You kissed him? When? Where?" She asked with wide eyes.

I bit my lower lip to contain my giggle. "In the hospital."

"Great!"

"Yeah. It was. I really want to know him better. I hope he feels the same."

"Invite him to dinner at your place. See if Sweetie likes him."

"I will. I'll call him tonight. And I'll ask him if he meant it when he said he'd help me train Sweetie."

Lucy looked like she was getting tired of hearing about my love life. Maybe I should be more interested in hers. "I saw you talking to somebody yesterday evening. Was that a date?"

"Yeah." She smiled. "I met a really nice guy at the SPCA the other day. We had dinner last night."

"So …" Now it was my turn to grin.

"So I plan to see him tonight, too."

"Great! Tell me about him."

Her eyes lit up. "His name is Peter Morris and he's a financial planner. This time I Googled him first thing. He's an honest, upstanding guy."

Who'd a thought.

*   *   *

Later that week, Dave, Sweetie, and I sat on the front porch after a home-cooked dinner at my place. Sweetie still wasn't herself. She lay down carefully next to her new best friend. Reaching down, Dave stroked her head. Her middle with the big white bandage around it was still tender and I had gotten a special doggie bed for her so she could sleep better at night and relax during the day. She hurt and sighed a lot. Despite the pain, she still looked at me with those loving yellow eyes. When I first saw those eyes last year they'd scared me. I couldn't have imagined that one day she'd save my life. And Dave—irritable, irritating, lovable Dave. His eyes looked loving, too.

Maybe they were.

T H E   E N D

ACKNOWLEDGEMENTS

This book has been a part of my life for many years. So many people have supported me in writing this. A few are of particular note:

- Jane for her support and helping me stay grounded in reality while I was lost in the world of Fort Madison, Virginia.

- Charlotte & Terry for all of their support and for Beta reading this book.

- Julia for cheering me on and being willing to talk writing.

- Nimrod Hall Arts Program for providing a place for Charlotte and Cathy to teach and enable us to write our best. To all my fellow writers who love our "Writer's Camp" as much as I do.

- Rachael Herron for her support and for providing a place to learn and to make friendships with other writers. And to all those wonderful writers I've become close to as we work toward our goals.